GUARDIAN OF EDEN SPRINGS

Jim Crowgey

Order this book online at www.trafford.com
or email orders@trafford.com

Most Trafford titles are also available at major online book retailers.

Note for Librarians: A cataloguing record for this book is available from Library
and Archives Canada at www.collectionscanada.ca/amicus/index-e.html

Printed in Victoria, BC, Canada.

ISBN: 978-1-4269-1389-1 (sc)

*We at Trafford believe that it is the responsibility of us all, as both individuals
and corporations, to make choices that are environmentally and socially sound.
You, in turn, are supporting this responsible conduct each time you purchase
a Trafford book, or make use of our publishing services. To find out how you
are helping, please visit www.trafford.com/responsiblepublishing.html*

*Our mission is to efficiently provide the world's finest, most comprehensive book publishing
service, enabling every author to experience success. To find out how to publish your
book, your way, and have it available worldwide, visit us online at www.trafford.com*

Trafford rev. 7/27/2009

 www.trafford.com

North America & international
toll-free: 1 888 232 4444 (USA & Canada)
phone: 250 383 6864 ♦ fax: 250 383 6804 ♦ email: info@trafford.com

The United Kingdom & Europe
phone: +44 (0)1865 487 395 ♦ local rate: 0845 230 9601
facsimile: +44 (0)1865 481 507 ♦ email: info.uk@trafford.com

This book is dedicated with sincere appreciation
to family and friends for their warm reception of my
first novel, The Battle of Eden Springs.

ACKNOWLEDGMENTS

With sincere thanks to:

Mary Beth Crowgey, my daughter, for offering her literary talents and creativity as my advisor, teacher, editor, and critic during the writing of this sequel to *The Battle of Eden Springs*. The long hours she spent helping me with the original manuscript for this book resulted in a much improved novel, and for this I owe her an enormous debt of gratitude.

Peggy and Jerry Aldhizer, and Paul L. Collins – Tinker Creek Images, my new friends, for providing the spectacular Civil War battle reenactment photograph which graces the cover of this book.

Hal Cantrill, my friend for many years, for providing computer and photography skills to adapt for publication the photographs used on the cover of this book and also my preceding novel, *The Battle of Eden Springs*.

28th Virginia Reenactors pictured on the book cover, for preserving our American heritage.

Left to right: Jerry Aldhizer, Mark Musick, Travis White, David Lawhorn, Jim Wood, Dan Baker, and others.

1959

	SU	M	T	W	T	F	S			SU	M	T	W	T	F	S
JAN					1	2	3		**FEB**	1	2	3	4	5	6	7
	4	5	6	7	8	9	10			8	9	10	11	12	13	14
	11	12	13	14	15	16	17			15	16	17	18	19	20	21
	18	19	20	21	22	23	24			22	23	24	25	26	27	28
	25	26	27	28	29	30	31									
MAR	1	2	3	4	5	6	7		**APR**				1	2	3	4
	8	9	10	11	12	13	14			5	6	7	8	9	10	11
	15	16	17	18	19	20	21			12	13	14	15	16	17	18
	22	23	24	25	26	27	28			19	20	21	22	23	24	25
	29	30	31							26	27	28	29	30		
MAY						1	2		**JUNE**		1	2	3	4	5	6
	3	4	5	6	7	8	9			7	8	9	10	11	12	13
	10	11	12	13	14	15	16			14	15	16	17	18	19	20
	17	18	19	20	21	22	23			21	22	23	24	25	26	27
	24	25	26	28	28	29	30			28	29	30				
	31															
JULY				1	2	3	4		**AUG**							1
	5	6	7	8	9	10	11			2	3	4	5	6	7	8
	12	13	14	15	16	17	18			9	10	11	12	13	14	15
	19	20	21	22	23	24	25			16	17	18	19	20	21	22
	26	27	28	29	30	31				23	24	25	26	27	28	29
										30	31					
SEPT			1	2	3	4	5		**OCT**				1	2	3	
	6	7	8	9	10	11	12			4	5	6	7	8	9	10
	13	14	15	16	17	18	19			11	12	13	14	15	16	17
	20	21	22	23	24	25	26			18	19	20	21	22	23	24
	27	28	29	30						25	26	27	28	29	30	31
NOV	1	2	3	4	5	6	7		**DEC**			1	2	3	4	5
	8	9	10	11	12	13	14			6	7	8	9	10	11	12
	15	16	17	18	19	20	21			13	14	15	16	17	18	19
	22	23	24	25	26	27	28			20	21	22	23	24	25	26
	29	30								27	28	29	30	31		

CONTENTS

CHAPTER 1

"This situation brings to mind a line from *Hamlet*," Robert Barker expounded in his deep voice, leaning forward in his chair, staring at the two men across the table from him. "Revenge should have no bounds."

Barker paused to pour two fingers of bootleg whiskey into his scratched tumbler. "But I've also kept in mind a lesson from the scriptures, 'There is a time for everything.' You must never let anger lead you to move recklessly.

"I've hunkered down and waited since 1952 for the right time to even the score with Bradford, Housman, and Jannsen. I've laid awake many a night in my bed remembering how they worked to deny me the Buchanan land to mine, and a chance to claim that enormous seam of coal." He paused, offering an opportunity for one of the younger men to show his understanding.

William Thorpe, who had been paying rapt attention to his short-fused boss, quickly agreed. "You were wise to be patient and plan carefully." Tipping his glass and swallowing quickly, obviously more accustomed to sipping premium eight-year old blended scotch than 100 proof corn whiskey, he continued. "There's been no need to rush. That hotshot district attorney,

1

Jack Bradford, wasn't able to pin you with any of the crimes that were committed during the move for the Buchanan farm.

"Bradford knew you were dead-set on mining the valley north of Eden Springs and had to have the Buchanan property to pull it off. But with the Buchanan nephew getting killed after swindling his uncle out of his land and selling it to you, and the two convict accomplices afraid to testify against you, Bradford knew that he had no witnesses and no case that would hold up in court."

Barker impatiently cut off Thorpe. "You're preaching to the choir. I already know all of that. And you don't need to remind me that I'm stuck with land next to the Buchanan farm that I paid far too much for."

Regaining his composure, Barker again took charge. "But it's not about the money. It's more personal than that. It's about losing. I recall when I was a youngster taking a beating from a bigger kid out in the schoolyard during recess. The next day I got hold of a fence paling, caught up with the boy behind the building after school, and evened up the score. I hadn't been whipped by anyone since then, until those three came along.

"I'm too old now to go after them and give them a good thrashing. But Barker Mining has acquired big money over the years. That's put a lot of politicians and public officials in our pocket. We've developed a cooperative relationship with members of a powerful family organization that's spread into West Virginia from up in New Jersey. They're running a profitable business just down the road, right under the eyes of the law. All of these connections will serve our purposes even better than a fence plank.

"It's been seven years now since the Buchanan farm debacle. I'm champing at the bit to settle an overdue account with that arrogant DA, and the attorney and doctor that put him on to me. I'll have my revenge. You can take that to the bank.

"Bradford's the easiest one to deal with. He's prosecuted a lot of people and sent a bunch of them away to the big house since he's been in office. He's made more enemies than Judas. People will be waiting in line to help take him down."

"Housman and Jannsen will give me more pleasure but will require more finesse. They're considered pillars of their community. That makes me really want to get them down on the ground and roll them around in the dirt. I want to make their lives miserable. Both of them, and all of their neighbors living in that valley who sided against me seven years ago and denied me the right to that coal."

Both men across the table from him shifted uncomfortably in their chairs. It had been years since either had seen Barker in such a vengeful mood, with such irrational malice in his eyes. Thorpe lifted his glass, this time not noticing the burning sensation in his throat.

Barker continued, "You're my most trusted confidantes. I want your opinions now, and I'll hold you accountable for them later. Are the plans we've just gone over well thought out? Do they provide the time and flexibility to assure success? Is this the right time to begin our payback?"

The tall, powerfully built man across from him looked him straight in the eye without blinking and spoke in a slow, deep drawl, "Yes, Pa. I think your plans will work. Now's a good time to even the score with the three of 'em." Barker's only son, Travis, had just bought in to his father's crusade for revenge.

William looked less certain but knew that he had no real voice in the decision. He had sold body and soul to Robert years ago, including the right to objectively evaluate his boss's irrational strategies and tell him when it would be wiser to pause and carefully rethink matters. He cast his lot with the other two, replying, "I suppose now's a good time to wrap things up."

The three men walked out of the hotel room together, Robert leaning heavily on his sturdy cane in severe pain, growling, "This damn gout is killing me."

*****

3

At that same moment, miles to the north in New Jersey, the leaders of the powerful family organization that Barker had mentioned were finishing a big dinner and wrapping things up in the back room of the Old Italy Restaurant. Seafood, pasta, and three bottles of imported wine had the Mengarelli brothers, Donatello, Fredo, and Giacomo, in a very pleasant state, the opposite of Robert's world of pain. The youngest, Giacomo, reached out to give the pretty, dark haired waitress a friendly pat on her derriere each time she came within reach, and knowing that a big tip would be left at the table, she held a smile and willingly played along with his game of tag.

The light-hearted atmosphere darkened a bit when the oldest and ranking member of the family, Donatello, the boss of bosses, brought up the family business. "We need to talk about cash flow here tonight. Some of our biggest sources of income were down toward the end of the year. Trash collection and disposal revenue is steady, and our special licensing fees for small businesses are coming in at the same rate, but our collections from the numbers game and income from our ladies outcall services are both off. That makes the beverage distilling and distribution business even more important. We've got a big payroll to meet in order to keep the politicians and law enforcement people happy. It seems like every time they come around to see us, they've got their hands out for more."

"What's the problem with the beverage business?" Giacomo asked. "I thought Angie, Carmine, and Dom all had their acts together."

"They each do OK on their part of the operation," Fredo replied. "But they're always fighting among themselves about small stuff. Angie's greedy and keeps trying to steal from the others. Carmine's always looking for a way to branch out into some new business on his own and keep the money to himself. Dom's just a hardhead who has trouble finding his way in out of the rain. It's like we're dealing with the Three Stooges."

Donatello turned to Fredo and handed out a work assignment

4

in his usual no-nonsense manner. "I want you to start keeping a closer eye on the beverage business, not only what's going on up here in Jersey, but also what's happening in West Virginia. If you think any of those three are going to screw things up, I want to know right away. You got that? You just let me know if we have a problem, and I'll fix it."

"I got it," Fredo replied in resignation.

The three remained at the table until the last of the wine was gone before departing. Fredo walked away with the familiar feeling that once again his imperious older brother had dumped on him.

CHAPTER 2

Ed quietly closed the side door, slipping into the kitchen behind Laura, who was standing with her back to him, peering through the back window into the early twilight. When he put his arms around her to sweep her off her feet, she let out a squeal of surprise, then turned her head to share a warm welcome home kiss. Almost immediately, they heard the sound of the front door opening and knew that six-year old Lizzie had bounded into the house.

"Better put me down now, Kong," Laura admonished him. "No time now for you to carry me to the top of the Empire State Building for whatever you had in mind. Our daughter just got home."

Lizzie entered the kitchen just as Laura was managing to get back to her feet and regain her composure. "Mom! Daddy! Are you two playing a game?"

"Yeah, honey, we were playing a game of Swinging Statues, and your mom just lost her balance. Did you have a good time after school playing with your friends?"

"Yes, Daddy." Taking off her coat, hat, and gloves and dropping them on a kitchen chair, she continued, her eyes flashing with excitement, "Karen and Tommy and I were making a playhouse. But my hands got cold and I decided to come in."

"Well, I'm glad you had the good sense to get in here where it's warm," Laura responded, wrapping her arms around the girl and giving her a peck on her cold cheek. "Are you ready for a good meal? We're having meatloaf tonight, and I fixed it especially because I know that it's one of your favorites."

"You're always ready to eat a good meal, aren't you, Liz?" Ed asked. "Did you know that your brother is coming over to have dinner with us this evening? He likes meatloaf as much as you."

"Doug's coming over!" Lizzie squealed with happy excitement. "I want to tell him about the new playhouse we're building. Maybe I can cut on the porch light, and he'll be able to see it."

"Great idea, Liz," Ed said enthusiastically. "Doug may be able to give you some ideas on how to attach that cardboard box to the tomato stakes I gave you. We don't want your playhouse to get blown down like the straw house built by one of the three little pigs."

A half hour later, Lizzie was still in the kitchen busily filling her mother in on everything that had taken place during the day, and Ed was seated in the living room watching the Huntley-Brinkley Report on television, when Doug came through the door. Ed glanced up, proudly registering how much Doug had grown since high school, noting that his six-one, one-ninety pound son was now considerably larger than he.

Doug slipped off his coat and tossed it on the sofa, then leaned over to give his dad a hug and his familiar affectionate greeting, "How you doing, old timer? Where are Mom and Liz?"

Laura and Lizzie had heard him enter and quickly came in to join them. Doug reached out to give Laura a big hug and whispered loudly, "Hi, Mom. Have Dad and Liz been behaving themselves today?" Then he turned to Lizzie and picked her up, swinging her around in a circle with her red pony tail trailing behind. "What have you been up to today, Squirt?" When he tried to put her down, Lizzie hung on to his neck and wouldn't let go.

"How did things go for you at Power Generation Controls today?" Ed inquired. "Isn't your workload a lot lighter now that you've made it through the year-end rush to get everything shipped out the back door?"

"It sure is, Dad. Our engineering staff was burning a lot of time in the factory back in December supporting quality control testers. But let's talk about something more fun. Has Squirt been staying out of trouble at school, or is she still getting sent to the principal's office for misbehaving?" Lizzie responded by grabbing Doug by both ears and grinding her face into his.

"You children behave yourselves," Laura chimed in, unable to keep from laughing at the two. "Doug, have you heard anything from Vickie in the last few days?"

Doug set Lizzie down on the floor, directing a smile toward Laura. "No, Mom. Vickie seems to have a busy life these days in the Big Apple, and she doesn't find time to write as often as she did. It seems as though her job as an assistant writer at NBC and her night school class at Columbia have her totally occupied. Must be a pretty exciting life. But I plan to call her tonight and find out how she's getting along."

Ed did not seem to pick up on anything out of the ordinary in Doug's remarks, but Laura was more perceptive. She sensed that things were changing between Doug and Vickie, and that her step-son was having trouble dealing with a new and more distant relationship with his former steady girlfriend. Changing the subject quickly, she spoke cheerfully, "Everyone in the dining room for dinner. My meatloaf you're having tonight is out of this world, even if I am bragging on my own cooking."

After serving the plates with her specialty, Laura remarked, "Your friend Freddie sold another house today, Doug. He's been doing really well recently. Several of his sales have been to outsiders moving into town to take new jobs at PGC."

"I'm glad to hear that. When Freddie dropped out at Marshall his freshman year right after Shirley Martin broke up with him, I was worried about how he was going to handle things. I'm glad to know that he's become your star real estate salesman."

"I don't think you or anyone has to worry about Freddie," Laura answered with a laugh. "Everyone likes him. He's just a natural born salesman. Introduce him to prospective buyers, and five minutes later, he'll be kidding around with them like he's known them all of his life." Taking a sip of iced tea, she continued, "He's approached me to see if he can buy into Housman Reality down the road, and I've told him that I'll sit down and talk to him when he's ready."

Setting her glass down, she added, "Freddie mentioned something that you all might be interested in hearing. He was driving up the highway north of town earlier today, and noticed some activity near the old Simpson and Henderson farms that have been lying vacant since Robert Barker gave up on his strip mine back in 1952."

Ed put his fork down and looked at her with curiosity, "What caught Freddie's eye?"

"He noticed there were a couple of pickup trucks parked together beside the road, and several men were standing in front of one of them. It appeared to Freddie that they were looking over a drawing spread across the hood, and he speculated that it might be a survey plat of the property."

"I'm curious myself about who those people were and what they were doing," Doug commented. "Does Barker still own that land?"

"I honestly don't know," Ed answered. "The Simpsons and Hendersons sold it to Copperfield Enterprises, a front for Barker Mining, seven years ago. I'm not aware that the land has changed hands since then.

"I do know that Madison County would require a change to commercial or industrial zoning on the property before any sort of non-agricultural business could be developed there. I'll inquire down at the courthouse and see if anyone is aware of what may be going on."

"We'll all be interested to hear what you find out, Dad," Doug observed. "Sorry to break up the dinner party, but I've got to get back to my apartment and go over some drawings this evening. Mom, thanks for having me over to eat. Your meatloaf was the best. I would have asked for seconds, but I could see that Liz had already eaten it all."

"Doug, don't leave until I show you the playhouse that Karen and Tommy and I built today," Lizzie pleaded.

"OK, Squirt. Bundle up and let's go outside and take a look. Dad, I need to borrow your flashlight, so I can to perform a preliminary design review on my kid sister's first architectural project."

Doug followed Lizzie out the front door and across the wide yard with the swinging beam of the flashlight creating a moving walkway of light through the darkness. When they reached a row of lilac shrubs near the edge of the yard, Lizzie exclaimed, "There it is. That's our new playhouse."

Doug could see the remains of an old cardboard carton that had once contained a Hotpoint washing machine, with haphazardly arranged tomato stakes holding up the open end. He got down on his hands and knees with her and examined the structure. "You kids have got a great start to your playhouse. The only thing I think you need now is a little reinforcement between the walls and the roof using a high-tech product that we engineers use to build all of our equipment. I happen to have some in my glove box, and I'll give it to you. It's called duct tape."

The two walked together to his car where Doug retrieved a roll of silver-gray tape from the glove box and handed it to her. Then he strode with her hand in hand back to the house. Picking her up in his arms, he kissed her on the cheek. "Goodnight, Squirt."

Lizzie stopped at the open front door and called out to him,

"Thanks for the duck tape." She turned back before going inside and added, "I love you, Doug."

Doug turned on the radio while driving back to town, tuning in to his favorite station just in time to catch the ending of Johnny Mathis's hit, *Misty*. Not sure I'm in the mood for that kind of sentimental song tonight, he thought, switching stations and hearing the unmistakable slow drawls of Amos and Andy. Gales of canned laughter following each of the comedians' lines, bringing a smile to his face.

Doug pulled into the parking lot in front of his two story brick apartment house and switched off the engine. He found himself in a pleasurable state of anticipation walking toward the front door, looking forward to hearing Vickie's voice again. The thought ran through his mind that they had talked a couple of weeks ago, and yet it seemed as if he hadn't spoken to her in ages.

He tossed his coat on the sofa upon entering the apartment, and went to the phone to dial her familiar number. After a couple of rings, he heard someone pick up on the other end. "Vickie?" he inquired.

A pleasant female recognized his voice and replied, "Sorry, Doug, this is Janice. Vickie's out for the evening and probably won't be back for a while. Would you like for her to call you when she gets in? It might be pretty late."

"No, Janice, that won't be necessary. Tell her I'll try calling again in the next few days. Are both of you getting along OK?"

"We're both doing fine, Doug. Constantly on the run between our NBC jobs and night school classes, but getting along just great."

"Well, have a good evening, what's left of it. Tell Vickie I love her, and that I said for her to stay away from all of those good looking men in town."

"I'll pass on your message, word for word. But just for the record, you're not likely to see Vickie or any of us hanging out at the Copacabana with Frank Sinatra and the Rat Pack. We stay way too busy to get into trouble. Bye now."

CHAPTER 3

"I should be home by 10:00," Vickie called out to her roommate as she went out the door. "Lock up behind me." Scurrying to the elevator, she pressed the button for the first floor, rushing into the lobby to join the young couple waiting for her when the doors opened. "Hope I didn't keep you waiting long."

"No need to hurry," Richard Hardy said pleasantly, smiling at her. "We've only been waiting here a few minutes. The shuttle is parked right outside, and we'll get to class in plenty of time."

"I'm really enjoying Dr. Peters' lectures in our Television Productions class," Karen Billings commented as they walked to the bus. "He just seems to know everything about the TV broadcasting business."

"It's one of the best classes I've taken since I entered grad school here two years ago," Richard replied to Karen, while looking at Vickie. "I'm glad both of you decided to sign up. I think Dr. Pete can be more entertaining than Jack Paar."

The lively conversation continued on the bus and into the classroom. Finding most of the seats for the popular class already taken, Richard steered Vickie to a vacant chair, taking the one beside her, while Karen selected a seat further to the front. The lecture was fast paced and engrossing. After the professor

13

dismissed the class with one of his trademark risqué jokes, the three rejoined outside the classroom.

"Let's go by Delano's Coffee Shop," Richard suggested, touching Vickie lightly on the arm. "I'll buy you girls a coffee and Danish." The three strolled into the coffee shop, crowded with students taking a welcome break from the books. Time seemed to fly by, and it was forty minutes later when they went outside to catch the shuttle back to their apartments.

Richard walked with them to the front door of their building to say goodnight, then continued on toward his apartment up the street. As the two girls headed across the lobby toward the elevator door, Karen commented, "It doesn't take Einstein to figure out that Richard has a thing for you. I wouldn't mind it if he gave me the same kind of attention. I think that he'd be quite a catch."

"He's all yours," Vickie replied with a laugh. "Richard's a good looking guy and a lot of fun to hang out with, but remember that I already have a boyfriend back home. Although Doug and I decided to give up going steady when he went off to VPI to take engineering, and I came here to Columbia to study journalism, I still haven't dated around very much. I guess I'm still sweet on him."

"Then I'll take Richard off your hands," Karen grinned. "I wouldn't mind ending up with one of your rejects. But I'm not sure hand-me-downs work like that when you're dealing with boys."

As Vickie unlocked the door and entered the small apartment, she could see Janice in the next room in her pajamas. "Glad you're back," Janice called out. "Oh, by the way, you got two calls while you were at class. Doug phoned right after you left and said he'll try to get you again in a night or two. He said to tell you that he loves you, and to stay away from all the good looking men around town. Then your mother called a little later. She wants you to give her a ring."

Vickie called home a short time later, and seventeen-year old

Tony, Jr. answered the phone in a voice now as deep as his father's. "Hey, TJ, Mom wanted me to give her a call. Can I speak with her?" Ingrid quickly came on the line and from the tone of her voice, Vickie knew that the call was about something serious.

"Your granddaddy was notified today that he's being sued for malpractice. Daddy has been a family doctor in this town for over fifty years and has never had anything like this happen before. You can imagine what a terrible experience it is, especially for a seventy-seven-year old physician approaching the end of his career. He's very upset, and so are all of the rest of us."

"What's going on, Mom?" Vickie inquired, concerned.

"Your granddaddy got a call late one night in June back in 1957 from a middle-aged couple named Dudley and Patsy Scaggs, asking him to rush out to their home and help deliver a baby. He had provided medical care to the Scaggs family before, and he was aware that the woman and her husband were dirt poor alcoholics. He realized from previous experience that it would be another of his many medical charity cases, but he went right out and attended to the woman. He told us that the birth wasn't difficult, and when he left, the baby boy and mother were both doing well. The couple was profusely grateful to him, as they should have been. Daddy didn't even bother submitting a bill to them for his services.

"Then this week, he was served with papers informing him that he is being sued for malpractice, alleging that the child suffered permanent brain damage due to his negligence following the delivery. The plaintiffs claim that he let the infant slip out of his hands following delivery, causing the child to strike his head on the foot of the bed. The couple has retained a lawyer in Beckley and is suing for a big damages settlement. Daddy said that the incident is a complete fabrication, and that there was no mishap of any kind during the delivery.

"Can you even imagine two people concocting such a horrible charge against a Good Samaritan who has just helped

15

them?" Ingrid continued. "Don't you wonder how they located an attorney who would take such a case?"

"Poor Granddaddy! Is he OK? What will he do?"

"He's taking this pretty hard, as you would imagine. He's talked to Doug's father, and Ed has already started to work on the case. But regardless of what happens, this malpractice suit seems so malicious. With all the good things your grandfather's done throughout his career for the people in Eden Springs, why is he having to go through something like this now, particularly so late in his life?"

"I don't know, Mom, but I do have confidence that it'll turn out OK. Doug's dad has a great reputation. I don't think that Granddaddy could have a better lawyer defending him."

"I agree that Ed Housman's the best person Daddy could have to defend him, but there is so much unpleasantness lying ahead for him and for all of us. I don't like giving you bad news like this tonight, honey, but I thought you ought to know. Now tell me, is everything going well for you at NBC and in your class?"

"Yeah, Mom, everything's going fine here. I hope things will be better at home soon. Tell Granddaddy he's in my prayers. And if you run into Doug around town, tell him I said hello, and that I miss him."

"I'll do that. Goodnight, sweetheart. Sleep well."

"Goodnight, Mom. I love you."

CHAPTER 4

"Good morning, Carolyn," Ed called out cheerfully to his versatile legal secretary as she entered the office and removed her coat. "I've already made a pot of coffee. I believe it's way too strong, and if you find it's undrinkable, we'll use it for varnish remover."

"A cup of hot coffee sounds mighty good on a cold morning like this, Ed. You know my taste in coffee, the stronger, the better."

Looking at Carolyn Carson's lined face and gray hair reminded Ed of how fortunate he was that she still enjoyed working at an age when many others would be counting down the days to retirement. When he had presented her with an IBM electric typewriter to replace her manual Underwood six months earlier, she had been as excited as though he had given her a new Corvette.

Carolyn settled in at her desk and began to review Ed's calendar for the day. "I've set up an appointment for you this afternoon at 3:00 with a small business owner in Hinton named Dominic Magino. He runs a small trucking company and hauls freight between West Virginia and several of the big east-coast cities. He wants to talk to you about converting his operation from a sole proprietorship to a corporation."

"Thanks, Carolyn," Ed responded. "I'll be ready to meet with Mr. Magino when he shows up."

That afternoon, Ed's visitor arrived on schedule, carrying a thick manila folder. After introductions were completed, Ed escorted him into the conference room and closed the door. He observed Dominic to be a heavyset, middle-aged man of Italian origin, with an olive complexion and long, black hair combed straight back and slicked down with generous amounts of Vitalis.

Dominic took a seat at the conference table across from Ed and opened the folder to display a collection of business documents. Speaking in a deep voice with a New Jersey accent, he explained that he was the owner of an eight-truck fleet. He related that most of his hauled freight consisted of West Virginia goods which were produced in the southwest corner of the state and delivered to customers in Newark, Philadelphia, and Baltimore. The decision to locate his trucking firm in Hinton had been driven by the opportunity to purchase an existing terminal at a bargain price.

"The reasons for incorporating are to limit personal liability, and make it easier for a couple of relatives to buy into the business," he stated. "The extra cash is needed to add new vehicles to my fleet. I've already picked out a name for the company, changing it from Magino Trucking Company to East Coast Transfer Company, Inc. That will sound impressive when I'm trying to drum up new business."

A discussion led to an agreement to proceed. Dominic passed his folder to Ed, remarking as the two shook hands, "I appreciate your taking this on for me, Mr. Housman. You'll contact me and let me know when you have the papers ready to go over?"

"Yes. I'll call you if I need information or have any questions. I would expect to have everything ready for you to sign before the end of the month."

The two men walked from the conference room to the door,

and Ed listened for Dominic's departing footsteps, saying to Carolyn, "It looks like we have a new client. From that accent, it appears he's from New Jersey. Judging by those two massive gold rings, I'd bet he's a successful businessman."

"I pictured him a little differently when he called on the phone to set up the appointment," Carolyn interjected with a laugh. "I believe after seeing him that he could have been cast in a role with Humphrey Bogart in *The Enforcer.* I don't think I'd want to run into him alone at night in a dark alley. But here I go again, judging a book by the cover."

"I'm a little curious how he found us," Ed mused. "I wish now that I'd asked him before he left. Oh well, let's get out of here and call it quits for the day."

*****

Ten miles up the road, at a small, dimly lit watering hole called Rusty's, Dominic Magino was also calling it quits for the day, standing in front of a pay phone with a cold Blue Ribbon in one hand, checking out the cleavage of the buxom redhead in the low cut blouse working behind the bar. "Vinnie? Everything went fine. Housman's going to be starting work right away to incorporate our business and have us operating as East Coast Transfer Company, Inc. Our trucks won't be running around much longer with Magino plastered on the side for everyone to see."

He paused to take in the reply from the other end, then added, "Yeah, I think we can also use him to collect the ten grand Angelo owes us, and at the same time make a few bucks on that deal Barker pitched to us. It'll be like killing two birds with one stone, where one of the birds is a legal eagle."

CHAPTER 5

Saturday morning, Doug drove his pride and joy, a bright red '57 Chevy, over to his folks' home and parked out front.

Lizzie spotted him driving up and came running out to greet him. "Doug, let me show you how Karen and Tommy and I fixed up the playhouse."

She led him across the yard, running ahead to stand proudly in front of the structure. Doug could not help but think how much it resembled a shelter that might have graced a hobo jungle during the Great Depression. The original Hotpoint washer carton was now flanked by two other equally large cardboard box add-on rooms, all covered with an overhanging piece of rusty corrugated sheet metal which projected out to make a roof for the wide front porch. The entire roll of duct tape he had given her had been used to wrap the collection of boxes and hold them together. "Do you like it?"

"Truthfully, I never saw anything quite like it," Doug replied. "That design would make even one of the greatest architects who ever lived, Frank Lloyd Wright, eat his heart out," he added. "Good job, Squirt."

Together, they walked back to the house and entered the living room. Doug watched as JR came streaking down the hallway and jumped up on his leg. The nine-year old beagle-terrier mix had never forgotten the teenage boy who had picked him up on the side of the road and brought him home seven years ago, even after the years Doug had been away at college.

"How you doing, fella," Doug exclaimed, dropping down on his knees to playfully rough-house with the dog. "You're the reason I'm here this morning. I've got to take you to the vet for your rabies and distemper shots. You want to ride along, Liz? First be sure it's OK with Mom."

It was only a short drive to the Eden Springs Animal Hospital, a flat roofed white concrete block building flanked on one end by a large open shed containing a dozen chain link fence dog runs. Doug clipped a leash on JR's collar, a wide leather strap with "JR Housman" engraved on the attached tag. "You want to lead him inside, Liz?" Doug asked.

Doug signed in JR at the front desk, then the three moved over to a bench near the end of the room to wait for their vet, Dr. Rollins, to appear. After Doug had thumbed through every *Reader's Digest* in the room, a slender, attractive young brunette in a white lab coat entered wearing a pleasant smile. Doug noted that her name tag read "Marilyn Nelson, DVM."

"I can see from the collar that this is the patient, JR," she observed. "I'm Marilyn Nelson, the new vet working here now with Dr. Rollins. If you'll follow me back to our examining room, we'll look this young fellow over, and take care of those booster shots."

Rising from his seat with Lizzie, and taking JR by the leash to follow her, Doug replied, "I'm Doug Housman and this is my sister Lizzie. It's nice to meet you, Dr. Nelson."

While Marilyn examined JR, preparing to give him his shots, Doug struck up a conversation with the pretty newcomer. "JR's a beagle-terrier mix who adopted me on the side of the road coming back from a Scout camping trip in 1952. He's Lizzie's best friend."

"He's my other brother," she corrected him.

"I wouldn't have known if you hadn't told me," Marilyn said to her with a laugh. " JR doesn't have red hair like you two. I take it that y'all are natives of the beautiful town of Eden Springs?"

"Lizzie and JR are. I moved here from Charleston with my dad when I was fifteen. I was away for four years at VPI in Blacksburg, studying engineering, and then came I back to take a job here with Power Generation Controls. May I ask where you're from?"

Interrupting her work with JR, she turned to Doug. "I grew up in rural Georgia and went to undergrad and vet school at the University of Georgia in Athens. Growing up in the country around livestock definitely influenced me to go into veterinary medicine. I love working with animals, but I decided to switch over from large to small animal practice along the way. When I found out about an opening here, I interviewed with Dr. Rollins, and when he offered me the job, I accepted it on the spot."

"I'm not the town mayor, but anyway, welcome to Eden Springs," Doug laughed. "It's nice to know JR will be in such good hands. Do you see anything that we need to bring him back for you to check out?" he inquired, sounding as if he hoped she would say yes.

"Nope. He looks to me like he's good for another year. Or another thousand miles, whichever comes first," she added playfully. "I'm glad JR's going to be my patient now."

Doug stopped at the counter on the way out to pay his bill, then followed Lizzie and the dog back to his car.

"Dr. Nelson's nice, isn't she, Doug?" Lizzie commented. "I like the way she talks."

"Yeah, she's right nice," Doug agreed. "I'm glad we have another good vet in town, particularly a pretty young lady with a great southern accent."

Doug returned to his apartment after driving Lizzie and JR back home. He tossed his jacket on a chair and headed toward the refrigerator to retrieve the other half of a deli sandwich he'd left there the previous evening. But he found something overriding all thoughts of lunch. He realized that Vickie had not returned his call from a few days earlier, and that he had not spoken to her in what seemed like forever. Wanting to hear her voice again, he picked up the phone and dialed her number. He was totally surprised when a male voice answered.

"I'm calling for Vickie Vicelli. Do I have the right number?"

"Yes. This is Richard. She's tied up right now and can't come to the phone. But if you'll give me your name and number, I'll have her call you back."

"Can I speak to Janice?"

"No, Janice isn't here. She's gone out for the day. Would you please go ahead and give me your name and number now, so I can leave Vickie a note?" Richard replied, a trace of impatience starting to show in his voice.

"Yeah. You can just tell her Doug called. She knows my number. And be sure to pass on that I said there's no need for her to bother calling me back." He put down the receiver and stood for a few minutes, feeling the resentment building up from within at the thought of his girlfriend being alone in her apartment with a man named Richard. What in the world had her so tied up that she couldn't come to the phone and take my call, he asked himself. Impulsively, he grabbed his jacket and headed out of the apartment. He could hear his phone ringing before he made it outside, slamming the door behind him.

CHAPTER 6

"Nice job, Freddie," Laura commented, as he wheeled the Houseman Realty station wagon back out of the driveway and onto the street. "I think you've obtained a couple of promising new home listings. Both houses are in good neighborhoods and priced to sell, particularly the brick ranch. How did you find out the owners were planning to put them on the market?"

"I had dinner with Mike and Ginny Rhodes a couple of days ago, and they put me on to both of them. They also gave me some other good news. Mike has just been promoted to assistant service manager at the Madison County Ford dealership, which means he'll be bringing in a bigger paycheck. With Jenny seven months pregnant and having to give up her job as a registered nurse, the timing was perfect."

"I'm glad to hear things are going so well for them. Doug told me that they were grade school sweethearts who had gone steady for ten years when they were married. And just think! You were the one who sold them their first home. It's such a beautiful place."

Freddie smiled, obviously appreciating the compliment from his low-key boss. "Mrs. Housman, while we're out this way, would you like to drive a little further and go by the old Simpson and Henderson farms where I saw those trucks parked a couple of weeks ago?"

"I think that's a great idea. And afterwards we could swing by the Buchanan farm to say hello to Gertrude, Daniel and Jonah, and take a look at Roseanna. I hear the family's made a lot of progress in restoring the old mansion."

There were neither people nor trucks to be seen when they turned in past the private road sign on the gravel drive running across the front of the two abandoned farms. But Freddie immediately noticed something that had changed since his last visit.

"The land along this road was completely overgrown with brush when I was out here the last time. Seeing the Simpson's and Henderson's cleared fields filled with weeds and briars made me think that nature really does abhor a vacuum. Obviously, someone's been in here recently with a bush hog and mowed it."

"I think they've done some work on the road, too," Laura added. "You can see where quite a few truck loads of pug and gravel have been spread, and it hasn't even had time to pack down."

"Do you know who owns this land now, Mrs. Housman?"

"Ed checked at the courthouse recently. The deed's been transferred from Copperfield Enterprises to a company called Mountain Ventures. He's still trying to find out more about the new owner."

Freddie made a U-turn in the loose gravel and started back toward the highway. Both he and Laura were surprised to see that a late model sedan was now parked near the entrance, apparently waiting for them to turn around and come back out. When they drove up beside the parked car, a tall, stocky man motioned for Freddie to roll down his window and spoke to them in a no-nonsense voice, "You folks see that sign over there saying private road? That means you aren't allowed to drive in here."

Laura spoke up, "We didn't see any posted signs, so we just

drove by to look at the old Simpson and Henderson properties. Is there some problem?"

"Yeah, there is. I don't want you or any other unauthorized people in here. You two clear out now, and don't come back again. I'll have no trespassing signs posted the next time you come."

Freddie rolled up his window without replying to the stranger and continued back out to the highway. "What a rude SOB," he exclaimed. "Pardon me for talking like that in front of a lady, but I'm calling a spade a spade."

"He certainly overreacted to what we did," Laura agreed. "I wonder what that was all about? Well, we may have to share our world with jerks like that man, but we don't have to let them get to us. Let's go on over to Roseanna like we planned. When we get there, I'd like to stop in for a few minutes and say hello to the Buchanans."

A short time later, they reached the old home. "Standing in front of this magnificent mansion makes up for that unpleasant encounter we just had," Laura remarked, observing the impressive restoration. "Look at all the improvements they've made! New wood and fresh paint have worked wonders. Too bad Gideon and Hester died before they could see this renovation."

"It really is. I was in my junior year in high school the winter they both passed away. Old Gideon didn't linger very long after Hester was taken, did he?"

"No. I think he lost his will to live after she was gone. We tend to forget that they too were young once. There's probably a great love story between Gideon and Hester that will never be written."

Laura and Freddie were greeted at the front door by Gertrude Buchanan. "How nice of you two to drop by. Come in the parlor. Dan, Joe, get in here and speak to our guests."

Laura was surprised to see the dramatic changes within as she and Freddie followed Gertrude into the house. Light now streamed in through the large, sparkling windows and flooded the formerly dingy rooms, illuminating the fresh paint on the walls, the sanded and varnished hardwood floors, and the updated furniture. Everything appeared clean and spotless. Undoubtedly, all of these improvements were made under the influence of the new lady of the house with her WAC and RN background, Laura speculated.

But she was even more taken aback by the appearance of the twins, Daniel and Jonah, as they entered the room. The two men, now in their sixties, were totally transformed. When Daniel had first started courting Gertrude Estep shortly after the death of Hester and Gideon, she had insisted on some changes. Heavy beards had been shaved with a straight razor in the Eden Springs Barber Shop, and fitted blue jeans from Belk had replaced their trademark faded, baggy coveralls.

Daniel and Jonah had become Dan and Joe to Gertrude. There was a strong bond between Dan and her that had led them to the altar less than two years after they had first met. Both could never forget that in the span of one terror-filled night back in 1952, she had saved his life, and he in turn had saved hers. To Dan and his brother, despite mannerisms still carried over from her days as a WWII WAC, Gertrude was an angel from heaven. Both were totally devoted to her and deferred to her in every situation.

"Do you know what's going on over on the abandoned farmland near Stony Creek?" Laura asked, during a break in the conversation. "A very unfriendly man just ran us off the property when we drove in to look around."

"A couple of men hunting quail with bird dogs got run off that property last week," Jonah responded. "I don't know why, but the owner doesn't want anyone coming on the place now. We've been curious about what's going on ourselves. From the cemetery on top of the hill, we can just make out their coming and going. We watched them mow those fields and do some road work recently."

"Please call and let us know if you learn anything more,"

Laura asked. "I think we ought to keep our eyes open to see what's going on. A surly man who doesn't want anyone coming around tends to makes me suspicious. I don't think he's the kind of person who'll make a good neighbor for you." She added, "Freddy, I guess we'd better be leaving now, if we're going to make any real estate sales this afternoon."

"I'm sorry that you have to run so soon," Gertrude remarked, disappointed, as she walked them to the door. "We don't get much company out here, and were really enjoying your visit."

"We'll get back out here to see you before long," Laura promised, as she and Freddie walked to the car.

On the drive back to the highway, Freddie commented, "I'm going to ride out this way from time to time. I suspect there's a reason that man was dead set on keeping us out, and I plan to find out why."

"Good for you, Freddy. But I caution you about stepping on his posted land. After our experience with him today, I think he'd call the law on you in a heartbeat if he caught you trespassing."

CHAPTER 7

Doug worked late at the office, staying at his desk after his friends had called out their goodbyes and left for the day. He wanted to recheck all the drawings for the revamp of the small hydro power generation station at Deep Creek, before submitting them for approval to Appalachian Electric Power Company. The pleasant anticipation of getting away from the office to meet with AEP engineers on site made the casual overtime seem quite bearable. Not a bad day at work, he thought to himself on the way home. I only wish I had someone waiting to have dinner with me when I get back to the apartment. Thinking of that someone suddenly made him feel very alone, and he pushed the thoughts of her from his mind.

Doug stopped to retrieve a stack of mail which had been delivered earlier that day. He rifled through an assortment of advertisements and the February issue of *Field and Stream* as he entered the house, then spotted a letter in a familiar small blue envelope. Sitting down on the sofa, staring at the letter from Vickie with a troubled conscience, he remembered how he had walked out the door rather than take her phone call a few days before. Turning the envelope over and observing that her familiar

29

affectionate SWAK was missing on the back, he tore it open and read the note inside.

"Dear Doug,

I was hurt that you would not pick up the phone when I called you back on Saturday afternoon. I'm sure that it was because you expected to speak to Janice or me when you called, and you didn't like hearing a man answer the phone. But I don't think that gave you any reason to hang up and leave a rude message that I shouldn't bother calling you back.

The man you spoke to was Richard Hardy, a classmate in my night school class. He and another friend, Karen Billings, were here at the apartment with me to go over a homework assignment. At the time you called, Janice was out for the afternoon with friends, and I was in the next room with Karen, who was still feeling sick from too much partying at a Columbia mixer the night before.

There is absolutely nothing going on between Richard and me. You and I agreed earlier that we could date other people as long as we were open about it. You knew that I went out a few times with Johnny Taylor last year, but I told you it was only to have someone to go places with. You told me back when you were at VPI that you were seeing a girl at Radford College, but that it was nothing serious. I confess that it bothered me at the time, although I never told you that until now.

If there's any problem facing us, Doug, it's the distance and difference in lifestyles separating New York and Eden Springs. I really enjoy the excitement of living in a big city and working at NBC, while you seem content living in a small town and working as an engineer at PGC. I honestly don't know how we'll ever be able to resolve this, but we don't have to come up with a solution right now. Let's just take one day at a time, and focus on not letting anything come between us, like a complete misunderstanding over simple phone call. Please call me back. I really want to talk to you.

Love,
Vickie"

Doug read the letter a second time, and with a lump in his throat, laid it on the table. He and Vickie had not had many serious disagreements since they had started going steady at the beginning of their junior year in high school. Each of the few times they had fought since then, he had come away regretting his actions, and this time was no different.

He went to the phone, dialed her number, and heard her pick up, answering the phone in the unmistakable voice he had been longing to hear again for days. "Vickie, I'm really sorry for the immature way I acted on the phone Saturday. I was a complete jerk. Will you forgive me?"

He could just make out her soft reply. "Yes. I'm glad you finally decided to call me back. I've really missed visiting with you on the phone and reading your letters the past few days. Tell me all about what you've been up to since we last talked. Don't leave out anything, sweetheart."

CHAPTER 8

"Have a seat and make yourself comfortable," Ed said to his old friend Arnold Jannsen. I don't think our meeting this afternoon will require much of your time, but I'm afraid that we may have a long slog ahead of us before we're through."

Arnold settled into a chair, replying wearily, "Thanks, Ed. I was out late on a house call last night, and I didn't get much sleep. Then all day long, there's been a steady stream of patients coming into the office. I think my age is finally starting to catch up with me."

"I don't think you've lost a step, Arnold. No one in this town but you could keep going day after day with your hours and workload. I'll try to push this discussion along, and maybe you can get out of here and home in time to grab a quick nap before dinner. Let's go over everything that we know to date. This process may be a bit unpleasant, but we need to be totally candid with each other all the way through this case.

"On June 1, 1957, you were called by phone and asked to come to the home of Dudley and Patsy Scaggs to help deliver a baby. Dudley is 50 years old, and Patsy is 49. The couple have two other children, ages 16 and 15, who appear to be physically and mentally normal. Dudley is employed part-time as a house painter, and Patsy is a full- time housewife. They live in a rented trailer in poor conditions. According to neighbors, they've always managed to scrape up enough money to support heavy drinking habits. You've provided medical services to the family whenever they've requested over the years, but you've not submitted bills, knowing that they're unable or unwilling to pay.

"The child, Harley, whom you delivered twenty months ago, is not showing signs of normal mental development for his age, a fact which seems to be incontestable. You have told me that the delivery was routine, and that there was no abnormal incident or accident involved in the delivery process. No one except you, Dudley, and Patsy was directly involved in the delivery. Neither of the two older children nor any outsider was present in the room during the birth. You've told me that the Scaggs were pleased with the outcome, and that both expressed their appreciation for your services on that evening. You also told me that you detected the smell of alcohol on Patsy and even more strongly on Dudley at the time, which cannot be proven, and which may or may not have any bearing on the case.

"You are now accused, according to the papers served, of having dropped the baby shortly after tying and cutting the umbilical cord, allowing the infant to fall and strike his head on the foot of the metal bed frame. It is alleged that this act of medical malpractice caused permanent brain damage.

"The couple has retained an attorney in Beckley, Samuel Lukins, to represent them. He in turn has hired Dr. Emil Heinz, a Beckley pediatrician, as an expert witness. No dates have yet been set for depositions or a trial. Have I missed anything?"

"No, Ed, I think that you summarized this whole sorry mess very well. What comes next? As you must know, I'm anxious to be acquitted and get all of this behind me."

"With your approval, I'm going to hire a Charleston private investigator named Andrew Stover to investigate the alleged accident and also the background of the Scaggs family. We need some solid evidence that we can present in court at the time of trial to help prove your innocence."

"Ed, I'm agreeable with any action you want to take that will help disprove these false allegations against me. Just do what you believe is best, and don't worry about the cost."

"I think that's all we need to go over today, Arnold. Why don't you head for home now and try to get some shut-eye? That's the attorney's prescription for the doctor. And give my best to Greta."

"I'll get out of here right now and try to get that prescription filled before dinner," Arnold replied, managing a weak smile. "I really appreciate all that you're doing for me."

Ed left the office, noticing how the early February days were becoming longer since the winter solstice had come and gone. He drove over to the Rexall Drug Store, and was walking inside when he heard someone behind him call his name.

"Ed. I haven't seen you for a while. How are you getting along these days?" Ed spun around and found himself face to face with his old friend, Sam Barry, who had been promoted to principal of Tyler High when Norman Stoner had retired three years earlier.

"Good to see you again, Sam," Ed responded, extending his arm for a warm handshake. "I was just stopping by the drugstore to pick up some crayons for Lizzie's latest school project. What a nice surprise running into you."

"That goes for me, too. I was going to grab a tuna salad sandwich and a Coke, before heading over to the court house for a meeting of the board of supervisors. You warned me when I took a seat on the board that it was going to seriously cut into my free time, and you were right."

"I'm glad that you accepted an appointment to the board despite my warning. We need more people like you serving in local government who have no political baggage and hold an informed opinion of what's right for the region. Anything coming before the board that's of interest?"

"Curious that you should ask me that question, because there is. A company called Mountain Ventures has purchased the old Simpson and Henderson properties, and the owners are petitioning for rezoning to permit the operation of a landfill. You may not be aware, but the existing landfill on the east side of town is almost full, and the town is searching for a new location. If the petition's approved, Mountain Ventures wants to bid on the contract to handle the town's refuse collection and disposal. Many of my fellow board members think this rezoning is a winner for both Mountain Ventures and the town. I'm reserving my opinion until I hear more of their plans, but between the two of us, from a board majority standpoint, the decision's already been made."

"That bit of information helps explain some other things that have occurred recently," Ed observed. "Laura and Freddie Palmer encountered a pretty unfriendly man out there a couple of weeks ago. I would imagine Mountain Ventures wants to get their rezoning approval before neighbors learn what business they're in. I expect neighbors would prefer an agricultural enterprise rather than a trash dump moving in so close to them, no matter how well it's operated."

"I'm sure you're right, Ed. I'll be asking a lot of questions about Mountain Ventures and their record of operating landfills before I vote for rezoning." Checking his watch, Sam added, "I'd better run now. Maybe Margaret and I can get together with you and Laura for a few hands of bridge some evening soon."

"Sounds good, Sam. Tell Margaret to call Laura and try to set something up. Hope your meeting goes well tonight. I'll watch the paper to see what action you and the other board members take on this petition. By the way, where does Mountain Ventures have their headquarters?"

"I think they're out of Beckley, Ed."

"I have an old Washington and Lee classmate, Phil Wine, who practices law in Beckley, and I may give him a ring to find out what he knows about Mountain Ventures. I'll let you know if I learn anything about the owners."

CHAPTER 9

"I'm really glad you could take the day off and come with me," Doug said to his long-time buddy Mike Rhodes as they pulled their fishing rods and tackle boxes from the back of his car. "I knew that it wouldn't take long to go over the drawings for the Deep Creek Power Gen revamp with the APCO engineers, since I mailed everything for them to look over weeks ago. We've still got a few hours to get in some good fishing before dark."

"That's all we should need to catch a bucketful here in Deep Creek," Mike answered. "This stream's loaded with smallmouth bass." Attaching a red and white Flatfish lure onto the snap-swivel at the end of his fishing line, he added, "I don't want to be too late getting home tonight, with Ginny going into her eighth month."

"I'm still having a hard time getting used to the idea of you becoming a father," Doug commented. Then stepping onto a large rock projecting out over the creek, he took a good natured shot at Mike. "If it's a girl, I sure do hope she looks like Ginny."

Mike stopped to pick up a small rock and sail it over Doug's head. "And when you have kids, Housman, assuming you can ever find a wife, I hope you adopt. I wouldn't want to see any innocent child afflicted with your looks."

Both were trying to keep from laughing as they cast their lures across the creek. They had kidded each other since becoming best friends during their sophomore year at Tyler High. But if an outsider had bad mouthed either of them, he would have answered to both. Mike and Doug were almost as close as blood kin.

Time slipped by unnoticed as they steadily caught and released a large number of smallmouth bass. Switching to night crawlers, they also pulled in several catfish, and one enormous carp. As the sun started to dip below the tops of the sycamores and poplars lining the banks, Doug commented, "I guess it's time to head back toward home. We can stop at the Country Boy Diner down the road and grab a burger and a chocolate shake to eat on the way."

Driving down the road beside Deep Creek with headlights turned on against the dusk, they passed the Universal Chemical Company plant, with bright flood lights illuminating the enormous facility. A tanker truck was waiting to pull out through the security gate onto the highway as they passed. Mike tried to make out the name of the trucking company on the door of the cab, but found the lettering illegible due to the build-up of grime. He turned to Doug and inquired, "You ever stop to think about what they're carrying in these trucks? Looking at them, you can't tell whether they're full of Coca Cola's secret formula syrup or concentrated hydrochloric acid."

"I wonder about that myself, since there's nothing on the outside to give you a clue as to what they're hauling. These heavy duty tanker trucks on the highway always make me a little nervous, particularly the ones you see making runs to and from chemical plants.

"I had an interview for a facility engineering job in a chemical plant last year. I found out that a lot of their products are classified as hazardous materials, and many of the processes produce toxic waste that's hard to dispose of. I don't know where they can find a place to dump it. Anyway, I sure wouldn't want to see us have a collision with a truck like that one. We might both come away looking like two of those weird creatures out of a Marvel comic book. It would probably be the last time that Ginny and Vickie would want to have us come around."

After stopping for take-out meals at the diner, Mike inquired, "What's the latest with you and Vickie? Do you think she'll ever want to come back down on the farm, now that she's seen Paris?"

Doug hesitated, then spoke quietly. "If I tell you something, Mike, will you keep it to yourself? Not even discuss it with Ginny?"

Mike nodded.

"I'm really worried that it may never work out between Vickie and me. We've spent the past five years apart, and we've seen very little of each other during that time. She seems to have no desire to pull up stakes in New York and come back to this area. I know she likes her job at NBC, but I'm not convinced that she really needs these night school classes in journalism that she keeps taking. It almost seems that it's a way for her to hold onto her apartment and her circle of grad school friends.

"She doesn't write every night the way she did when she first left for New York, and when we talk on the phone, I feel like we don't have as much in common or as strong a connection as we used to. She admits that we have a big problem facing us, and neither of us seems to have a clue as to what we can do about it. I can't help but recall how quickly Ronnie Myers and Wayne Miller broke up with Barbara Ann and Mary Pat Stevens after the twins left for school at Florida State."

"I'm glad I didn't have to walk in your shoes, Dawg," Mike said, using the old nickname he had hung on Doug their sophomore year. "When I went off to Charleston after high school to study automobile mechanics, and Ginny left to get her RN at the hospital in Bluefield, we never doubted for a minute that we were going to be married when we got back home. I'm sorry that the connection between you and Vickie seems to be changing."

"Thanks for saying that. When I think about what Vickie and I once had, and where we are today, it hurts. Just keep all of this to yourself."

"Sure. We'll just talk fishing the rest of the way. You know, I must have caught at least three bass to every one you pulled out this afternoon, same as always." Glancing over, he was glad to see that he had Doug smiling again.

When they drove up in front of Mike's house, lights poured out their welcome through every window. Ginny obviously had been waiting up for them to get back, coming out on the porch to wave. Doug watched Mike jog up the front steps and envelope his pregnant wife in his arms, then follow her into the house.

There was little traffic as Doug headed across town, and pulled into his customary parking space next to the building. He remained in the car for a few minutes after turning off the engine, reflecting upon how dark his apartment looked. Once inside, he went straight to the refrigerator, took out a quart of milk, a cheese sandwich wrapped in wax paper, and a stale doughnut, carrying them into the living room. Seated in front of the TV set with his meal on a folding metal tray, he watched network shows until the Jack Paar Show went off the air, then went to bed, but not to sleep.

CHAPTER 10

"Mr. Magino's here for his 3:00 meeting with you, Ed," Carolyn said, from his office doorway. "He's waiting in the conference room."

"Thanks, Carolyn," Ed replied, taking a folder containing an array of papers from his desk drawer and following her into the hallway. "He's right on time."

Ed shook hands with Dominic, settling across the conference table from him. "Let's go over these documents together. Then I'll ask Carolyn to come in and notarize our signatures. If we don't need to make any changes, we should be able to file the papers immediately, and we'll have you doing business as East Coast Transfer Company, Inc. before you know it."

The signing of the incorporation documents completed, Ed picked up the folder and was preparing to slide his chair back from the table when Dominic spoke up. "Mr. Housman, I really like the way you handled this matter for me. I'd like to start using you for other legal work. Right now, I'm holding a number of uncollectible bills that I submitted throughout last year to a wholesale food and beverage outfit in New Jersey called Universal Restaurant Supply Company. I want to start legal action and put some heat on them to settle up, so I can recover ten grand they still owe me. You think you could you handle that for me?"

"That's certainly something we could talk about, Mr. Magino. If you'll get all your records together, we can make an appointment to discuss the best plan of action to collect on that delinquent account."

Ed hesitated, then inquired, "If I may ask, how did you happen to pick an Eden Springs attorney like me, when there's at least one well qualified lawyer practicing right in Hinton?"

"I've heard good things about you for quite a while, Mr. Housman. You have a reputation for doing good work and charging reasonable fees. To me, it's worth the driving time to come over and work with someone I have confidence in."

Dominic left the office shortly afterward, and Ed resumed work, until he sensed the presence of someone close by. He saw Carolyn standing in the doorway as he glanced up. "What's on your mind?" he inquired.

"I'm not sure, Ed. There's something about that man that makes me uncomfortable. Maybe it's his New Jersey accent, or the way he looks with all that dark hair slicked straight back. I can't put my hand on it." Carolyn returned to her desk, and called back, "Forget what I said. It's probably just me. Maybe I've had one too many cups of coffee today."

*****

Dominic Magio had also consumed a prodigious amount of black coffee during the day and was sipping still more from a cardboard cup while barreling along at seventy miles an hour up the highway, hurrying to get home. He continuously scoped out the road ahead for signs of a radar speed trap, knowing that another conviction would cost him his license, but did not slow to the speed limit until he arrived at the outskirts of Hinton.

Dominic turned his car into a gravel parking lot completely surrounded by a gated chain link fence topped with barbed wire, and drove up next to the entrance of a large unpainted concrete block building with *Magino Trucking Company* painted in large black letters across the front. I've got to remember to get that sign repainted, he thought as he got out of the car and was greeted by the agitated barking of three German Shepherds chained to nearby barrels. He proceeded up the concrete steps two at a time to the front door and went straight to his office.

His brother-in-law Vinnie Vitale was waiting for him, seated at his desk, checking out the centerfold of a well-worn copy of *Playboy*. "How'd it go, Dom?"

"Better than good. I have that Eden Springs attorney, Housman, getting lined up to start handling stuff for us that the lawyer in town, Bill Patrick, wouldn't touch with a stick. It looks like we may be able to collect some of the money that's been owed to us for a while by our friend in Newark, and at the same time help Barker take care of that matter he's so obsessed with.

"But I have to tell you, I don't want to get much better acquainted with Housman. Sitting in his conference room today I could see that he's a decent guy. If he had any idea that trying to collect money from Angelo Vinciano is like pushing your face up against the muzzle of a pit bull, he'd drop me like a hot potato. You and I both know that Angelo hates lawyers worse than the devil hates holy water, ever since his first wife and her divorce attorney took him to the cleaners, and then disappeared together somewhere down in the Caribbean. But Housman hasn't wised-up to that. And what he doesn't know could come back and hurt him pretty bad."

Vinnie tucked the centerfold back into the magazine and set it down on the top of the desk, looking at Dominic with a grin. "I thought that was the whole idea, Dom. Isn't that how we collect the two grand from Barker?" Then a more serious look came across his face, and he added, "I hope this doesn't boomerang on us. You don't think Angelo would ever try to come after us for putting Housman on him, do you?"

"He's way too smart to try anything like that. The family up in New Jersey would come down on him hard if he started anything that threatened to screw up their operation. Carmine Nardelli runs the production plant over near Keystone, I've got the hauling covered from here in Hinton, and Angelo does the distribution out of Newark. It's been a smooth money-making machine ever since we started, until Angelo started getting greedy. The family would be all over us if this dispute ever headed to court and got in the newspapers, but Angelo knows he's in the wrong trying to stiff me out of the money he owes me, and I'm sure that he won't let it get that far."

"I hope you have the right reading on how he's going to take this legal action thing, Dom," Vinnie added, picking up the magazine again to take one last look at Miss March. "You'd better be sure you know what you're doing this time."

CHAPTER 11

Doug paused in the cool afternoon air as he approached the entrance of the Fresh Harvest Supermarket, reflecting upon how much the store had grown in the seven years since he had first worked there as a bag boy. He passed through the automatic sliding glass door, observing that the floor space had doubled and the number of cashier lanes had increased from one to four, since the store expansion a few years earlier. Three of the lines were busy, with customers standing behind full grocery carts waiting to be checked out. But one thing seemed to be the same. He could still pick up the same pleasing aroma of fresh produce and ground coffee that carried him back in time to his teenage years.

Ingrid Vicelli saw him enter and came over to greet him with a warm hug. "Doug, it's so nice to see you again. Every time I look at you, I can't get over how much you've grown up since you used to work here! How in the world are you doing today?"

Doug wrapped his arms around her and held her for a moment. In the days after he and Vickie had begun going steady, he and Ingrid had bonded. Maybe he was not as close to Ingrid as he was to his stepmother, Laura, but he felt closer to her than to any other woman of his parents' generation. "I'm doing great, Mama V. How about you? How's the boss?"

"Tony and I are both doing well, thanks, and so's the family. I spoke on the phone with Vickie a couple of nights ago, and we talked about you."

"That explains it. I felt my ears burning about that time."

"You got it all wrong, Doug. We were saying a lot of nice things about you. She asked me to give you her love." Then Ingrid laughed. "You were just pulling my leg, weren't you? You know that Vickie's still crazy over you."

"I sure hope so, Mama V."

Tony also had seen Doug enter the store, and he came over to greet him affectionately. "Grab an apron, son, and get to work. What am I paying you for?"

Doug shook hands with Tony, replying, "I assume you're planning to pay me the same half dollar an hour rate. You always wanted to pay me what I was worth, but I told you before that I wouldn't work for nothing."

"Nah- I'm going to do better than that by you, boy," Tony said, eyes twinkling. "I'm raising you to sixty cents an hour, right here on the spot."

Doug momentarily reflected that when he first starting to work for Tony at sixteen, he never dreamed the day would come when Tony would treat him as a peer, joking with him in such a friendly way.

"I picked up those duck eggs you wanted out at the Buchanan farm yesterday," Tony added. "You want to come with me and get them now?"

Doug followed Tony down the aisle, calling back to Ingrid, "See you later, Mama V. Don't take any wooden nickels." He could hear her laugh, and it seemed like an echo of Vickie's voice.

Tony instructed Doug as he handed over four duck eggs in a small brown paper bag, "Don't shake them around, don't wash them, and once you start the eggs to incubating, keep the temperature at 98 degrees. If you do all that, you should be in the Mallard business in 28 days. Oh yeah, you need to rotate the eggs several times a day, like their mama would."

Tony refused to take Doug's money, saying, "I always told you when you took Vickie out that you were responsible for keeping her safe. Now you've got my duck eggs, and the same thing goes for them. I expect to be invited over to see four ducklings around the middle of March."

He put his arm around Doug, slapping him warmly on the shoulder, and walked away, throwing his hand up in acknowledgment when Doug called out to him, "Thanks again, Tony."

Doug drove out to the home place on the hill later that evening and quietly opened the door, setting the cardboard box on the floor in the foyer. Then he walked into the living room where Lizzie was seated on the sofa between Ed and Laura, reading to them from her first grade primer. "Don't stop," he requested.

Lizzie was far too excited to remain seated, jumping up to run to him, bubbling over, "Did you bring me a surprise?"

"You know that your birthday doesn't come for another month, Squirt. But, yes, I brought you a surprise Stay right here and I'll bring it in." Doug retrieved the box, setting it on the floor for all to see.

"What is it?" Lizzie asked.

"It's your new duck factory," Doug replied. "You've been wanting pet ducks, but first you've got to make them. Here's the deal."

Doug showed Lizzie the duck egg incubator he had made, consisting of a ten watt light bulb with a thermostat regulator to maintain constant temperature. "You need to rotate each egg a quarter turn several times a day, and if you are a good duck factory operator, you'll have four little Mallards hatch on your birthday in exactly four weeks."

"Good Lord," Laura said in a low voice. "Oh well, at least there won't be any Lucilles running around in the yard."

Ed laughed, as they both remembered how he had teased her

earlier about the color of her auburn hair resembling that of his childhood pet Rhode Island Red hen, and Laura's remark coming back from their honeymoon: "I'm going to spend the rest of my life competing with the ghost of a chicken."

The four worked together situating the apparatus down in the basement. Then Doug plugged in the power cord, and Lizzie switched on the incubator light. "The production line is running, now," Doug commented. "Your ducks are on the way."

"I can't wait for them to hatch," Lizzie replied. "This is the best birthday I've ever had! I'm going to start picking out names tonight. Daddy, maybe I'll name one of them Lucille."

"Good choice," Ed said cheerfully.

"Good grief!" Laura echoed in resignation.

CHAPTER 12

A gray-haired gentleman wearing a dark overcoat entered the front door of Ed's office suite on Wednesday morning and spoke to Carolyn. "It's been a long time, Mrs. Carson. How've you been getting along lately?"

"Andrew Stover!" Carolyn exclaimed as hugged him. "Don't act so formal around me, when we've been on a first name basis since day one. You haven't changed a bit since the last time I saw you." She continued her friendly chat while taking his overcoat to hang in the coat closet. "Regarding your kind inquiry, I'm doing quite well, considering my age and mileage. Now tell me all about my favorite private eye."

Carolyn observed again, as she had the first time they met, that Andrew did not fit the mold of a Sam Spade or Mike Hammer, the stereotypical hard-drinking detective equally good with his wits, his fists, and the ladies. Andrew seemed more like a quiet, scholarly professor who might teach history at a small college.

Ed had overheard the conversation and came in to greet him. "Andrew, I appreciate your coming down here from Charleston today to help us out. Let's go back in the conference room, and maybe Carolyn will make coffee for the three of us."

Ed brought Andrew up to speed on the malpractice lawsuit

initiated by Dudley and Patsy Scaggs, including their allegation of brain damage to their young son resulting from Dr. Jannsen's mishandling of the baby. Andrew took copious notes on a pad.

"You say that the attorney, Lukins, and the doctor, Heinz, are both out of Beckley, Ed?" Andrew inquired. "That will certainly make it convenient for me."

After a thorough discussion, Andrew said, "I guess that about wraps things up for me. You've certainly given me plenty of information this morning to get started. You and I are together on one thing. There's a bigger player in this law suit than that alcoholic couple. Now it's up to me to find out who's pulling the strings."

Ed walked Andrew to the door. "I'll look forward to hearing from you when you find who and what is behind all of this. Good luck."

"Thanks, Ed. I'll take all the good luck I can get. I'll be in touch with you soon. Tell Carolyn I said goodbye, and thank her for the coffee."

The first thing Andrew did after leaving Ed's office was to drive past the edge of town to a run-down trailer park marked by a rusty metal sign lettered *Green Meadows Mobile Home Court*. He turned in just past the sign post and cruised slowly down the gravel road fronting a long row of trailers until he spotted the one with the tarnished brass numerals 37 mounted beside the front door. Slowing almost to a stop, he observed a middle-aged man wearing a worn canvas hunting jacket and faded jeans lethargically sprawled in a metal lawn chair on the plank deck out front. The man looked up at him with disinterest, then his head nodded toward his chest again, as if he were dozing.

Snooze on, Dudley, and dream about all that money you and the missus are planning to come into, Andrew thought. You obviously have enough antifreeze in you to keep from chilling down too badly in the sunshine today. But I sure hope Patsy remembers to drag you back inside before nightfall. I wouldn't want to have you freeze to death in the cold February air before I find out who's putting you and your wife up to all this mischief.

Andrew turned around in the alley and started toward Beckley, deep in thought. It's time now for me to start finding out more about that attorney, Samuel Lukins, and his sidekick, Dr. Emil Heinz. I bet that somewhere in one of their offices, there's a folder with confidential information, including the medical records of young Harley Scaggs. And somewhere in that same office, there's probably a disgruntled, hard-up employee who has his price for loaning that file to me.

The old gray fox had picked up the scent of his quarry, and with his nose close to the ground, he was now off and running. Andrew had known from day one that he'd never get rich working as a PI, but also knew that he'd never be happy in mundane job behind a desk. He lived for the thrill of the hunt.

CHAPTER 13

"Phone call for you, Mrs. Housman," the young receptionists called out to Laura, who was reviewing a new home listing with Freddie in her office. "The lady says she won't tie you up but just a minute." The identity of the caller was unmistakable to Laura as soon as she picked up the phone and heard the distinctive voice on the other end.

"Hello, Mrs. Housman. This is Gertrude Buchanan. Pardon me for bothering you this morning, but you asked me to let you know if Dan, Joe, or I saw any work starting over at the old Simpson and Henderson farms. This morning, they took a walk up to the top of cemetery hill, and they were able to make out a crew of men working with a bulldozer and a grader, excavating the big field near Stony Creek, the spot where Barker Mining was working before they abandoned their strip mine venture in 1952. I thought you'd want to know."

"Gertrude, thanks for calling to tell me. Freddie and I may drive out later this afternoon to see if we can tell more about what they're doing. We learned a few things since we were at your house, and if you have a few minutes, I'll be glad to share them with you.

"We've discovered that the farms are owned by a company

called Mountain Ventures. The owners have successfully petitioned the board of supervisors to rezone the property for industrial use in order to develop a regional landfill. They're now well on the way to signing a contract with the town to handle residential and commercial waste disposal on that property. I hate to bring you this bad news. If there's a bright side, it's that the landfill will be well away from Roseanna and your farm."

"It really distresses me to learn that, Mrs. Housman. I don't suppose there'd have been any way we could have stopped them even if we'd known earlier. But I'd certainly appreciate your sharing anything else you hear going forward."

"Grab your coat and let's take a drive," Laura called out to Freddie as she hung up the phone. "We've just got time to go out to the Simpson and Henderson farms before I have to be home when Lizzie gets in from school. I'll tell you what I just heard from Gertrude Buchanan on the way."

A short time later, Freddie slowed to pull the station wagon off the shoulder of the highway, just past the private road sign marking the gravel drive into the Mountain Vemtures property. Two conspicuous red *No Trespassing* signs had been tacked to fence posts since their last visit. "No sign of any southern hospitality around here, is there?" Freddie wryly joked.

"No, they definitely don't want anyone driving in to watch them work," Laura rejoined. "But we can see quite a bit from where we're parked. I'm quite curious as to why they're crowding Stony Creek with their excavation. You'd think that they'd want to start work further across the field in our direction, and avoid any potential problems with the stream. It overflows almost every year during the rainy season."

"I'm inclined to agree with you. I remember reports about Barker Mining doing some blasting around that spot back in '52, and people thinking that was what caused the muddy water to show up at the Eden Springs spa. A lot of folks think there must be an underground stream running under this property carrying water down to the mineral springs at the resort. I hope

Mountain Ventures doesn't create a big problem for the resort with this landfill. But we'd better get you back to town, Mrs. Housman, if you're going to beat Lizzie's school bus."

"Thanks for reminding me, Freddie. Now that you're making real estate sales your career, and showing an interest in buying into the Housman Real Estate business, I think it's high time for us to drop the formality, and for you to start calling me Laura."

"Yes, Ma'am. I mean, Laura," Freddie stammered, appreciation showing, as they started back to town.

Back at the office Laura made a quick phone call to Ed. "Honey, I'm just on the way out the door to meet Lizzie when she arrives home. Anything exciting going on for you today?"

"Nope, pretty much business as usual. I spent part of the morning with that new client I told you about, Dominic Magino, the one who owns a small trucking company in Hinton. He's trying to collect payment on a delinquent account with a wholesale food and beverage distribution outfit in New Jersey."

"I remember your telling me about him, and how he stood out from the native West Virginians around here. Did you get him squared away?"

"I've just sent the business owner a letter requesting that he contact me with his payment plan in order to avoid legal action. So you see, like I told you, nothing very exciting going on with me today."

"I'm glad to hear that, Ed. We're getting to the age where we don't need a whole lot of excitement. Anything you want to tell me before I hang up?"

"Yeah, sweetie, three things: first, leftovers are fine with me for dinner tonight. Second, please remind Lizzie when she gets home to turn those duck eggs again. And third, I love you more than the day we were married."

"I like the third one best, honey. See you tonight after work."

CHAPTER 14

"**Two of the eggs had** hatched when I got up this morning, and the other two hatched before I got home from school!" Lizzie exclaimed, while Ed, Laura, and Doug looked over her shoulder at the four fuzzy mallard ducklings. "How can I tell if they are girls or boys?"

The three adults glanced at each other with nonplussed looks, then Ed replied, "Liz, we may have to wait until they get a little older and develop feathers. Then we'll see that the female ducks have mottled feathers, while the male drakes have bright, contrasting colors."

"Or we could build two little bathrooms for them, one marked Boys and one marked Girls, and watch to see which room each one visits," Doug suggested. Laura quickly reached behind his back, out of Lizzie's sight, to pinch him on the arm.

"You're kidding me, aren't you, Doug?" Lizzie inquired, looking up at him and trying to read his face. Then she added indignantly, after realizing that he was pulling her leg, "Everyone knows that ducks don't use bathrooms. I'm just going to give them all girl names, and I'll change them if I have to. I hope they're all girls, anyway."

"Girls don't stir up near as much trouble as boys," Laura agreed. "What names have you picked out?"

"I changed the first one's name from Lucille to Lucy. The other three names I picked out are Lulu, Lena, and Lori."

"I sort of wish that one of them was still called Lucille," Ed remarked, with a covert look at Laura. "I really like the name Lucille a lot." Laura reached behind his back and grabbed a handful of flesh on the back of his arm, giving it a hard squeeze.

"Here's some starter rations for ducklings from the Purina Feed Store," Doug said, handing a small brown paper bag to his kid sister. "When Lucy, Lulu, Lena, and Lori get a little bigger, the four of us will take them over to the branch and let them take a swim. It'll be fun watching them go in the water for the first time, won't it, Squirt?"

JR took in everything that was going on, lying on his favorite rug in the corner. Occasionally, he wagged his tail to thump the floor when he sensed it was appropriate to join in on the hubbub. The four ducklings were an interesting new curiosity to him. He couldn't possibly have realized that they would soon imprint on him as their surrogate father, and that down the road he would have an entourage of four noisy, quacking, web-footed sons and daughters following him around wherever he went.

Doug happened to glance at his dad's dime store wall clock (which Laura had immediately relegated to the basement), and quickly said goodbye to his family, starting up the basement steps two at a time and out the door. He was out of breath when he rang the doorbell of the Rhodes home, greeted warmly at the door by Ginny, now only a week away from delivery and looking very pregnant. He reached out to gently hug her at arms length, unable to keep from showing mild astonishment at the striking change in her appearance since he had last seen her.

Ginny's irrepressible sense of humor kicked in, and she asked, "Notice anything different about me since we used to dance together at the canteen, Doug? Mike thinks that I may have swallowed a watermelon seed."

Mike walked up in time to catch the exchange, and added his two cents, "I think Gin may have swallowed a whole pack of Burpee Jumbo's. She looks quite motherly now, doesn't she?" He backed away as Ginny gave him her patented fisheye.

"Come inside, Doug, so I can sit down and take a load off my feet while we visit. Mike, why don't you make yourself useful for once. Please go in the kitchen and bring us some Cokes and that plate of Ritz crackers and some cheese spread."

One more week now, Ginny?" Doug inquired, already knowing the answer, as they settled comfortably into upholstered chairs in the warm living room.

"One more week, Doug. Please, Lord, let it be just one more week," Ginny said wearily. "The first few months of this pregnancy weren't bad except for the morning sickness, but now I'm ready to bring this child into the world, and not have to carry it around with an aching back twelve hours a day. I wish you men could enjoy the child bearing experience for nine months. It might make you think about having smaller families."

As Mike came into the room with the refreshments, Ginny changed the subject. "I bet you're looking forward to Vickie's visit in May, aren't you, Doug? She hasn't been back here since last summer. It's seems like she's been away even longer than that. We write each other every week, but letters aren't the same as visiting face to face."

Ginny abruptly stood, exclaiming, "Excuse me. I need to visit the ladies' room again." She made it as far as the hallway, then stopped to call out tersely, "Mike, I think my water just broke. We better call Dr. Jannsen now, and tell him I may be starting into labor early."

Mike jumped to his feet, "Dawg, do me a favor to save us some time. Call Dr. Jannsen and tell him I'm taking Ginny straight to the hospital to get her checked in. Then please get hold of both of our folks and let them know what's happening. Lock the house up for me, and follow us on over if you want to."

Looking back later, the three would all recall how quickly

things happened at that point. Mike and Ginny were out of the driveway and on the way to the hospital within minutes, with Mike pushing the speed limit the entire way. Dr. Jannsen and Doug arrived at the hospital shortly afterward, followed by Ginny's parents. An hour later, with Ginny settled in, Doug said goodbye.

If things went quickly at first, afterwards they slowed to a crawl for the young Rhodes family. It was twelve long hours from the time Ginny went into labor until she delivered. The birth process was not an easy one for her. A very subdued Mike told his wife afterward that one child was enough for him, and that he never wanted her to go through such an experience again.

When Doug got the anticipated call later, he heard his best friend exclaim, "Dawg, Ginny's OK. She had a pretty hard time delivering an eight pound boy, but they're both doing fine now. You'll be relieved to hear that he looks a lot like her. We named him Mike, Jr." But to family and friends, the newest member of the Rhodes family had already acquired a nickname, and would forever be known as Mikey.

Doug then called Vickie as Ginny had asked. He would have called her anyway, both to pass on the good news, and also to satisfy a compelling need to hear her voice again. "Vickie, Ginny's had the baby, and she's doing fine! It's a boy, and they named him Mike, Jr."

"I'm so glad to hear that good news! Ginny told me she's been terribly uncomfortable lately. Have you seen the baby?"

"Not yet, but I'm going over to the hospital in a little while. Anything you want me to pass on to the new parents?"

"Yeah, please tell Ginny I'll be calling to hear all about the new baby, and that a gift will be in the mail to her tomorrow. I was waiting to see whether to buy blue or pink. Let her know that I just can't wait to get home in May to see Mike, Jr."

"I hope there's someone else you can't wait to see. It's been a long time since we've been together."

"I'm looking forward to getting back home to be with my

family and friends in Eden Springs, Doug. But you're the one I've missed the most. You're the one I'm dying to see."

"Then why don't you just move back to Eden Springs? You could see me three-hundred and sixty-five days a year."

"I don't know, Doug. I still enjoy living and working in New York so much. But we'll talk about it when I get back. I still love you."

"Then I'll just keep taking it one day at a time, hoping you'll come back, Vickie. You owe it to me to make your decision soon, and not keep me waiting around forever."

"I realize it's not fair to you. I'll make up my mind and give you an answer before too much longer. I promise."

CHAPTER 15

Andrew Stover worked quickly with his Nikon SLR camera under the bright desktop light, snapping pictures of each document from the brown manila folder. Behind him, the skinny, white-haired building custodian shifted nervously from foot to foot, glancing anxiously toward the windows and door, still clutching five crisp new twenty dollar bills in his sweaty hand. He was obviously extremely anxious for the detective to depart the premises, so he could lock up again before Dr. Heinz might come back to attend to some sick child emergency. "Can't you move along a little faster?" he pleaded.

"I'm just about there," Andrew replied calmly, although his heart was also racing. "Just three more sheets to go." He knew that he would face criminal breaking and entering charges if apprehended in the doctor's office at midnight, rifling through private medical records. When the last sheet had been photographed, he returned the folder to the steel file cabinet opened earlier with his special key, then followed the custodian down the stairs to the back entrance of the building. The headlights remained off until he was halfway up the block and had started on the sixty mile drive from Beckley to his home in

Charleston. Rest well, Dr. Heinz, he thought. Your good works make you a credit to the medical profession.

He stopped for coffee at the all-night Oak Hill Diner, chatting with a pleasant middle-aged waitress over coffee and a slice of cherry pie, then proceeded on, arriving at his small home on the south side of town in the early hours of the morning. His wife called out to him as he quietly entered the house, "Andy, is that you? I'm glad you're finally in. I couldn't sleep for worrying about you." A few minutes later, he smiled as he heard her begin to snore lightly.

Andrew developed 8 x 10 glossy black and white prints in the basement darkroom beside his office the next morning. When the prints had dried, he inspected them, relieved to see that there was a sharp, detailed photo of every sheet in the folder borrowed from the doctor's file cabinet.

Andrew meticulously studied each print, using a large magnifying glass to discern all of the typewritten text, cursive notes, and reproduced photos. By the time the review was complete, it was apparent that he had underestimated his adversary, and possibly wasted a hundred dollars attempting to peek over the doctor's shoulder. The folder marked Harley Scaggs seemed to contain nothing that would compromise the Scaggs family's lawsuit against Dr. Jannsen if subpoenaed and presented in court.

The one possible exception was the photographically reproduced x-ray picture of a young child's skull. Upon close study, it appeared that there was a barely discernable hairline fracture on the right side of the child's forehead.

As he continued to stare at the picture, something about it began to register as out of the ordinary. There was something that differed from the x-ray picture of a similarly aged child that he had obtained during an automobile accident investigation six months earlier. Andrew retrieved the other picture from his file cabinet, placing it side by side on the table with the photo copy of the Scaggs child's skull. It struck him that the Scaggs child had much smaller eye openings and noticeably flatter cheekbones, and he noted these observations on his pad. Picking up the phone, he dialed a number recently penciled on his desk blotter.

Ed took the call on the first ring. "Andrew, I've been waiting to hear from you. Have you made any progress?" He listened for a few minutes, then called to Carolyn in the next room, "Please get on the other line and ask Dr. Jannsen to meet with Andrew Stover and me here at 5:30 this afternoon."

Andrew's report on the current condition of the Scaggs family held few surprises. Dudley was still performing small house painting jobs, working only enough hours to put meager food on the table and keep cheap liquor in the cabinet. The oldest son had dropped out of school at sixteen, and the fifteen-year old was following in his brother's footsteps. Neighbors reported that the state of young Harley's development appeared to be far behind what they felt was normal for a child his age.

Then Andrew spoke of his midnight visit to Dr. Heinz's office, displaying the collection of photographed documents from the Scaggs folder. He withdrew the x-ray photo of young Harley and placed it on the table side by side with his reference x-ray. "Compare the skulls of these two youngsters, and tell me if you see anything different about the Scaggs child."

The room was still as Arnold and Ed studied the two pictures, then Arnold broke the silence. "This anterior view of the Scaggs child's skull shows an early hairline fracture of the frontal bone that has since closed with new bone growth. It would appear that the child fell or was otherwise struck in the forehead on the right side. It does not appear to be the result of a major blow, or I would expect the fracture line to be larger." He hesitated, and then continued. "I'm seeing something else here that I've encountered before, although I've never read any published papers on the subject in JAMA.

"The Scaggs child shows deformity in the sphenoid bone, or the eye socket. The eye opening appears abnormally small. In addition, the zygomatic bone, or the cheekbone, appears abnormally flat. I've seen similar features in x-rays of two other young children who were born to mothers known to be heavy drinkers. Both children were diagnosed as mentally retarded due to some unknown hereditary condition. I've speculated privately that large amounts of alcohol in their mothers' systems during pregnancy was the principal cause of their birth defect."

Andrew replied excitedly, "I thought that a light bulb might come on when we reviewed these pictures together. I believe Dr. Jannsen just threw the switch."

"I believe he did," Ed agreed. "And another thought comes to mind. If young Harley had been dropped while Arnold was cleaning him up right after cutting and tying the umbilical cord, his skull fracture would have been at the back of the skull, not the front. I don't think that even the Scaggs family members have belly buttons on their backs."

"I think you just switched on another light," Andrew interjected, smiling at Ed. "Now how do you use this information to build a case for the defense?"

"I think we should prepare a three-pronged defense strategy. We need to discredit the plaintiffs's claims regarding the alleged accident, following with a valid explanation of the real cause of the child's mental condition.

"We start by demonstrating that the fracture to the frontal bone of the skull as shown by the x-ray is inconsistent with the allegation that the child was dropped against the metal bed frame while the doctor was wrapping up the umbilical cord procedure.

"Next, we bring in an expert witness to challenge the timing of the injury shown by the x-ray. Our expert should also be prepared to testify that a blow to the head causing only a slight fracture would be unlikely to cause permanent brain damage.

"Finally, we provide the real explanation for the child's retarded mental development, alcohol in the mother's bloodstream while she was carrying the child. Our expert witness should testify that a mother's heavy consumption of alcohol throughout pregnancy would be likely to damage the developing brain of a fetus, resulting in permanent mental impairment.

"We should also line up neighbors prepared to testify that Patsy was a chronic alcoholic during the time she was carrying Harley. Andrew, it would be extremely helpful if we could show that Patsy was not a heavy drinker when she was carrying her two older boys, Lonnie and Marvin. They both seem to have average intelligence, since they were able to stay in school until they were sixteen. Do you think you could you get that information for us?"

"I'll go to work on it, Ed. Then I'll start digging around to see if I can find out who's bankrolling the Scaggs family lawsuit and paying off Samuel Lukens and Dr. Heinz. I'm sure Lukins isn't investing his valuable time gambling entirely on a winning verdict and a percentage of the damages award."

"Can we all get back together here again within a few weeks and see how everything's coming together?" Ed asked.

Arnold nodded, and Andrew replied, "Let me know exactly when you want to reconvene. I'm sure that I'll have more to report by that time."

Ed walked Andrew and Arnold to the door, then turned back to his desk, suddenly remembering one other task that he had planned to complete that day. It was now been two weeks since he had contacted Universal Restaurant Supply Company by registered mail, asking for a payment plan to settle the delinquent account with his client. Having received no response to the earlier letter, he now drafted a much stronger one, giving a deadline of thirty days for receipt of the first of six equal monthly installment payments in order to avoid the certainty of a lawsuit.

Ed handed the document to Carolyn, requesting, "Would you see if you can get this typed for me to sign before closing time, and make a copy for Dominic. I would appreciate your dropping by the post office on your way home, and sending this letter by registered mail. Maybe we can expedite the collection of this debt by lighting a fire under Mr. Vinciano."

CHAPTER 16

"I appreciate both of you meeting me for lunch today," Preston Cline remarked, as he, Ed, and Sam Barry sat down in a booth near the back of the Rexall Drug Store. "Running a hardware store and serving as mayor of this town makes it hard for me to work everything in."

After the waitress had taken their orders and brought coffee, he continued. "I'd like to talk to you about the upcoming Cen Plus Ten celebration for the 110th birthday of the town of Eden Springs. We're only six months away from the event, and the town council is in high gear making preparations for activities to take place the last week of September. We're hoping to draw quite a few visitors from around the region.

"My wife Edna was talking with her sister Marlene, and they came up with a terrific idea. They want the culminating event for the weeklong celebration to be a reenactment of the Battle of Eden Springs out on the Buchanan farm near Roseanna. That skirmish took place in 1862, only thirteen years after the town was founded in 1849. Edna has learned that several battleground states are now well along in planning reenactments as part of their upcoming Civil War Centennial commemorations. She made a few phone calls, and found there are some Civil War reenactors who are willing to help us out with uniforms and other props. What do you think of the idea so far?"

"I think I know where you're heading with this discussion," Sam replied. "You're about to ask Ed and me to enlist, aren't you?"

"Close, but no cigar. I'm asking you and Ed to take over as co-chairmen of the event. You can flip a coin to see who gets the role of Confederate Captain Jason Taylor Early. The other of you goes into the service as Union Major Horace Dunford. Whoever gets the role of Captain Taylor gets to perform the dramatic death scene."

Ed glanced at Sam in resignation, remarking, "I know if we turn down the job, we'll never be able to get any more help with our home repair projects at Cline Hardware. I guess I'm in if you are, Sam, just as long as I get the Rebel part."

"Then I'll go along and take the commission in the Union army for this event. But I'm never coming to lunch with Pres again as long as he's town mayor and still married to Edna. If he was going to snooker us like this, he could at least have taken us to the Eden Springs Resort for a fine meal, instead of getting us the dollar blue plate lunch special here at the drug store."

"Thanks for accepting the co-chair positions, both of you," Preston responded. "I hate to see two grown men cry, so I'm going to ask that cute little blonde waitress to bring each of you a piece of her cherry pie for dessert."

Sam glanced sideways at Ed and winked, "Mayor Cline has always been a big spender."

As the three said their goodbyes, Preston added, "I'll have Edna mail both of you a list of her Civil War reenactment contacts, so you can get started with your preparations. You've got some work ahead of you, particularly lining up your military recruits."

With Preston out of earshot, Sam looked helplessly at Ed, asking plaintively, "Housman, what have we just gotten ourselves into? I'm a vet and should know better. You learn in the army, never volunteer for anything."

Ed, however, was starting to have a different take on things. Driving to the courthouse afterward, he felt more enthusiastic about the prospect of commanding a company of Rebel troops. He imagined how Laura and Lizzie would feel watching him and the other men in town show their gallantry in battle. He felt even better when he spotted Jack Bradford, District Attorney, and three other friends taking a smoke break outside the building. It took him only ten minutes to enlist all four into the CSA Army.

"Do we each get issued a horse?" Jack asked facetiously.

"Nope, we're going to be like Stonewall Jackson's foot cavalry. But most of you will get to fire a musket several times. And a lot of pretty southern belles in hoop skirts will be seated nearby, holding mint juleps, checking y'all out and noticing how dashing you look in your gray uniforms."

"I guess we'll march off into battle with you, Ed," Jack replied, "but it's a good you got us to sign up before Sam tried to recruit us. In the courtroom or on the battlefield, we'd all prefer to be on the winning side."

"Better check your history book again. Remember that in the Battle of Eden Springs, there weren't any winners." As Ed entered the courthouse, he turned and called back, "Welcome to E Company. I'm naming it after Captain Jason Taylor Early. Jack, if you really want to help win the war, maybe you could start with that Cessna you keep out at the airfield east of town, and organize a Confederate Air Force."

He could just make out Jack's parting remarks before the door closed. "Yeah, I could water balloon the hell out of Sam and his Yanks. By the way, Housman, you better not have been lying about all the pretty southern belles who'll be holding mint juleps to refresh us when the fighting's over."

CHAPTER 17

Ed and Arnold Jannsen drove to Charlottesville on Monday afternoon, parking in the visitors lot beside the University of Virginia Pediatric Medicine Building on Jefferson Park Avenue. "I guess things look quite different than when you were here getting your MD degree in 1908," Ed remarked, glancing at his friend.

"If I hadn't been back for class reunions over the years, I probably wouldn't be able to recognize the place," Arnold replied. "Some of the old academic buildings from my era have been torn down, and a lot of these impressive new buildings weren't even standing when I was here. Fortunately, the grounds of Thomas Jefferson's Academical Village have been preserved, which is one thing that makes this university so unique."

Together they entered the building and took the elevator to the second floor, making their way to Room 203, where Dr. Eugene Rosenthal, Professor Emeritus of Pediatric Medicine, was waiting for them. Arnold shook hands with Eugene, then introduced the tall, gray haired pediatric surgeon to Ed, who was surprised by the strength of the older man's grip. "Gene and I have been friends for many years," Arnold commented to Ed, as the three took seats around a small conference table. "For quite a few years we would get together at the UVA-Duke football games. We cheered the Wahoos on to many victories, didn't we?"

"I think we may have lost a few to the Blue Devils over the years, Arnold, but we won't go there today," Gene laughed.

The three then settled down to business. Ed explained the lawsuit which had been filed against Arnold, and the facts which had been compiled to date in preparation for his defense, including information about the Scaggs family. He laid the x-ray showing the anterior view of the Scaggs child's skull on the conference table in front of Gene, but as he and Arnold had discussed in the car, purposefully withheld any opinions regarding the moderate nature of the hairline fracture or the abnormal features. Arnold wanted no information to be provided which might interfere with an independent expert opinion from his associate.

Gene picked up the photo and studied it for several minutes, then glanced up and remarked, "This x-ray is dated Dec. 5, 1958. You've told me that this male child was born June 1, 1957, which makes him about eighteen-months old at the time this view of his skull was filmed." He took a final look and laid the photo back on the table. "You want me to give you my opinion regarding this child's injury, as far as I can tell from this one picture?" .

"This child does not appear to have experienced a severe cranial injury as far as I can tell. The hairline fracture seems to have occurred quite some time prior to the date of the x-ray, based on the growth of new bone since the break. I can't rule out that the fracture occurred immediately after birth, although I would be quite surprised to find out that it did. I occasionally see these types of mild skull fractures on toddlers who have begun to walk and have tumbled forward, striking their heads against a hard, unyielding object like an iron stove or a brick fireplace. As you know, most children walk between nine and fifteen months, and unless there are problems, almost all walk by eighteen months. Since you have told me this child is not developing normally, I would doubt that he fell and sustained this injury. I would speculate that he was injured by some occurrence such as slipping from a parent's arms and striking his head against a hard surface. It's uncommon to see permanent brain injury result from such a blow.

"But there is something else obviously wrong with this child, and I'm sure you are already aware of it, Arnold. I suspect you didn't comment to me before now because you wanted an independent professional observation. This child shows a congenital deformity, exhibited by undersize openings for the eyes, and abnormally flat cheek bones. If you'll excuse me for a few minutes, I'll show you x-rays that I have on file of several other children with similar deformities."

Gene disappeared into the next room, and returned shortly carrying three x-ray films of children's skulls. He arranged them on the table next to the one of Harley Scaggs. All exhibited similar abnormal bone structure.

"What do you think we found to be the one significant common denominator for these three children?" he asked.

Arnold looked directly at him and answered, "Alcoholic mothers."

"Bingo! These children were all exposed to sustained high levels of alcohol in the mother's bloodstream during the fetal stage. And I'm 90% certain that the Scaggs child was, too. I believe that Harley Scaggs' central nervous system was severely damaged by alcohol, not by physical trauma to his head."

"Would you act as an expert witness for the defense and testify on behalf of Arnold when this malpractice suit goes to trial?" Ed asked.

"I certainly will. Malicious and fraudulent law suits against medical professionals really frost me. And I feel even stronger when it's an old friend of mine being attacked."

Arnold commented to Ed as they were leaving Charlottesville, "I feel better now than I have since I was served with the lawsuit. I'm beginning to think that we'll prevail when we go to trial."

"Our meeting with your friend went even better than I'd hoped it would, and right now, I'm starting to feel the same sort of confidence. But this isn't the time for us to let up for a moment. Let's take this opportunity to roll the rock over and see what kind of slimy creatures come crawling out in the light. We should be able to identify the people who are pulling the strings and expose their motive for attacking you. I'd like to be able to turn things around, and put the plaintiffs in the position of defending themselves against criminal charges before we're through."

"I can see where your competitive instincts serve you well in the field of law, Ed. As a doctor, I'm committed to providing medical care for everyone regardless of merit. But there's a need in this world for people like you who are equally committed to assuring that justice is done."

CHAPTER 18

Vinnie Vitale pulled up to the front gate at Magino Trucking Company on Friday morning long before daylight. He was feeling a nagging need for that first morning cup of black coffee to shake off the cobwebs and jolt him awake, while realizing that the old brown-stained GE percolator in the office would not be fired up for a while. Java would have to wait. There was too much that had to be done right away.

Five of the company drivers needed to be on the road by 6:00, and he wanted to look over the manifest for each truck to be sure it was filled out to his liking, before they were dispatched. The manifests were a necessary part of the company's accounting records, purporting to be accurate, current, and complete statements of each truck's cargo. Vinnie knew that in actuality the itemized list of contents on the clipboards differed significantly from what was actually stowed on board, in or out of sight. After all, that was how the Magino Trucking Company (soon to become East Coast Transfer Company, Inc.) made most of its money.

Vinnie pulled out his keys to open the padlock on the gate, and the silvery cobwebs of sleep instantly disappeared, as he realized that there had been visitors since he and Dominic had left the previous evening. He saw where the stainless steel shackle of the padlock had been cut with bolt cutters, and the lock left hanging on the gate hasp like a Christmas tree decoration. Vinnie called out loudly to the three German shepherds, "Rocky! Boomer! Taz! Get over here now!" But there was no response from the canine night watchmen. Vinnie could not know that on the other side of the building, all three were sprawled on the ground, sleeping off a heavy dose of barbiturate seasoning contained in an earlier serving of delicious ground beef patties.

Vinnie had a dilemma. The only available phone was inside the building, so he could not contact Dominic through his wife at home, or at over at his girlfriend's house, whichever place he had slept last night. There was no way he was about to drive over to the Hinton Police Department and ask for help. The last thing he and Dom needed was a local policeman poking around their building and looking inside the trucks.

Since there was no sign of a suspicious vehicle in sight, and no evidence that an intruder might still be on the property, Vinnie made a strategic decision. He went back to his car and pulled the sawed-off Louisville Slugger from under the front seat with his right hand, feeling the adrenaline rush he had experienced many times before a barroom confrontation.

He made his way across the parking lot toward the entrance, tapping the bat against his open left hand, like a Roman soldier striking his sword against his shield while approaching the enemy, with the goal of both frightening his adversary and reinforcing his own courage. Although he could handle himself in a brawl against almost anyone his size, his heart was pounding a mile a minute as he unlocked the front door and stepped inside, holding the bat ready to strike.

The interior of the building was as dark as a coal mine, and just as still. Vinnie stood for a moment, running his left hand along the wall next to the door, probing for the light switch. His hand located the electric conduit, which he followed downward to the attached switch box, and then to the switch mechanism on the cover. Another fraction of a second, and he would have flipped it to flood the room with light. But time ran out on him when a heavy work sock full of dimes struck him across the temple, causing him to crumple to the floor like a sledge-hammered steer in a slaughter house.

Vinnie could hear the sound of two men talking when he first regained consciousness, but the world around him was completely black. His arms and legs were almost completely immobile, and he could not see or speak. What he could not see was the half roll of duct tape encasing his extremities, and the two wide strips across his face, one over his eyes and the other across his mouth. Straining his ears to make out the conversation between two men, he heard one of them say, "Looks like he's starting to come around now."

"Nod your head, yes or no, if you understand what I'm telling you," one of them spit out, obviously now talking to him. Vinnie nodded yes, and instantly felt splitting pain as he moved his head.

"You don't want to play hardball with us anymore. See how easy we got to you? It's just as simple for us to get to any outsiders you're thinking about bringing in to help you get back at us. You listening to me carefully? You understand what I'm saying?" Vinnie again responded affirmatively. He was already starting to think of payback, but that would have to wait.

"You pass along to your buddy Magino what I just told you. Tell him not to act stupid again. Next time we don't go so easy with you. You got that?" Vinnie nodded again.

"There better not be no next time," the other man growled, giving Vinnie a hard kick in the gut for emphasis.

Vinnie heard the door slam and hoped the two men were gone, but he could do little except lie on the floor and wait until Dom or one of the drivers showed up for work.

Although it seemed like an eternity, it was only a half hour later when the first driver, Skeeter Ratliffe, arrived to take his truck out on the route to Baltimore. When he stepped through the door and saw Vinnie trussed up on the floor, he panicked and bolted back outside. Then, after summoning up enough nerve to re-enter, he leaned over and pulled the tape off of Vinnie's mouth and eyes, removing most of Vinnie's eyebrows and eyelashes in the process. "What happened?" Skeeter inquired excitedly.

"Nothing you need to get involved in. Dom and me will handle this situation. Just cut this damn tape off my arms and legs."

Dominic drove in from his girl friend's house an hour later and waited with Vinnie until the last of the five trucks had pulled out through the gate, heading up the highway.

"You gonna be OK?" Dom asked. "You really look like crap without no eyebrows or eyelashes. You remind me of some kinda weirdo creep that just came up out of a subway tunnel."

"Yeah, I'm gonna be OK," Vinnie answered. "Thanks for your kind flattery. Maybe I'll borrow a Maybelline eyebrow pencil and some Magic Mascara from my girl friend Loretta and draw me some eyebrows and eyelashes back on, if that's what it takes to please you. But I swear, I've never been hit that hard before," he muttered, gently exploring the goose egg on his forehead. "It was Angelo's boys, wasn't it? They told me we don't want to be stupid and play hardball with them again."

"No doubt about it," Dom replied. "Angie was behind this. He sent his first installment payment to Housman right on time yesterday morning. It was all in cash: seventeen crisp one-hundred dollar bills rubber-banded together, in a cardboard box sent by registered mail. Guess what else was inside?"

"I don't have a clue. My head still hurts too bad to be worrying about bullshit like that."

Dominic hesitated, then looked at Vinnie with a faint smile. "Housman said there was a framed photo of his wife and daughter, taken just a few weeks ago, as the kid was getting off the school bus. The glass in the picture frame was busted like something had hit it right in the center. Our new attorney wants to know just what in the hell is going on."

"What do we do now?" Vinnie asked, carefully rubbing his chest, checking for cracked ribs.

"We don't have to do nothing. Angie's paying me back the money he owes me now. His boys roughed you up a little bit, but after you draw some eyebrows back on, you'll be as good as new. I don't see why we have to do nothing."

"We don't always see eye to eye on things, Dom," Vinnie replied, gingerly rubbing the goose egg again. "Doing nothing just don't seem to cut it for me right now."

CHAPTER 19

"**It didn't take your dad** long to draft all three of us into the Confederate Army," Mike commented to Doug, as the long-time friends entered the front door of the Thimbles and Thread custom apparel shop on Saturday morning. "These uniforms are going to cost us a lot more than we privates are going to be issued for our uniform allowance. I think we may be looking at close to sixty bucks each by the time we buy the whole works."

"Who cares?" Freddie cracked. "The paymaster's going to pay us in Confederate money anyway, and there aren't too many places around here that'll still take that stuff. But maybe these ladies will."

Abigail Garrett overheard their conversation, approaching them with a big smile. "I take it that you're three more of Ed Housman's recruits. So far there's been about the same number of Rebs and Yanks coming in here to get fitted. I bet you're Ed's son Doug, and his friends, Mike Rhodes and Freddie Palmer. He told me that you three would be dropping by this morning to see about getting your uniforms made."

Abigail, Agnes, and Anne were the three matronly sisters who owned and operated the shop. All were equally proficient as seamstresses and tailors, capable of altering garments or making them from scratch to custom fit their patrons. As Abigail talked to the three young men, her sisters continued their work on busily humming sewing machines in the next room, while curiously watching the activity through the open doorway.

"We're making the uniforms in only three sizes: medium, large, and extra large," Abigail continued. "I think that two of you boys will need a large," she said, addressing Doug and Mike. "And you will definitely need the biggest size we make," she added, turning to Freddie.

"It's all muscle, Mrs. Garrett," Freddie replied. "I work out a lot." Doug and Mike rolled their eyes, while Abigail smiled pleasantly, and Agnes and Anne giggled quietly.

"Here's a picture of the uniform," she commented, holding up a sketch of a Civil War veteran in baggy gray wool trousers and a jacket with a single row of brass buttons. The only other clothing item you'll need is a soldier's cap and a belt, and I can order both of them for you. Everything together will come to fifty dollars, so it's not quite as bad as I heard you guess when you came into the shop. But we will insist on being paid in Union currency, and not your Confederate money."

Agnes and Anne laughed aloud. They had probably heard Abigail deliver that line twenty times before in the last few weeks, but the three sisters had always been a good audience for each other's jokes, and the two on the sewing machines were holding up their end of the deal again today while their sister was on stage.

"Do you want us to pay you now?" Doug inquired, reaching for his billfold.

"That won't be necessary. We'll collect the payments from you when you pick up your uniforms, which should be ready soon. And remember, we'll expect you to wave gallantly to the three of us, before you go off to reenact the Battle of Eden Springs."

Doug, Mike, and Freddie walked from the shop down to the Cricket Diner beside the theater, and parked on three adjacent stools to have their usual nutritious lunch, which consisted of a large hot dog and a fountain Dr. Pepper.

"I learned something yesterday you two may not have heard yet," Freddie commented, spooning a line of mustard down his foot-long. "Our local NBC affiliate radio station, WESP, has gotten a license to begin television broadcasting on Channel 8. They've obtained approval to erect a tower on the high end of Pine Ridge, and they expect their signal to reach viewers all across the southwest part of the state, including Beckley, Princeton, and Bluefield- maybe even Charleston."

Doug put down his drink, and stared at Freddie. "Are you serious? Where'd you hear something like that?"

"I talked to Charlie Goins, the station manager, at our Kiwanis Club meeting Thursday. You'll probably be reading about it in the paper anytime now. Charlie said they hope to start transmitting a test pattern around the first of August, and be on the air with network and local programming a couple of weeks later."

"Do you think they'll be hiring a lot of new people to staff up for television? All they have now is a small radio broadcast operation."

"I would think so, Dawg. It's going to be an entirely separate operation from their radio station. Why? Are you looking to get away from Power Generation Controls? Think you might be the next Edward R. Murrow?"

"Nope. I don't see me becoming a famous news commentator. The thought just crossed my mind that there might be a job coming open that might interest Vickie."

"You really think so, Dawg?" Mike inquired. "Do you really think that some kind of TV station job out here in the boondocks would interest her after she's had a taste of working at NBC Headquarters at Rockefeller Center in New York?"

"I can't answer that, Mike, but she's coming here to visit after her night school class at Columbia wraps up next week. I hope she might have enough interest to talk to Charlie Goins.

Work isn't everything. Vickie's got a close-knit family and lots of friends here, not to mention a boyfriend who's been patiently waiting around for a long time for her to decide what she wants to do with her life."

"Good point, Dawg," Freddie chimed in, trying to lighten up what was rapidly becoming a serious discussion. "Maybe those Garrett ladies can put your Confederate uniform on the front burner, so it'll be ready for you to wear when you meet Vickie's plane. It would be like Ashley Wilkes coming together with Melanie Hamilton in *Gone with the Wind*, right there on the tarmac in the Charleston airport. After she sees what a gallant military figure you cut, no way she'll 'evah go back up nawth' with those damn Yankees again."

Doug and Mike both laughed. "We're never going to be able to carry on a conversation that makes a lick of sense as long as Frederick Palmer is around, are we?" Mike commented to Doug.

"Yeah, Freddie and you are like Abbott and Costello. I'd have to say, once a comedian, always a comedian," Doug agreed, putting an arm around each of his two best friends. But in the back of his mind, he was still thinking about the television station coming to town, and about a much missed girlfriend four-hundred miles away.

CHAPTER 20

"**I think this is a** good time for us to be getting back together," Ed said to Andrew Stover, as the private investigator joined Arnold Jannsen and him in his conference room. "I don't feel comfortable in discussing over the phone some of the things that we've discovered. Arnold, why don't you start things off by telling Andrew what we learned from Dr. Rosenthal at UVA two weeks ago?"

Arnold summarized his friend's expert opinion that the abnormal features of the Scaggs child's skull did indeed indicate fetal alcohol damage as the most likely cause of mental impairment. "Gene's prepared to provide expert testimony, including corroborative evidence from his medical research activity," Arnold concluded. "And one other thing: Gene agrees with me that the severity of the hairline fracture shown on the x-ray does not indicate a cranial injury severe enough to cause permanent brain damage. He's prepared to offer that opinion at trial also."

"Your turn now, Andy," Ed continued. "What have you uncovered since our last meeting?"

"It will be hard to top Arnold's report," Andrew observed, "but I have some valuable information that you asked me to go after. We wanted a timeline on when Dudley and Patsy became alcoholics, and here it is. Dudley has been drinking heavily since he dropped out of high school when he turned sixteen. Patsy didn't touch the stuff until Christmas in 1955, when she was driving her twin sister Emma home from work, hit a patch of black ice, and skidded into a tree. Her sister was killed, and Patsy was emotionally devastated. She started hitting the bottle then and never quit. It seems to corroborate our theory that the older two sons are normal because they weren't exposed to alcohol during pregnancy like their younger brother Harley."

"It's hard to celebrate after hearing something that tragic," Ed replied quietly. "But I think that puts a key part of our defense strategy in place. Do we have neighbors or friends of the Scaggs that will corroborate Patsy's problem with alcohol from the time of her accident until now?"

"Got that base covered," Andrew replied. "There's an elderly couple, Rupert and Deloris Conner, living in the trailer next to the Scaggs, who've known the family since moving into the trailer park in 1950. The Conners seem to be good folks. They've agreed to testify if we need them, and both would appear to make credible witnesses."

"Excellent! I'll see that they're subpoenaed. Anything else you have to tell us?" Ed inquired.

"Yes. We wanted to discover who's bankrolling the plaintiff's legal team. I did some snooping around and found out that the Beckley attorney, Samuel Lukins, cuts checks to his employees at First City Bank in town. In my business, you try to make friends and help people out wherever you can, because you never know when you'll need them. Anyway, there's a high level employee at the bank that I helped to investigate an unfaithful wife situation, pro bono. I called in the favor and learned that two large cash deposits were made to Lukins' savings account within the last six months. The deposits happened to be two months apart. That still doesn't tell us a whole lot, does it?

"But I think someone may have gotten careless and slipped

up after that. A third deposit for exactly the same amount was made after another two months went by. This time the deposit wasn't cash. It was a check from Copperfield Enterprises right in Beckley, signed by William P. Thorpe, Jr. Does that name mean anything to you?"

Ed and Arnold looked at each other, and replied almost simultaneously, "Robert Barker!"

Andrew looked at them quizzically. "Who's he?"

"A psychotic man who's apparently still trying to get back at Arnold and me seven years after we denied him a strip mine north of town. I don't think he'll give up trying to get even with us while there's life in his body. Now we know who we're up against."

"Do you want me to keep digging around and trying to find out more about Barker's involvement?"

"Most definitely. See if you can come up with a credible witness and concrete evidence linking Thorpe and Barker to this case. That could turn things around one-hundred and eighty degrees. If we can prove that this is a malicious lawsuit deliberately initiated to destroy Arnold's reputation, we'll put both of them in the hot seat. We'll have them facing both criminal charges, and a civil suit for defamation of character. The thought of taking Barker to the cleaners makes my mouth water. Arnold, you could endow a few Jannsen scholarships at your alma mater in Charlottesville to make up for what you've gone through."

"Where are we now concerning the trial, Ed?" Arnold inquired. "Do you know if a date's been set?"

"We're now only six weeks away. It's scheduled to start on July 20th in US District Court with Judge Winston Averhart presiding. I plan to start taking depositions the first week of June. The trial will probably drag out for the better part of a week. With the developments we've just gone over, I'm getting more and more optimistic about the outcome."

"Give me a little more time to see what else I can uncover," Andrew asked, as the meeting concluded.

"Just be careful, and watch your back, Andrew," Ed warned. "Barker and Thorpe sent their goons after us seven years ago. Two of them are now serving life terms in Moundsville for trying to take me out in a car wreck, and later attempting to trap us in a house fire. Barker plays for keeps."

"I appreciate your warning me, Ed. Unfortunately, in my profession, you encounter psychopaths like that from time to time. That's why I carry a .38 snub nose strapped to my ankle under this suit, and sleep with a loaded .357 magnum in the drawer of my nightstand. Rest assured, I can take care of myself."

CHAPTER 21

"**Thanks for giving up your** Saturday morning and going with me," Doug called out as Freddie came down the steps of Owen's Boarding House and out to the car. "Did Mrs. Owens put out her usual big breakfast spread for you today?"

"You better believe it," Freddie replied. "Bacon, eggs, waffles, the works. Meals are the big reason I stay here. I think Nell's a better cook than my mom." Then he reached across the back of the seat to give JR a pat on the head. "Why do you need me to help take your pooch to the vet this morning? He looks fine to me."

"I just thought I might need another set of hands. JR has a cyst on his back, and I thought the vet might want to take it off today while we're there."

"I haven't been over to the Eden Springs Animal Hospital since the last time I took my cat Minnie there a couple of years ago," Freddie commented. "How's ol' Doc Rollins getting along?"

"He stays pretty busy. He just recently brought in a new vet to work with him, a University of Georgia Vet School grad."

"Great. I'll probably be able to sell the new guy a house while we're there," Freddie replied. "I'll just tell him I've always been a big University of Georgia football fan. Go Dogs!"

"How about taking the leash for JR while I check in," Doug asked as they entered the waiting room. Stopping at the front desk, he told the young girl behind the counter, "I've brought my dog JR in today to have Dr. Nelson check out a cyst on his back."

Freddie was busy watching a lop eared rabbit hop around inside its cage when Dr. Nelson entered the room behind him. She bent over to rub JR's head, speaking in a soft drawl, "Good morning, JR. How's my favorite patient today?" The dog looked up at her with soulful brown eyes and wagged his tail.

Freddie spun around at the sound of an unfamiliar female voice with a strong southern accent and found himself face to face with a strikingly pretty young brunette in a white lab coat.

Doug hesitated for a moment, enjoying the surprised look on Freddie's face, before greeting Marilyn and making the introduction. "Dr. Nelson, I'd like for you to meet my friend, Freddie Palmer. He came with me this morning to help handle JR. Freddie's in the real estate business. He mentioned on the way over here that after you finish examining JR, he'd like to sell you a house."

Doug observed that the normally quick-witted, wisecracking Freddie Palmer was suddenly very red-faced and at a total loss for words. "While he's getting his sales presentation together, I have JR here this morning so that you can check out a cyst on his back."

Marilyn could read Freddie's obvious discomfort. She quickly picked up on the fact that Doug had set him up and went along with the gag. "I'm glad to meet you, Mr. Palmer. What kind of house did you have in mind to sell me this morning? Maybe a mysterious old Victorian mansion with a widow's walk on the roof? Or possibly an affordable cozy little gingerbread cottage with flower boxes under the windows and a white picket fence in front?"

Fortunately for Freddie, nature had blessed him with a high degree of common sense and a quick wit. He was never behind the pitch again after the first swing, and he staged his usual fast comeback. "Having gotten to know you now, I believe the home that would best suit your needs and tastes would be a Georgia-style antebellum mansion situated in a grove of magnolias. I'll have to check my listings, but I believe I have the perfect place for you."

Amused and impressed by Freddie's fast recovery, Marilyn laughed. "I think we better take JR back to the examining room now, and take a look at that cyst. I don't think he likes having to wait around while we conduct our real estate transaction."

With JR standing on the white enamel table under a bright light, Marilyn conducted a thorough inspection, concluding, "Mr. Housman, I don't think the cyst is malignant. It appears to be a simple lipoma which I could remove today, but I question that it's necessary to excise it unless it becomes larger and starts to cause a problem, particularly in light of JR's age. Let's just continue to watch it a little longer before we put this fellow through a surgical procedure."

"I'd prefer to have you call me Doug instead of Mr. Housman, if you will, please. Being called mister makes me feel really old. I just wanted to be sure that JR doesn't have something that could turn out to be serious. Now that I know the growth isn't cancerous, your recommendation to forego surgery makes a lot of sense to me. I don't think he's looking for any alterations to his hide that aren't absolutely necessary."

As Doug and Freddie prepared to leave, Freddie remarked, "Nice to meet you today, Dr. Nelson. I'll go to work now and start keeping an eye out for that perfect home."

'Thanks, Freddie. Nice meeting you, too. Just let me know if you can find a queen's palace that I can purchase on a commoner's budget."

Doug had put JR in the back seat of the car, ready to head home, when Freddie commented, "Marilyn isn't wearing an engagement ring or a wedding band, but you'd already noticed that, hadn't you?"

"Yep, I had noticed that when I was here earlier to get JR's shots and saw her for the first time. She's an attractive lady, don't you think?"

"You brought me out here this morning just so I could meet her, didn't you? This whole thing was a set-up. You didn't need any help from me with JR."

Doug smiled, replying, "Now what would make you think something like that? You never know when you'll need an extra set of hands, taking a dog to the vet."

"Wait on me just a second," Freddie exclaimed, as he got out of the car and strode back over toward the animal hospital entrance. He returned in a few minutes, smiling and holding up a small piece of paper with a number scrawled on it. "I got her phone number," he said proudly.

"How'd you do that?" Doug inquired with genuine curiosity.

"I told her my cat Minnie seemed to be stiff and lethargic, and I thought it might be something serious. I said that I might need to get in touch with her about Minnie's condition after her normal working hours."

"You told her what?" Doug exclaimed incredulously. "Your cat's been dead for two years! She's buried in the flower bed out behind your folks' house!"

"I told Dr. Nelson that Minnie seemed to be stiff and lethargic, but I never said whether she was alive or dead," Freddie replied, grinning ear to ear. "I think that Dr. Nelson's gorgeous, and she seems to have a great sense of humor. I'm going to ask her out."

He continued more seriously, "You know, I haven't dated anyone around here but a couple of times since Shirley Martin sent me that Dear John letter right before I dropped out at Marshall. You have no idea what it's like not having a special girl."

"I may know a lot more about how that feels than you think," Doug confided. "Being over four-hundred miles away from your girlfriend for five years is a little like not having one at all."

His spirits rising, he added, "Yeah, I did set you up by bringing you with me this morning. I was really impressed by Marilyn the first time I met her. I hope that something works out between you and the new vet. Let me know how she does treating Minnie's condition. The last patient who recovered from something like that was named Lazarus."

CHAPTER 22

Freddie wasted no time in following up on his plan, and later that day, he dug out the scrap of paper from his billfold and dialed Marilyn's number. When he heard a young woman answer, "Dr. Nelson speaking," he launched his pitch.

"Dr. Nelson, this is Freddie Palmer. I apologize for bothering you at home this evening, but thought I ought to check with you about another problem my cat's having. Could you spare a few minutes to talk with me?"

"I don't know how much help I can give you over the phone with an animal I've never examined, but I'll try," Marilyn replied. "What seems to be the problem with Minnie now?"

"Minnie's not eating her Friskies. It used to be her favorite food, but she doesn't seem to have an appetite any more."

"Freddie, I'm afraid that this could be something serious. Better bring your cat over to the clinic Monday morning, and I'll take a good look at her. How old is Minnie?"

"I got her as a kitten back in 1949, so I guess she'd be about ten years old now."

"Well, she's getting a few years on her. You definitely need to bring her in, so I can give her a good checkup, before I start trying to guess what's ailing her. Anything else I can help you with this evening?"

"Yes, ma'am. I was wondering if I could drive you around the area tomorrow afternoon and show you houses in some of the nicer neighborhoods. I promise that this would just be an introductory home tour and a not involve any high pressure real estate sales pitch."

Marilyn had gotten plenty of male attention before, from the time she had entered grade school and continuing all the way through college, and she was starting to smell a rat, or possibly a long-dead cat. But she was also starting to enjoy Freddie's little charade, and rather than cut him off at the knees, she decided to play along and see how far he was prepared to go in his effort to get her attention. "How does the home tour tie in with your sick cat?"

"I thought this tour would work well for two reasons. It would take my mind off Minnie for a few hours while I'm showing you around. And it would give us the opportunity to find you that Georgian mansion in a magnolia grove that we talked about." Sensing an opportunity to strike while the iron was reasonably warm, he tried to close the deal, continuing, "I'll need to get your address, so I can drive by and pick you up. Does 2:00 sound OK?"

"I don't normally give my home address to people I've just met, Mr. Palmer. But in this case, I'm going to make an exception, just to help get your mind off Minnie. I have an apartment in the Reston Building at 204 South Elm Street, and I'll be looking for you at 2:00. Will you be driving your Mercedes?"

"No ma'am. I'll be driving my Olds 88. I'll look forward to seeing you tomorrow." As Freddie put down the phone, pleased with the outcome of the conversation, he momentarily thought about Marilyn's inquiry about whether he would be driving his Mercedes, wondering if she saw through him. Then he reassured himself, convinced that Palmer Charm School 101 had worked again, that he had slipped a high, fast pitch right by her.

Freddie pulled his freshly washed and waxed car up to the curb at 204 Elm Street just on time Sunday. He watched Marilyn walk toward him in a yellow print dress, holding the car door open for her to slip inside before returning to the driver's seat.

"Any change in Minnie's condition, Mr. Palmer?" Marilyn inquired, smiling, but speaking seriously.

"No change, either for the better or worse," Freddie replied, innocently returning her smile. "Could we use first names? I'm like my buddy, Doug. I'm a lot more comfortable being addressed without the mister."

"Well, Freddie, I'm sorry your cat hasn't taken a turn for the better since we talked. You definitely need to bring her to the hospital tomorrow for a checkup."

Freddie managed to direct the conversation away from sick cats to the subject of homes for sale. "I'll start out by driving you over to a nice neighborhood of smaller homes where two of my friends, Mike and Ginny Rhodes, live. Three bedroom, two bath homes there start in the low twenties." As they cruised up the street, Freddie spotted Ginny meandering up the sidewalk, pushing eight-week old Mikey in a stroller. "May I pull over and introduce you to one of my best friends?" he asked. When she nodded in agreement, he pulled up and stopped beside Ginny.

Freddie handled the introduction, using Marilyn's title of Dr. Nelson, but she corrected him and gave her first name to Ginny as she extended her hand. Her pleasant smile and unpretentious personality would have undoubtedly won her a new friend anyway, but when she took Mikey from the stroller and commented on what a handsome young man he was, she sealed the deal right on the spot. Before they left, Freddie and Marilyn had received a guided tour of the Rhodes' new home and an invitation to come back for a visit as soon as possible.

"You have some nice friends," Marilyn observed as they pulled away. "I like Ginny, and Doug Housman, too."

"I think you'd like a couple of other members of my old high school gang if you met them. Ginny's husband and Doug's girlfriend are both former classmates and a lot of fun. But enough chatter from the bus driver, let's get on with the Madison County home show."

As they proceeded further out of town, Freddie continued, "I'd like to show you the nicest neighborhood around here before we finish our tour. It's situated on top of Logan's Hill. Some of the locals refer to it as Snob's Knob. Homes up there run in the forty to fifty range."

"A little too rich for my blood at this point," Marilyn replied. "But let's go take a look anyway. I'd like to see how the rich and famous of Eden Springs live."

"Not many rich people, and nobody famous living in this backwater town," Freddie laughed. "But I'm like you, I enjoy looking at those big piles of rock, wondering what it would be like to live there. Something about the thought of looking down at people from a big house on the top of a hill really captures my imagination."

There aren't many hills in the part of Georgia where I grew up. I think that's one of the things I like best about living here in West Virginia. The countryside seems so much more three-dimensional."

The two drove by rows of impressive homes winding around the top of Logan's Hill, all with beautifully landscaped grounds and terraces, and large picture windows taking in the panoramic view of the small town below. Each tried to pick out a favorite place to live, only to change the selection upon seeing an even more spectacular home.

"I don't think I should have come up here with you today," Marilyn commented. "Now I'll never be content with anything I can afford." As they were driving away, she made a suggestion that let Freddie know this would be a day he would never forget. "Would you like to stop by Gil's Drive-In and get a hamburger and shake?"

Sitting at the drive-in, Freddie and Marilyn talked, opening up about themselves in a way that neither would have dreamed of only hours earlier. Freddie told the story of how he had dropped out of Marshall, not only because of poor grades, but also because of the hurtful breakup with Shirley Martin. Marilyn talked about the period of depression she had experienced when she was a college student, and how she had managed to battle through it to graduate. Finally, Marilyn asked the question that Freddie had known was coming, sooner or later. "What's the real story with Minnie?"

"She's in cat heaven," Freddie replied. "I buried her two years ago in the middle of my mother's flower bed between two rose bushes. I loved that little calico cat, and cried like a baby when she died. It was crummy of me to use Minnie, trying to get to know you, but I did it. You were on to me before I told you, weren't you."

"I was beginning to sense a hoax. But Minnie brought us together today, and made us friends. I suppose all's well that ends well."

Later, when Freddie took Marilyn back to her apartment, he told her, "This has turned out to be the best day I've had in I don't know when. Could I call you some time soon and make a real date to go out with you?"

"That would be nice, Freddie. I think you've already conned me into a first date today, so we'll call it a second. I had a great time, too."

As Marilyn walked away, Freddie continued to follow her with his eyes until she entered the building and the door closed behind her, feeling an exhilaration unlike any he had ever known before.

CHAPTER 23

"E Company, fall in!" Ed called out to the forty men and high school boys who were lounging in folding chairs and carrying on noisy conversations in the church fellowship hall. "I appreciate all of you turning out here today to help the Confederate Army get ready for battle. To help us organize for this reenactment, Buddy and Beau Preston from Richmond have kindly volunteered to join us this morning. Later today they'll also work with Sam Barry and the Yanks. Both have been heavily involved in preparations for the upcoming Civil War Centennial reenactments in Virginia. Buddy and Beau, the floor is yours."

The two brothers, dressed in gray wool Confederate Army regalia, explained how E Company should plan and train for the upcoming event. They suggested that the scaled-down company be organized as a single platoon made up of five squads, each headed up by a vet with military drill experience, and they recommended that each squad start to hold weekly close order drills.

The brothers discussed safety at length. "Beau and I are going to act as your safety officers right up through the reenactment," Buddy informed them. "Many of you will be issued a borrowed 1862 CS Richmond .58 caliber musket, but only men with previous experience in shooting black powder firearms will be allowed to load and discharge their weapons, and then only after we've gone through safety training for shooting during a battle reenactment."

Beau picked up the presentation from his brother, adding, "The same safety rules apply here that you follow while hunting: assume all weapons are loaded. Remember that firing a musket loaded with black powder and patch at close range is still dangerous. You must always point your rifle in a safe direction before you pull the trigger. The spectators watching the show will never know the difference."

"Today, we've talked a lot about preparation to be sure your reenactment is as safe and authentic as you can make it," Beau said in closing. "The other thing that my brother and I want you to do is go out and put on a good show. Enjoy yourselves. Holler those Rebel yells, and cut loose like you would if you were a bunch of kids playing capture the flag. You enactors should have a better time than any of the spectators watching the show. We'll both be back here in August to see if we can help you with final preparations, and to be sure that you're ready to give those damn Yanks a good whuppin.'"

Buddy added, "And pray for cool, cloudy weather the day the battle is staged. Your wool uniforms are going to be hot as hell on a sunny afternoon. They'll make you sweat like a horse and smell like a goat, and those pretty southern belles won't come within fifty feet of you."

Doug was heading for his car when seventeen-year old TJ Vicelli came running up to him. "Doug, I'm glad I'm going to be in the same squad with you, Mike and Freddie. Dad wanted to get in on the reenactment, too, but he couldn't afford to be away from the store for all the practices. Mom told me to invite you over for supper after we got through here. It'll be some of her fried chicken and mashed potato left-overs."

"That's the best offer I've had today," Doug replied, throwing an arm around TJ's shoulder. "I'm finally going let you get behind the wheel of my '57 Chevy hardtop to drive us over house." He moved his hand up to give TJ a knuckle rub on the top of his flat-topped head, adding, "But I warn you, if you put a scratch on it, you won't live to finish your junior year."

Tony Vicelli looked up from his favorite chair to give a friendly wave to Doug and his son as they entered the house, remaining totally absorbed in the Sunday afternoon performance of the Metropolitan Opera, which was booming out from the radio only a few feet away.

"I have no idea what he gets out of listening to that that opera crap," TJ commented, as the two walked through the living room toward the kitchen. "You can't make out a single word that they're yowling back and forth at each other."

Ingrid overheard her son's remark as she turned off the oven and crossed the room to give Doug a hug. "TJ thinks nothing's worth listening to but rock and roll," she said laughing. "He definitely prefers Elvis Presley to Mario Lanza. I hope some of his dad's passion for opera comes out in him some day, but I'm not going to hold my breath waiting until it does." Flipping TJ playfully with a dish towel, she added, "Would you two please help me carry some of these hot dishes into the dining room?"

"Just think! Vickie's flying into Charleston less than two weeks from now," Ingrid mentioned during the meal. "Won't it be good to have her home again? I wish she were staying longer than a week, but that's all the time she could take off from her job."

"Good of you to meet her at the airport and drive her home," Tony interjected, glancing over at Doug. "But I guess that isn't the most unpleasant work assignment you've taken on, is it?"

"No, I've had worse," Doug replied. "Although I might have to borrow a recent photograph in order to pick her out from the other passengers when she gets off the plane. I've almost forgotten what she looks like."

"Yeah! Right!" TJ chimed in. "I believe that back during the fall you got a long, close-up look at her. I saw y'all sitting out in the car with your faces glued together." He would have continued if his mother hadn't kicked him in the shins under the table.

Doug quickly changed the subject. "I just learned something from Freddie Palmer that I think you'll be interested to hear. It hasn't come out in the newspaper yet, but our local NBC affiliated radio station is planning to begin television broadcasts in August. The station will be called WESP, and it'll broadcast on Channel 8. They're planning to build a transmission tower on Pine Ridge."

Tony Vicelli put down his fork and joined the conversation. "I heard something about that last week from one of my customers. I wasn't sure whether the story was true, or just another of those rumors always going around about a new company coming to Eden Springs."

"I hadn't planned to say anything about this," Doug continued, "but I'll go ahead and tell you something if you'll please keep it confidential and not discuss it with Vickie until she gets home. I took an hour off from work two days ago and went over to talk to Charlie Goins, the station manager. I wanted to see if there might be some position at WESP that would appeal to Vickie and fit her education and experience. I haven't told her anything about this yet, and don't want her to think I'm trying to run her life behind her back."

"I don't think you have to worry about that, Doug," Ingrid interjected. "Please go on and tell us what you learned. I promise that our lips are sealed until you've had a chance to discuss it with Vickie."

"I told him all about Vickie's BA degree in journalism from Columbia, and her grad school class in television production. Then I told him that she's working at NBC headquarters. By the time I showed him her picture, he seemed very interested in talking to her. If Vickie's agreeable, he'll work her in for a job interview while she's home."

Ingrid rose to hug him. "Doug, if something should come of

what you've done, and Vickie should decide to move back to this area to live, I'll spend the rest of my life trying to repay you."

TJ chimed in, "Mom, don't get so carried away. But I agree that it would be kind of neat having Sis living here in town. Then Dad would have someone else to keep his eye on besides me."

CHAPTER 24

Dominic Magino walked through the door of Lester's Café just past noon, spotting Carmine Nardelli in a booth in the rear with a bottle of Carling Black Label in front of him. As he walked back and took the opposite seat, Carmine greeted him with a curt, "You're late."

"I know. I got caught behind a couple of old geezers in their big clunkers, afraid to pass a loaded dump truck that was creeping along holding up traffic. I couldn't get around them for five miles; it seemed more like fifty." When the fat, bald proprietor, Lester Hanes, waddled over to take his order, Dominic said, "I'll have what he's drinking." As soon as Lester brought him a long-neck bottle of beer and meandered back out of earshot, Dominic inquired, "Why'd you ask me to come here today?"

"Angelo Vincieno is plenty PO'ed about you bringing in a lawyer and threatening to take him to court over the ten grand you claim he owes you. He said that you've cost him a lot more than that in lost business with your crappy missed deliveries over the last couple of years. He went ahead and sent his first payment, but it really burned him up. Angie wants you to drop the whole matter right now, and call off the Housman guy who's dunning him."

"Why's he bringing you into all of this? It's between the two of us. He should have called me. You know that he had a couple of punks come down and rough up my brother-in-law Vinnie don't you? He also dropped Housman a not-too-subtle hint that he knows where his wife and kid live."

"Dominic, you're dumber than I thought you were. Your trucking outfit plays a small part in the business we're running. I have a lot more at stake in making the product, and Angelo in distributing it, than you do in hauling it a few hundred miles up the road. As long as you don't do something really stupid like wrecking one of your trucks or getting the state police curious about what you're carrying, you're clean. Angelo and I both pay off the politicians and law enforcement people in our neighborhoods to look the other way, but at any time, we could see new guys get elected who won't play along. That's why Angelo wanted me to talk to you, before a small timer like you really screws things up."

"What if I don't let him off the hook for the rest of the ten grand he owes me? What's he going to do?"

"I don't know, and I don't think you want to find out either. Have you leveled with your legal hot shot about getting out on some mighty thin ice? I doubt you're paying him enough to make him want to put himself and his family in the middle of this dispute." Shifting impatiently in his chair, he drained the last of his Black Label, adding, "I don't plan to sit here all day and debate this with you, but you'd do well to consider my friendly advice and drop this bill collection thing you've got going. That's all I'll say. I'm outta here now."

Dominic retorted, "You can tell Angie I'll split the ten grand debt with him. If he'll pay me another thirty-three hundred, I'll settle for the five grand and call off Housman. If that gives him heartburn, tell him to call me, and keep you out of this."

As Carmine walked away, he turned back and called out contemptuously, "Like I said, Dom, sometimes you can be dumber than hell."

Carmine's remark burned up Dominic all the way back to Hinton. When he reached the truck terminal, with the sign across the front of the building now freshly painted to read *East Coast Transfer Company, Inc.*, he went inside and caught up with Vinnie, sitting at his desk reading the newspaper.

"Put that thing down, and listen up," Dominic commanded. "I just came out of a meeting with Carmine. I've decided to settle up with Angelo and let him off the hook by only collecting five of the ten grand he owes me. Carmine says I can expect Angie to balk at paying another dime."

"Dom, you sure you want to get something going with Angelo?" Vinnie inquired nervously. "He's got a lot of muscle on his payroll to back him up."

"I know Angie's not stupid enough to mess with our drivers making deliveries up his way, and end up with reporters writing embarrassing stories for the front page of his local paper," Dominic replied. "Even a dog won't crap in his own yard. But he might try to do something here to get his point across. I'd like for you and your two brothers to take turns sleeping over here in the terminal at night with a shotgun, in case he tries something to get back at me."

"What about Housman? What do you think Angie might do to get back at him?"

"I don't know what Angie may do. Personally, I like Housman. But if something should happen to him, we'd collect that two grand bonus from Barker, which leaves me with mixed emotions about the whole thing."

"I can't believe you said that, Dom. You wouldn't want the priest to hear you talk like that. Father Thomas told me that there's a limit to the stains on your soul that that you can get washed off by confession."

"You let me worry about my soul, Vinnie, and you worry about protecting our business from Angelo. That reminds me of something. I need to call Housman and have him send out a letter with my new offer to settle up with Angelo for fifty cents on the dollar."

Dominic was quick to follow through. When the phone rang in Ed's office, Carolyn picked up for him, knowing he was gone for the day. The strong New Jersey accent told her who was calling, even before Dominic identified himself. Carolyn listened closely and made shorthand notes on a steno pad while Dominic outlined his request.

"Tell Mr. Housman that I want him to send out a revised settlement letter to Universal Restaurant Supply Company, conveying my offer to settle the delinquent account for half the amount owed. I'm giving the company owner a break because I'm still doing business with him."

Nothing in Dominic's words or tone set off any alarms as Carolyn recorded the details of what seemed to be an ordinary business transaction. When he was finished, she said, "Mr. Housman will be back in the office tomorrow, Mr. Magino. He'll need your written authorization to change the terms and conditions of the previous settlement letter to agree with those you've just dictated to me. I would expect that he'll have something drafted for your final approval and ready to send out before the end of the week."

Dominic sat back in his chair after the phone call, deep in thought. The conversation had gone exactly the way he had expected, and things seemed to be proceeding the way he had planned, yet he felt disturbed. In the back of his mind, there was a clear recollection of a Bible lesson taught to him by a nun when he was a boy. He recalled the story of a treacherous man who had betrayed his friend for money, and he could still remember the reward despite all of the years that had passed, thirty pieces of silver.

Then his street-hardened character took over again, pushing thoughts of nuns and childhood Bible lessons from his mind. In the tough world he lived in, it was every man for himself.

He'd look out for Dominic Magino, and Ed Housman was on his own.

CHAPTER 25

"I'm glad to have the final exam behind us but really sorry to see our television production class end," Richard Hardy said quietly to Vickie and Karen Billings as the three turned in their examination blue books to the professor at the door.

"I enjoyed your class, Dr. Peters," he called back from the hallway. He turned to Vickie and Karen, adding, "Let's go by Delano's and have one last cup of java to celebrate. Are you two up for it?"

Sitting at a table with a steaming mug of coffee before her, Karen remarked to Vickie, "I guess you're flying out for home in the morning. It's going to be awfully quiet here next week without having you around, but we've got something really special planned when you get back. Tell her, Richard."

"I got tickets for the three of us to see *Gypsy*! Samantha Spiro plays Fanny, and Ethel Merman plays Mama. The show's getting great reviews. Being able to take in these Broadway plays is one of the best things about living here in New York, don't you agree?"

"Yeah, I sure do," Vickie replied. "Richard, you'll have to let me pay my way. I know that those tickets must have set you back quite a bit of money."

"I wouldn't think about doing something like that. This show is my way of saying thanks to both of you for all the great times we've had together this semester." Richard spoke the words "both of you," but Karen was keenly aware that all of that time he was looking at Vickie.

The three walked back to the apartment arm in arm, all laughing as they recalled the many good times in Dr. Peters' class. Karen quickly said good night when they arrived at the door and went straight toward the elevator. Vickie was preparing to follow, when Richard asked, "Do you have a moment for us to talk?"

Richard said hesitantly, "I suppose you've known for weeks that I have feelings for you, haven't you?"

Vickie was momentarily at a loss for words. She had noticed almost from the beginning that Richard was extremely attentive to her every word and action, while often seeming oblivious to Karen's presence. And Karen had earlier speculated with certainty that "Richard has a thing for you." But this conversation was heading in a direction that she did not wish to go, and she replied gently, "I'm not sure I did. Hearing you say that is a high compliment indeed. But you're aware that I'm still committed to my high school sweetheart."

"You told me about him. But if you decide to stay in New York and work at NBC, I believe we'd have a wonderful opportunity to share a happy life together. Think about what I've said. You don't have to make any decisions tonight. I just want you to know that I'm another man who's crazy about you." Richard leaned over and gave her a light kiss, then wheeled around and was gone, leaving Vickie surprised and filled with mixed emotions as she took the elevator back to her apartment.

Janice excitedly came to greet her when she entered. "Did you pass the final exam?"

"I think so. The questions didn't seem too hard. But the exam wasn't what has me in such a tizzy right now. What would you say if I told you that Richard Hardy came awfully close to proposing to me at the front door downstairs just now?"

"I'd say you're a lucky gal. Richard's a really smart, likeable guy, and doggone good-looking to boot. I've heard his dad is chairman of the board of some big company headquartered in Fairfield. Look's like Doug's got some serious competition here in Metropolis from a young Clark Kent trying to win Lois Lane's heart."

"Janice, you're not helping me at all," Vickie laughed. "All I wanted to hear you say is that I should steer clear of Richard from now on and stay faithful to my boyfriend back home. I'd like to talk about this some more, but I guess I'd better turn-in and try to get some sleep. My flight's out at 7:00 in the morning."

Vickie was up early and waiting at the door when the cab arrived to take her to LaGuardia. She boarded the plane at 6:45 and was in the air and on the way to Charleston right on schedule. The cabin attendant handed out boxed breakfast meals to go with the Coke and peanuts she had received shortly after boarding, and she reclined her window seat to watch the silver-gray clouds slipping by beneath her. Occasionally, she could feel turbulent air shake the plane and hear the rattling sound of the plastic interior of the aircraft, but her mind was focused on only one thing. Doug would be meeting her when she landed to drive her home. All she had to do now was sit back and wait.

Doug arrived at the airport late that morning. It always surprised him to drive uphill to reach a commercial airport, but he knew that the precious flat area for the runways was created by excavating the tops of two mountains and pushing the fill into the valley between them. Flying in and out of Charleston had always reminded him of taking off and landing on the flight deck of an aircraft carrier. He noticed that the scattered clouds overhead were breaking up, which should mean that Vickie's plane would have no trouble landing on schedule.

Doug watched a small silver dot appear in the northeast sky, gradually transforming into a twin engine aircraft making its approach to land. The plane touched down and taxied to a stop, the door opened, and a dozen passengers filed down the steps and walked across the tarmac in his direction. Still, he caught no sight of her. Finally, he saw a tall, slender blonde wearing a brown skirt and tailored leather jacket exit the plane and walk toward the terminal, obviously looking for someone. Her blonde hair was now shoulder length, longer than the last time he had seen her. "Vickie! I'm over here," he called out.

She broke into a wide smile of recognition, running toward him, her pocket book swinging on her arm. "Doug, I was looking around for you, but I didn't see you," she called out. As she came through the gate, he ran over to hug her, lifting her off the ground. He caught a faint hint of her favorite cologne, holding her in his arms for a few moments before sharing a long kiss.

They retrieved both pieces of her luggage from the baggage claim area, then walked arm in arm to Doug's car. Inside, she slipped over in the front seat to snuggle against him. "Doug, it's so good to be with you again. I was counting the minutes all the way down. I kept wishing the plane would go faster."

"You'll never know how much I've missed you. It's been really hard living so many miles away from you for so long, and only being able to visit by phone calls and letters."

Neither was aware of other travelers coming and going around them, as they tried to make up for the long days of being apart since they had been inseparable, in a time that now seemed so long ago. It didn't end until they heard a car pull in next to them and saw several high school kids staring in their direction.

"I guess we'll have to hold the rest of our reunion celebration for later, and head for home now," Doug said, disappointed. "We'd have a lot more privacy if we were to go back to our favorite parking spot during our high school days, the one overlooking Sander's Pond. You remember all those summer nights we spent out there together, watching the submarine races."

"Yeah, I remember them well," Vickie replied softly. "I'd like to go back there some night this week and try to recapture the past. I haven't been to a good submarine race since we graduated."

As Doug drove out of Charleston and turned toward Eden Springs, Vickie wanted to hear all of the news. She pressed him for information about family and friends that he and her mother might have overlooked during their weekly phone calls. "I can't wait to see Ginny and Mike's little boy. She sent me some pictures, and I can't decide whether he looks more like his mom or dad."

"Mikey got lucky," Doug cracked. "He's a cute kid and a dead ringer for her." Vickie wasn't about to play along with a joke about one of her favorite male friends, turning on the car radio, immediately hearing Connie Francis's plaintive rendition of *Among My Souvenirs.*

Doug changed the subject from home town happenings to gingerly broach a new topic. "I've got some exciting news to tell you. Guess what's coming to town?"

Vickie looked at him with a grin and inquired, "The circus?"

Doug took his hand off the wheel to put his arm around her neck and give her a gentle squeeze. "No, Gracie, not the circus," he replied in his best George Burns impression. "A TV station. The local NBC radio affiliate has gotten a license to carry NBC television programming, broadcasting as station WESP on Channel 8."

"Actually, I already knew that. Janice Gilmore heard it from her dad a few weeks ago. I'll bet the locals are pretty excited about this, aren't they?"

"Yeah, and your mom and I are two of them. What would you think about coming back and going to work for the new station?"

"Gosh, Doug, that thought never even crossed my mind when Janice and I talked. Remember that in New York, I'm an assistant staff writer, and that's probably not what WESP management is going to be looking for."

"What if I told you that Charlie Goins, the station manager, thinks your degree and experience make you an excellent candidate to work at WESP?"

"How would you know that?"

"Because I spoke to him about you. I told him that I hadn't discussed this with you, and I wasn't even sure you'd be interested, but I just wanted to take a preliminary look to see if there might be some sort of fit. After I showed him your picture, he seemed to think there might even be an opportunity for you to do some work in front of the camera."

"Mom's in on this big secret, too?"

"Yeah. I'm not going to beat around the bush. We'd both turn handsprings to get you to come back home."

"I appreciate what you've done, Doug, but you've really caught me cold with all of this. "What do you and Mom expect me to do?"

"Just call the station day after tomorrow and talk to Charlie. It's an opportunity for you and Charlie to see whether any of the WESP openings match your career interests. If they should, then you could give him your resume and arrange a formal job interview later. That's all there is to it. I'm not putting any pressure on you." Doug hesitated, then continued openly, "OK, I'm handing you another pitchforkful of BS. Actually, your mom and I are both hoping some opportunity at the new station will knock your socks off, and that you'll want to come back here to live."

CHAPTER 26

"A registered letter just arrived from Universal Restaurant Supply Company with the thirty-three hundred dollar balance owed to Dominic Magino," Carolyn commented. "I don't think we've ever dealt with anyone who paid off such a big account in cash." She handed the letter to Ed, adding, "The cover letter from the company owner is pretty short and sweet. I don't think Mr. Vinciano considers you to be his new best friend."

"I'm glad to be wrapping up my services to Dominic," Ed replied, looking over the terse message from Angelo, which read: "Here is payment in full of the remaining balance on this account. The only reply I want is a statement showing a zero balance." It was signed simply "A. P. Vinciano".

"You're not going to handle any more work for Mr. Magino, even if he asks you?" Carolyn inquired.

"Definitely not. I'm planning to tell him I have a work overload situation, and that he'll have to find a new attorney. I don't think Dominic has been up front with me about his business and personal relationship with that restaurant supply outfit in New Jersey. It's pretty obvious that Vinciano has no use for Dominic, and that his displeasure has now been extended to me. I wonder how he got hold of that picture of Laura and Lizzie that he sent along with his first payment. The whole business of dealing with these people gives me the creeps, particularly when it starts to involve my family. I've even thought about hiring Andrew Stover to investigate what's going on behind the scenes. But I guess that's all moot, since I'm getting out of the middle right away."

He happened to be looking over one of Andrew Stover's investigative reports that afternoon when Arnold Jannsen came by to go over preparations for the upcoming trial. The two settled in together across his desk and spent the afternoon meticulously reviewing the defense plan. Carolyn had long since departed when they finally wrapped up their discussion. Ed saw Arnold to the door, then returned to his work, after calling Laura to apologize for standing her up again for their family dinner. "That's OK, honey," he heard her say in her usual understanding way. "All you're going to miss tonight is my macaroni and cheese casserole. See you in a little while."

On the way home, he watched the sun dropping close to the mountain ridge in the southwest, bringing twilight to the valley, and he thought about Laura and Lizzie waiting for him, and that single cold bottle of Miller High Life in the fridge. Everything seemed to be falling peacefully into place at the end of a long, tiring day, until he noticed the rhythmic thumping sound of his left front tire and felt the car beginning to pull toward the center of the road. What a time for tire trouble, he thought as he steered the car completely off of the pavement and stopped on the right shoulder. The train of irritated introspection continued as he turned off the engine and climbed got out of the car, confirming the flat.

Ed took the jack, tire iron, and spare from the trunk, jacked up the car, and removed the wheel, observing two roofing nails stuck side by side in the center of the tread. He'd mounted the spare, and was in the process of tightening the lug nuts, when he heard the sound of a vehicle approaching at high speed from behind. Being well off the road, he felt no cause for alarm, but some nagging sixth sense warned him to stay alert.

The following events happened so quickly that they seemed a blur. A dark sedan suddenly sped by, crowding the edge of the pavement where he had pulled over, with the right door swinging open as it came alongside. Ed straightened, starting to dive across the fender of his car, but at that instant the open door struck his right shoulder, knocking him to the ground in front of his car. He looked up in intense pain to see the car speed out of sight. There was no chance for him to read the license number. The best he could determine, he had just been struck by a dark blue late model Buick sedan with out of state tags and two occupants.

Climbing back to his feet, Ed realized that he could not move his right arm without excruciating pain. He managed to lower the car off the jack using only his left arm, then climb into the car, make a U turn, and drive to the hospital, placing a call from the front desk.

"Laura, I've had a minor accident, and I'm over at Madison General. No, I'm not seriously injured. Great, I'll be watching for you. Take your time driving over; I'm not going anywhere for a while. I love you, too."

Laura rushed into the hospital a short time later to be with Ed for a few minutes before he was taken back for x-rays. She embraced him gently and held on to his hand, inquiring anxiously, "Ed, what happened to you? I saw your car out front, but I didn't see a scratch on it."

Ed quickly filled her in on what had just happened, but he was unable to answer many of her questions. "All I'm sure of is that there were two men in a dark blue '58 or '59 Buick two-door sedan, and they deliberately tried to hit me. I need to report this to Sheriff Daniels. Could you make that call for me?"

It took Laura only a few minutes to report the incident to the deputy pulling the evening shift at the sheriff's office.

"We'll put out an alert immediately to be on the lookout for a dark Buick two-door sedan with damage to the right door," she heard the young man reply. "Sheriff Daniels will be in touch with your husband in the morning to get more information."

Ed and Laura received good news from the young intern staffing the emergency room. Ed had gotten off with no broken bones, but did have a dislocated and severely bruised shoulder. The doctor managed to manipulate Ed's arm and return the ball back into the socket, with only a loud expletive from Ed, and a quiet groan of sympathy from Laura. As the two slowly made their ways to their cars, Ed turned and said with a wan smile, "Can I have that Miller High Life when we get home?"

Laura smiled and nodded. "You've earned it, sweetheart. I heard your shoulder pop when he was manipulating it back in place. I'm wishing there was another cold one in the fridge for me."

*****

The day's action was over for Ed and Laura but just getting ready to begin for Vinnie Vitale, who had drawn night watchman duty at the East Coast Transfer Company terminal in Hinton. He was kicked back on an old davenport with his feet propped up on a scarred coffee table, which held a utilitarian center piece consisting of a Remington Model 1100 semiautomatic 12 guage shotgun loaded with five high-brass 00 buckshot shells.

The table also carried refreshments and recreational items intended to help a man pass the time while pulling a long night shift in a dark, drafty warehouse. After all, it could get a little lonely just sitting there hour after hour, listening to the wind whistling around the corners of the building and the occasional spate of barking from Taz, Rocky, and Boomer in the parking lot.

But tonight there was a stack of girlie magazines, which Vinnie had borrowed earlier from Skeeter Ratliffe, and a fifth of high quality bootleg whiskey. He had discovered that happy little surprise inside a truck which had completed a beverage delivery run from Keystone to Newark, bringing back a truckload of empty bottles to Keystone to be refilled with the local product. The bottles, carrying the labels of various premium whiskeys, were packed in cardboard cartons. To his delight, one Old Cabin Still bottle refilled with Keystone beverage product had been shipped back inadvertently among the empties, as though it were some divine gift from Providence. Vinnie couldn't help but feel that the evening ahead was shaping up to be about as good as a night shift in that miserable location could be.

Two hours later, Vinnie had enjoyably consumed a third of the bottle's pale brown elixir and carefully pored over half of the magazines with all of their anatomical astonishments, when he thought he heard a faint noise, as if something were moving about outside. He stopped and listened intently for any reaction from the dogs, but he could not hear the agitated barking which might signal intruders on the premises. What he did not know was that the disturbance he had heard was the sound of three hungry German shepherds once again jostling for fresh hamburger patties being provided by their new friends standing just outside the gate.

Vinnie was totally engrossed in savoring his stock of gustatory and visual delights when he was startled by the sound of breaking glass, seeing a single stick of dynamite with a brightly sparking fuse sail through the window into the center of the open terminal.

His panicked cry, "Oh, shit!" echoed off the walls as he dove over the back of the davenport to the floor behind, hugging the concrete and contemplating whether Dom should be offering him combat pay. His last thought was, where the hell are Rocky, Boomer, and Taz? Then a deafening blast blew out every window in the building, and Vinnie's world became peacefully still as he blacked out from the concussion.

CHAPTER 27

"**Best country ham I've had** in a long time," Tony Vicelli complimented his wife, between bites. "What do you think, boys?"

TJ, who was busy polishing off another ham biscuit, responded with a couple of words that sounded something like "really great," delivered through a mouth full of half-masticated food.

Doug, who had been holding hands with Vickie under the white linen tablecloth overhanging the round oak table, chimed in, "Best country ham I've ever tasted. Mama V, you and my mom are the two best cooks in the world!"

Ingrid smiled and passed the bowl of potato salad around the table for the third time. "I only wish Sandra could be here tonight. She's finishing exams at Radford and won't be home until next week."

"What do you two have cooked up for tonight?" Tony asked, looking at Doug.

"I want to see how he answers that," TJ whispered to Vickie, receiving almost simultaneous kicks in the shins from both his sister and his mother.

"We're going down to catch the second show at the Lyric,"

Doug replied. "They're showing *Rio Bravo*, a western starring John Wayne and Dean Martin. Freddie took Marilyn Nelson, the new vet in town, to see it last night. He said it was pretty good, but every time there was a scene with the young gunslinger, Ricky Nelson, he kept expecting Ozzie and Harriet to ride up."

Ingrid served her trademark homemade coconut cake topped with a scoop of vanilla ice cream for dessert. Afterward Vickie volunteered, "Doug and I will do the dishes tonight, Mom. It'll be like old times for me to put on an apron again. Y'all can go on out in the living room and watch TV." The dishwashing chore should have been completed in fifteen minutes, but it took twice that long, and when they were through, Vickie needed another minute or two to wipe the last traces of her lipstick off Doug's face.

On the way to the theater, Doug asked, "You're still planning to meet with Charlie Goins in the morning?"

"I told him I'd go to lunch with him. This is really just a chance for us to get acquainted and to see whether I'd be interested in any of the station openings, and more importantly, whether he'd have any interest in considering me for a job."

"You're going to knock him for a loop. I just hope you'll give the job situation a serious look."

Freddie's movie review turned out to be accurate. *Rio Bravo* would not win any Academy Award, but the lead actors were obviously having fun. Dean and Ricky sang some good songs, and Angie Dickinson was easy on the eyes in her role as Feathers, the female lead and major set decoration.

After stopping next door at the diner for a cup of coffee, Doug and Vickie took a trip back in time to their high school days, driving out to Sander's Pond, parking at their favorite overlook. Vickie turned on the radio, and after dialing back and forth across the band several times, she finally found a station playing popular songs from the Hit Parade. The first they heard was the Platters' nostalgic hit *Smoke Gets In Your Eyes*. "I don't see any submarines out on the water tonight," she said softly, turning to face him.

"Me neither," Doug replied, pulling her closer. "I guess they don't hold races every night." A silver curtain of fog forming on the inside of the windows gradually masked the outside world. "We couldn't see 'em now even if they were running on the surface," he grinned, burying his face in her long blonde hair.

Later, Doug started the car and switched on the headlights, while Vickie ran a comb through her hair, touched up her lipstick, and cleared the fogged windows with his handkerchief. Then, with Doug's arm around her while he steered using his left hand on the necking knob spinner, and with Vickie shifting gears, they pulled away from the overlook and started on their slow drive back toward town.

The next morning, Vickie was still in bed when her mother called to remind her she had only an hour and a half until her lunch interview. She showered and dressed quickly, arriving at the Eden Springs Resort promptly on time. Walking through the foyer into the dining room, she spotted a tall, brown-haired man, who appeared to be almost the age of her father, looking toward her from a table on the other side. The hostess at the door nodded in his direction and remarked quietly, "I believe Mr. Goins is expecting you."

Charlie rose to greet her, looking at Vickie with unabashed interest as she followed the hostess across the room to his table. He stood to extend his hand, saying warmly, "I'm Charlie Goins, Miss Vicelli. I recognize you from a picture that Doug Housman showed me. It's very nice to meet you."

"Thank you. It's a pleasure meeting you, too, Mr. Goins," Vick said, smiling back at him before taking the seat that he offered.

"You're taking night school classes toward a master's degree in journalism from Columbia, while working days as an assistant staff writer at NBC?" Charlie asked. "How in the world do you manage to juggle that kind of schedule?"

Vickie relaxed, laughing, "It's pretty demanding, Mr. Goins. I really don't have much of a personal life."

"Call me Charlie, and may I call you Vickie, so we don't sound so formal?" Vickie nodded, and he continued, "How do you like living in New York, compared to your home town?"

Vickie soon revealed that she enjoyed the fast pace and cosmopolitan perks of life in New York, yet regretted the separation from her boyfriend and family back in Eden Springs. "Deciding what to do has been a huge problem for me. I guess I'm guilty of wanting to have my cake and eat it, too."

Charlie described the need for the new station to hire newscasters, reporters, and writers, positions which he felt she was academically qualified to fill, only requiring actual on-the-job training and experience. "In the short time we've talked here this morning, you've impressed me more than a dozen other job applicants I've screened to date, and some of them have work experience with other TV stations," he told her candidly. "I'd like for you to submit a full resume. And before you go back to New York, I'd like to have you come down to the new WESP studio, and let us film you in a simulated news broadcast situation. Would you be willing to do that?"

Vickie was momentarily speechless, but composed herself quickly. "Yes, Mr. Goins, I mean Charlie. Things have started to move a lot more quickly than I had expected. I guess I'm going to have to face my dilemma soon, and decide whether I'm ready to give up the bright lights of New York and come home."

"That's a decision no one can make but you," Charlie said sympathetically. "But I talked to your boyfriend. I found him to be a very likeable young man who seems to have a solid engineering career here in this area, and I know which way he's pulling. Your mother has also called to learn more about career opportunities at WESP. She and your boyfriend would like to see something work out for you here."

"I already knew that," Vickie replied. "I'll work up my resume the first thing after I return to New York. When would you like me to come by the studio for a test shoot? I'm flying out at the end of the week."

"Drop by my office tomorrow about 4:00 PM. I'll give you a script to study, and then we'll put you on camera. After we look over the taped interview together on a monitor, we'll give you a chance to do it a second time, if you care to."

As Vickie and Charlie walked to the parking lot, he offered her a little fatherly advice. "Life's a wonderful adventure, Vickie. Don't try to over complicate it, and tie yourself up in knots. Make your decision based on what you think is best for you in order to have a rewarding and happy life, and then put it behind you."

CHAPTER 28

"**How's my tough old war** horse this morning?" Laura asked, as Ed limped into the kitchen with a days growth of salt-and-pepper stubble and his hair uncombed, still wearing the T-shirt and pajama bottoms he had slept in the night before. "I guess you must be an old pinto war horse, since your arm and shoulder are still black and blue."

"Trying to be another Carol Burnette this morning, honey?" Ed inquired, grinning at her good-natured ribbing. "Try showing a little respect for your husband. After all, how many offensive linemen in the National Football League have ever thrown a body block on a Buick?"

"I said you were tough, sweetie. Maybe not too bright, but tough. Are you feeling any better today? Would you like for me to bring you a couple of Bayers?"

"I'm way beyond aspirin. But if you see a new arm and shoulder in the medicine cabinet, I'd definitely like to have them."

Laura walked over to the percolator on the counter beside the kitchen window and poured him a cup of coffee. Glancing outside, she remarked, "I see that JR's taking his new family out for a walk around the yard. Lizzie's four ducks follow that poor dog everywhere he goes."

"Yeah, it's quite a show. They apparently think he's their daddy. Lizzie still calls then Lucy, Lulu, Lena, and Lori, but you can clearly tell now that two of them are drakes. I hope it doesn't cause them to have any gender identification issues when they get older."

Laura gave Ed a playful swat on the head with the morning paper. Then she recalled something she had just read. "There's a small item on page two about some excitement late Friday night over in Hinton at a truck terminal. Apparently, a can of gasoline exploded and blew out a bunch of windows. There was no mention of anyone being injured."

"Can I see that article? Dominic Magino owns a truck terminal in Hinton. I'll bet it's the same one."

A quick scan of the article confirmed his intuition. "Looks like a strange coincidence that he's just had the same run of bad luck that I did," Ed observed. "But, actually my injury had nothing to do with being unlucky, except for my being in the wrong place at the wrong time. Someone deliberately tried to hurt me. Magino's trouble sounds more like some kind of freak accident."

After glancing at the paper, Ed asked, "Anything going on around here today that I should know about?"

"Actually, there is," Laura replied. "Doug's getting off from work early this afternoon to go over to the TV station with Vickie. It sounds likes the manager is offering her an introductory look at their operation and an on-camera tryout rolled into one. Doug has his fingers crossed that something good will come of this."

Doug did indeed have his fingers crossed when he rolled into the Vicelli driveway. Vickie spotted him through the window and quickly came out to join him, dressed in a pale blue suit and heels, with her hair swept up. "You look great," Doug commented, as he opened the door for her to slide into the front seat. "Is that your NBC business outfit?"

"Not really. Working as an assistant writer doesn't put me in front of the public. The other writers and I come to work dressed pretty casually. But I thought that since I'll be going on camera today, I'd go for the successful business professional look."

Charlie met them in the station lobby, then led them on a tour of the facility, including the staff offices, and the rooms where broadcasts would later originate before the TV cameras. "This station probably doesn't look like much compared to NBC headquarters in New York," Charlie commented to Vickie, "but our facility has advanced communications technology comparable to any TV studio in this region."

The three entered the room set up for news broadcasting, with a long desk and seats for up to four people to work together as a team before the camera. Two technicians joined them to operate the lights, camera, and recording equipment. Then Charlie handed Vickie a script containing three brief paragraphs, instructing her to familiarize herself with the news story, then deliver her interpretation into the camera without looking back at the text again.

While Doug and Charlie stood to the side, Vickie spent five minutes reading the script over and over. Only the slight rattle of the paper revealed her nervousness. "I guess I'm ready," she finally said. "Let's do it."

Looking directly into the camera with a smile, and radiating confidence, Vickie delivered the simulated news story almost flawlessly. Then at the end she broke into a wide grin, and ad libbed "th-th-th-that's all, folks!"

Charlie, Doug, and the two technicians gave her a friendly round of applause, and Doug whispered, "I'm so proud of you." Replayed afterward on a monitor, her performance looked as good as it had when she had delivered it live. "You're a natural," Charlie said sincerely, as they left the room and walked toward his office. "Anything else that I can show you here at the station?"

Vickie shook her head, and he continued, "I'll take this opportunity to tell you about the salary bands and benefits for newscasters, reporters, writers, and producers who come to work here. Later, if we both decide to go forward, I'll ask you back for a formal interview to discuss the specific position that we both think would be the best fit, and if things work out, make you an offer of employment, including a starting salary."

Charlie walked with them to the door. "I appreciate both of you coming by today. Vickie, I don't mind telling you that you've made a great impression on me. I hope that we can keep things moving forward in trying to find a place for you on the team here at WESP."

On the way home, Doug asked, "Did you hear what Charlie said about you back there? That was a pretty high compliment to pay someone he hasn't talked to but a couple of times. How do you feel about the way things went?"

"I was shaking like a leaf getting ready to shoot that simulated broadcast, but I tried not to let it show. Normally, newscasters are reading from notes or prompters and don't have to recite news bulletins from memory. But still, I had fun. Charlie and his crew are very likeable."

"What do you think? Could you be satisfied working here in town? As happy as you are working at NBC headquarters in New York?"

"It's like trying to compare two very different things, Doug. Going into work at 30 Rockefeller Plaza, you may walk past celebrities like Bill Cullen, on his way to emcee *Name That Tune.* Here it would be entirely different. But on the plus side, it looks like there's an opportunity to be a much bigger fish in a small pond. There are pros and cons for both." Then noting the crestfallen look that came over his face, she slipped across the seat to sit close to him and added, "Coming back here to be near you is WESP's biggest pro."

CHAPTER 29

"The week really flew by, didn't it?" Doug observed quietly, as they arrived at the Charleston Airport parking lot. "Everything seems to happen in such a hurry. Your flight's out in an hour and a half, and you'll be back in New York City by 8:30, if you don't run into some kind of air traffic delay in Philadelphia."

"It went by way too fast, didn't it?" Vickie replied. "Still, we got to be together almost every night. Going over to Mike and Ginny's house for dinner yesterday, and having Freddie there with his new girlfriend was especially nice. It seemed like old times, having so many of our high school gang back together again. No one seems to have changed all that much. And Marilyn seems to fit right in, almost like she went to Tyler and graduated with the rest of us."

They entered the terminal building, finding their way to a booth in the small food service area. A Marine Corps sergeant sitting nearby got up to feed the jukebox, and they found themselves listening to the beautiful, plaintive voice of Brook Benton crooning *It's Just A Matter Of Time.* "What did your mom and dad say when you were getting ready to leave?" Doug asked. "It looked like both of them were pretty choked up when I came by to get you."

"They just said that they miss me and wish I didn't live so far away," Vickie answered, turning aside to hide blue eyes now filling with tears. "Daddy thinks I'm still his little girl, and that he should be looking out for me like he used to. Some things never seem to change, do they?"

"Your dad's always kept an eye out for you and Sandra. I think he lets TJ run on a lot longer leash now. Tony and I get along great, but when I was bringing you home from our dates around midnight this past week, I noticed that his bedroom light was always still on. I think he'll try to keep you under close surveillance until he walks you down the aisle. But I honestly believe he'd be OK with my being the one standing at the altar when he gives you away. I guess I stack up pretty well when he remembers that you used to go out with Len Hacker."

"I wish you'd never mention Len Hacker's name in my presence again," Vickie said in disgust. "Daddy despised him from the very start. If you and I ended up together, I think he'd be incredibly pleased. My whole family thinks the world of you. You already know how I feel. There's only one thing I still need to get sorted out, and we both know what that is."

As her flight time approached, they settled into chairs near the window to hold hands and watch the planes come and go, their shiny wings reflecting the late afternoon sun.

Finally, the boarding call came, and Doug went with her to the departure gate. He pulled her close to share a long kiss, then whispered in her ear, "I'll be counting the days until you come home." She wheeled around and started quickly toward the aircraft, not turning to look back, trying to hide her tears.

Doug took the long way coming out of Charleston, so he could drive back and stop to look at the neighborhood where he had grown up. He gazed at the brick bungalow where he had lived until he was fifteen, the last home that his mother had shared with his dad and him before she was stricken with cancer. Everything looked so much smaller than he remembered it from his childhood. His house and others nearby showed their age, and all looked as though they were in need of maintenance. Thomas Wolfe had it right, he thought to himself, with a lump in his throat. You can't go home again. Then he started the car, trying to picture the neighborhood of his happy boyhood as it had been in those earlier years, and not the forlorn way it appeared to him now.

Doug continued on the lightly traveled highway south toward Eden Springs, turning on his headlights as daylight faded to twilight, then yielded to darkness, as he drew closer to home. Passing through Abner Gap into the north end of the valley, he caught sight of a glimmer from the crest of a knoll to the east, and knew that he was seeing the lights of Roseanna in the distance.

Then he looked west in the direction of Pine Ridge, where he spotted activity at the new landfill on the former Simpson and Henderson farms. Two small trucks could be seen in the distance, parked so that their headlights illuminated a section of landfill not far from the bank of Stony Creek. It appeared that the contents of a much larger truck were being transferred into an excavated shallow pit, while a second similar vehicle waited in line to unload, and a Caterpillar Bulldozer stood by, ready to cover the dumped material with dirt.

Something about a large crew of men working on a regional landfill at night struck Doug as highly out of the ordinary. He slowed to a stop at the private road leading into the landfill, remembering his mom's story of how she and Freddie had been ordered off of the property earlier. Killing his lights, he continued to watch the crew at work, unable to tell what they were unloading. Curiosity overcame him, and he turned onto the gravel road and slowly drove closer, shifting down into second gear, aware that he could not touch the brakes without the lights giving his position away. He realized that he was now legally in violation of the clearly posted No Trespassing signs adjacent to the entrance, recalling the effect of curiosity on cats.

When he was within a half mile of the work scene, he could get a better look at what was going on, and it was not what he had expected to see. The crew was unloading something from flatbed trucks, not the Mountain Venture trash collection vehicles he was accustomed to seeing making their rounds each week through town. Although he had no way to be certain, common sense told him that material being hauled on flat beds and dumped into the landfill at night was in no way related to trash trucked out from the Eden Springs area.

Doug's thoughts were interrupted when one of the two pickup trucks providing makeshift floodlights at the work site suddenly moved in his direction. Unsure as to whether the truck driver had spotted him, he slowly turned around and started back toward the highway, still running with his headlights off. Seeing that the truck was closing on him quickly, he decided it was time to swap stealth for speed and flipped on his lights, shifting into high gear, and flooring the accelerator.

Doug watched through the rear view mirror as dust from the unpaved gravel road billowed behind him like a smoke screen, and the lights of the pickup truck begin to fade in the distance. It seemed unlikely that the state police would be running a speed trap at night, and much more probable that the pickup truck would continue to follow, so when he reached the state highway and turned south toward home, he kept the pedal down until he hit the town limits.

Doug dialed up his dad when he arrived, reporting what he had had seen on his return trip home and the events that had followed.

"Something sounds fishy about what's going on over at the landfill tonight," Ed agreed. "Sam Barry's a member of the board of supervisors, and was involved in giving Mountain Ventures the go-ahead to develop that landfill. I'll tell him what you saw and ask him to find out what kind of work their crew is doing out there at night.

"You're aware that you broke the law going on posted private property tonight. I make a living defending people who do things like that without thinking out the consequences of their actions. But I believe you had your heart in the right place when you spied on those men. It sounds like Mountain Ventures may be breaking a law that's a lot more serious than trespassing."

CHAPTER 30

"Ya gotta shake it off and just get over it," Dominic yelled at Vinnie, as the two stood arguing on the shipping dock in the early morning air. "What's done is done. Besides, look on the bright side. The way it worked out, I collected a grand from Barker yesterday. He only paid half of the bonus he'd promised me because Housman was just hurt and not permanently injured."

"Easy for you to feel good about how things are going, Dom. You're collecting money while Housman and me are the ones getting the crap knocked out of us by Angie's boys. My ears haven't quit ringing since they tried to blow me up the other night. I'm not going to roll over and let them get away with it." Gaining courage as he continued to preach retribution, he added, "This time Angie's screwed with the bull, and he's going to get the horns."

"That's stupid talk, Vinnie. Carmine says the head of the family in New Jersey is getting fed up with all this infighting. Our West Virginia bootleg operation is their big moneymaker these days, and if we screw it up, we'll all end up taking a long nap at the bottom of a mine shaft, and they'll have someone else down here running things."

"I'm not going to screw up the family business, Dom, but I'm not through with Angie. I owe him, big time. I swear by all that's holy, he hasn't heard the last from me. "

Dominic turned away in exasperation, then heard Vinnie call out. "I'm going to need a few days off, Dom. I've got to go out of town and visit my aunt. Her old man's in a bad way with congestive heart failure, and he isn't going to be around much longer."

Dominic probably should have asked Vinnie where his aunt lived, but he failed to do so. It might have caused an alarm bell to go off in his head if he had known Vinnie had already lined up a trip to Newark.

*****

Vinnie sat back in his old Caddie four hours later with an unlit cigar butt clamped between his teeth, watching the road unwind in front of him at fifty-five miles an hour. It was a lot more enjoyable to be sitting back in his fat-ride luxury sedan than standing around all day on hard concrete floors at the truck terminal with two flat, aching feet. He thought about what he had told Dom without a trace of remorse about lying to his brother-in-law and best friend. After all, he did indeed have an Aunt Emma in Newark, and he would be spending the night at her house. But not before he conducted a little business.

Vinnie mentally inventoried the assorted materials he had stashed in the enormous car trunk before departing: his battered suitcase containing a fifth of Seagrams 7; a long handled bolt cutter with the jaws nicked from earlier work on some hardened steel alloy high-security locks; Dom's four-foot long steel crowbar; his wife's one gallon lard can, now holding four pounds of cheap ground beef laced with enough prescription sedatives to put a trophy size Kodiak bear into early hibernation; the rusty five gallon metal gas can from his garage; and a bath towel borrowed from Howard Johnson's. Then he remembered one other item in the trunk: a two pound box of Whitman's chocolates for Aunt Emma.

Vinnie entered the south side of Newark around 11:00, driving straight into the inner city, where factories, repair shops, and warehouses in rundown turn-of-the-century buildings fronted the streets, flanked by parking lots, and in a few places, neon-lit bars. He turned down a narrow side street illuminated by widely spaced street lights and soon spotted his destination: a two-story brick building converted from an old mattress factory into a food and beverage distribution center. A sign on the gated chain link fence identified the business as *Universal Restaurant Supply Company*.

Vinnie backed into an alley diagonally across the street, turned off his lights, killed the engine, and began to scope out the scene. His adolescent years, including a stint in reform school, had prepared him well for a life of living on the edge of the law, and he could break, enter, and commit grand larceny with the best.

Floodlights near the top of the building lit the parking lot outside, but no interior light escaped from the building through the dirty windows. A dozen delivery trucks were lined up close to a dock on the west end of the building, with *Shipping* painted above two tall overhead doors. A dock further to the rear of the building was similarly marked *Receiving*. Staring for a moment between the two docks, Vinnie thought he glimpsed a sign of movement. Finally, he was able to distinguish two Dobermans and a bull-mastiff moving around in the shadows. Almost time to feed the pooches, he thought. They'll enjoy a nice hamburger dinner as much as Rocky, Boomer, and Taz.

It was good that Vinnie sat and waited a bit longer, for at that moment a black Lincoln Continental pulled up in front, and a stocky, gray-haired man in a dark suit got out to unlock the gate. The three dogs ran toward him with fangs bared, growling ominously, until the man yelled at them sternly, "Get the hell away from me." All three then skulked away, looking back at him with gums still pulled back to display impressive canine teeth. He drove through the gate, stopped to relock it, and then pulled into a parking space next to the building. When the passenger door opened, a well-stacked blonde-haired woman in a fur coat and stiletto heels stepped out to take hold of the man's arm and walk beside him up the steps to the front door. He unlocked it, and they both disappeared inside.

Angie's got a hot date tonight, Vinnie thought. She's quite a bit younger, and a helluva lot better looking than his old lady. I don't think either of them will be getting up and coming to the window to look around for a while.

He had carefully removed the bulb from his car trunk light earlier, so that nothing lit up when he lifted the trunk lid to take out the gallon lard can full of dog treats. The dogs growled at him as he crossed the street and approached them, but soon became silent as burger after burger came sailing over the fence to their waiting jaws. "No jostling, boys," Vinnie said to them in a soft voice, like a mother gently reprimanding her children at the dinner table. "There's plenty of good food to go around." Within minutes of the banquet, all three were lying unconscious on the ground.

The padlock on the fence was even less of a challenge than Vinnie had expected, and he felt a twinge of disappointment that his bolt cutter broke it so easily, without giving him a chance to demonstrate his considerable skill in working with hardened alloy.

The next part was the easiest. Wearing gloves, Vinnie used the towel to wipe off all his fingerprints from the gas can. Then he carried the can and towel to the parking lot, where he poured a trail of gasoline from the gate to the back of Angie's Continental. Just behind the car, he soaked the towel with gasoline, stuffing one end down the spout, leaving the other end trailing to the ground.

The last step was the fastest. Vinnie struck a match and held it to the puddle of gasoline at the gate, bounded across the street into his Caddie, started the engine, and quickly accelerated up the street. He didn't wait to watch the trail of flame slither across the parking lot like a blue snake, set fire to the towel, and ignite the jumbo Molotov cocktail. He was a full block away when the explosion occurred, transforming Angie's brand new 1959 Lincoln Continental into an enormous ball of fire and twisted metal.

Vinnie was grinning like a kid as he sped away, noticing that his ears no longer seemed to be ringing so badly. He thought to himself, I'm really sorry if I spoiled your little romantic rendezvous tonight, Angie, but Dom says sometimes we all have to shake it off and just get over it. Sure hope your car insurance is paid up.

Then he was off across town to deliver the two pound box of chocolates to Aunt Emma. But first he would remember to tell her not to answer the phone for a few days.

CHAPTER 31

Ed walked into the courthouse for the depositions on Friday morning, taking the winding staircase up to the second floor, stopping at the water fountain for a quick drink. When he entered room 204, he was greeted by his good friends, court reporter Betty Blankenship and court clerk Arlene Smith, who were already seated at a table near the front of the room.

At the back of the room, he saw three people, all of whom he recognized from photos provided to him by Andrew Stover. Dudley and Patsy Scaggs, wearing their Sunday-best clothes, stood nervously talking to Samuel Lukins, a graying, middle-aged man in a dark three-piece suit. Ed surmised that Dudley and Patsy were anxious to get the whole business behind them, so they could get home, take off their uncomfortable clothes, and have a stiff drink, climbing back down off the wagon that their attorney had put them on a full day earlier.

Ed walked back to them, smiling pleasantly, and introduced himself. Dudley and Patsy did not make eye contact, but Samuel stared back at him expressionlessly during the get-acquainted formality. As they stood across from each other, Ed was reminded of the meeting between two prize fighters before a bout, each trying to size up the other and establish psychological dominance.

"If you all are ready, we'll get started," Ed said. "I'd like to depose Mrs. Scaggs first."

A look of consternation flashed across Patsy's face, and she looked at Samuel for direction. He tried to reassure her, nodding for her to take the witness chair. "Swear her," Ed directed Arlene, who then picked up the bible on the table and quickly administered the oath.

Ed started by asking Patsy questions that were intended to disarm her and put her at ease, inviting her to talk freely. They were all questions to which he already knew the answers.

Then he sprung the first unexpected query: "Did you consume alcoholic beverages during your first two pregnancies?"

Patsy reponded quickly, not bothering to first look to her attorney. Samuel was caught off guard, with no opportunity to object, as she answered, "I didn't drink back then. I never touched a drop."

Ed gave no indication that there was any significance attached to her answer, and he continued rapidly with other questions from his list. "What did Dr. Jannsen's bill you for his services the first time he treated you? How much for delivering your first child, Lonnie? How much for the second child, Marvin? How much have you ever paid Dr. Jannsen for medical services provided to yourself, Dudley, and your three sons?"

The answer to each question was an embarrassed "Nothing."

"Mrs. Scaggs, you've testified that you didn't drink alcoholic beverages during your first two pregnancies. When did you first begin to consume alcohol?"

Samuel Lukins entered the deposition for the first time. "Objection. The question is immaterial."

"Let me rephrase the question to Mrs. Scaggs. Did you consume alcohol during the time you were pregnant with Harley?"

"Objection. The question is still immaterial."

Ed turned to Betty, "Let the record show that Mrs. Scaggs has been instructed by her counsel not to answer whether she consumed alcohol during the time she was carrying her third child, Harley.

"Mrs. Scaggs, did Harley ever take a fall and strike his head while he was in the care of you or your husband? I'm talking about something like a tumble from a high chair or maybe a grocery cart?"

Patsy froze in alarm, looking nervously at her attorney. He silently signaled for her to answer, and then she perjured herself for the first time. "No."

"Describe the events that occurred the night Harley was born, beginning immediately after the delivery."

Patsy again looked at Samuel Lukins, who gave her an almost imperceptible nod to proceed. "Dr. Jannsen took the baby right after I delivered him, and set him across my belly on his back. He tied and cut the umbilical cord, and started to clean up some blood off his tummy. Then something went wrong, and the baby slipped out of his hands. Harley hit his head on the foot of the bed and started crying."

"So Dr. Jannsen was working with your son while the child was lying across your belly on his back near the center of the bed?"

"Yes." Then, gaining unexpected self-confidence from previous coaching, she added, "He did everything with Harley just the same as he did with Lonnie and Marvin."

Ed saw Samuel make a motion with his forefinger across his throat.

Seizing the opening which Patsy had unexpectedly given him, Ed pressed the attack. "If Dr. Jannsen was working with Harley while he was positioned near the center of the bed, lying across your belly, on his back, how could Harley fall and strike his head on the foot of the bed? What reason would Dr. Jannsen have to lift the child and carry him toward the foot of the bed?"

Patsy's self-confidence seemed to evaporate. "I don't know. He just lifted him up and somehow or another dropped him on the foot of the bed. That's what Mr. Lukins said." Looking over at her attorney, Patsy could see that she had just blown the scripted delivery of her lines and now had a very upset director.

Ed didn't push Patsy's deposition much longer. He really didn't need to. She had just self-destructed under oath, and there was nothing that a livid Samuel Lukins could do to recant her testimony.

Dudley's deposition held fewer surprises. Other than perjuring himself on record, he did not put his foot in his mouth, at least not until Ed threw out a couple of unexpected questions.

"How did you happen to hire a lawyer practicing in Beckley, whom you had never met before, to file this lawsuit against Dr. Jannsen?"

For one moment Dudley was completely honest, answering, "He came by the trailer to see me."

"How did Mr. Lukins know that you needed his services?"

Dudley followed with another honest answer, also born of inadequate coaching, "I don't know."

When the proceedings were over, a very unhappy Samuel Lukins quickly escorted Patsy and Dudley out of the room. Ed could hear Samuel's raised voice lecturing them as they went down the hallway, and it reminded him of a coach chewing out his team in the locker room after a lousy first half. He was almost certain he heard Samuel asking Patsy, "What the hell were you thinking in there?"

Ed gathered his papers and slipped them back in his briefcase. At the same time, Betty Blankenship was also getting her belongings together, and putting them in a large manila envelope. He heard her call his name. "Housman-"

He looked at up to see her smiling at him from across the room. In a very low voice, she delivered a remark that was strictly off the record. "Nice work."

Arlene Smith, who was walking toward the door, pretended not to hear the comment but was smiling as she went out into the hallway.

CHAPTER 32

"Hey, Vicelli, I need to talk to you for a few minutes." Vickie looked up to see young unit manager Rob Bournes standing beside her desk, smiling down at her.

"Is there some kind of problem?"

"Nope. I just need to talk over a few things with you. Norma can take your phone calls. Follow me on back to my office. Please."

Rob invited her to take a seat across the desk from him and inquired, "How was your trip back home to see your family? Everybody doing OK?"

"Everything's good at home. But I know you didn't call me in here to talk about the latest news from Eden Springs."

"You're pretty sharp, Vicelli. I noticed that from the first day you started reporting to me. So I'll get right to the point: What's this I hear about you interviewing with some new start-up TV station back home?"

"Who told you that?"

"I have hidden cameras and microphones all over 30 Rockefeller Center, and I know everything that goes on. Seriously, you're not looking to jump ship on me, are you?"

"I still would like to know how you heard about that."

"OK, I'll level with you. I've been working out at the gym for the past few months with a secret admirer of yours, Richard Hardy. We were talking about you the other night, and he told me you'd spoken with the new station manager back home and submitted a resume after you got back up here. What's that all about, anyway?"

"I think that Richard ought to have his head examined and get a swift kick in the pants for discussing my private affairs with my boss in a public gymnasium. Having said that, I'll level with you, Rob. Everything he told you's true. I didn't go searching for a job situation back home, but my long-time boyfriend did. He arranged for an introductory interview while I was home, and after the interview, I agreed to submit a resume."

"Why in the world would you do that, Vicelli? You know that I'm fast-tracking you here to become an associate staff writer and grooming you for a future promotion into TV production. There's no way any West Virginia boondock TV station can offer you the advancement opportunity you have here."

"You're part of my problem, Rob. You've a great boss, and you've always treated me first class. I know you're looking out for me from a career standpoint. This is a terrific job situation. I enjoy my work, and I love living in New York. But on the flip side, my family and a lot of my best friends are back in Eden Springs. And I'm still in love with a man back home."

"Well, Vicelli, I'm sorry about your dilemma. But you're a special person, and I'm going to do everything I can to see that you stay here. And you can kick Richard Hardy in the seat of his pants if you're so inclined, but I know he thinks a lot of you."

"How much do you know about Richard? I bet he's never told you that his family's one of the wealthiest in Connecticut, and that his folks are big philanthropists. Have you ever heard about those endowed four-year Hardy Scholarships at Harvard, Yale, and Princeton? His grandfather was the one who set them up."

Vickie returned to her desk, but her mind was now a million

miles away, or more precisely, four-hundred. That morning, just before she had left the apartment for work, she had gotten a phone call from Charlie Goins, requesting a time that he could call her back that evening. He had told her that the station was prepared to offer her one of several positions and that that they needed to work together to find out which one would be the best fit. He also wanted to determine her salary expectations. It was the toughest decision Vickie had faced in her entire life, and no one but she could make it.

That evening, back in the apartment, the phone rang, and it was Richard. "Vickie, I just called to see if you're free to go out with me for a cup of coffee?"

"I'm sorry, but I can't make it this evening, Richard. I'm expecting an important phone call, and I need to be here to take it."

The second phone call came an hour later, and this time, it was the one she had been expecting. "Vickie, this is Charlie Goins. Is this a good time for us to talk about the job opportunities that we discussed earlier?

"We're looking for an anchor who will not only present the evening news, but also cover special reporting assignments and have heavy involvement in the writing and production of the daily newscasts. We want this person to become a well-known personality and almost a personal friend to our viewers. We hope to employ someone who will evolve into the ambassador and face of WESP TV to our part of the state. Does that sound like something you'd like to take on?"

"What about the hours, Charlie? Would this person be required to live at the station twelve hours a day, seven days a week?"

"The hours probably wouldn't be any longer than those you're currently working, but they wouldn't be nine to five, as I imagine yours are now. You'd have to be flexible and prepared to work evenings. We would expect to have back-up staff to handle the weekends, leaving you free on Saturdays and Sundays, unless a special story broke."

"Charlie, how long can you give me before you have to have my answer? I've got a really tough decision facing me."

"I'm putting myself over a barrel if you don't accept, but I want you badly enough to take that risk. I'll give you three weeks. But I absolutely must know something before the Fourth of July."

After saying good-bye to Charlie, Vickie dialed Doug. "I just got off the line with Charlie Goins. He made me a job offer. Here's the scoop." She filled him in on everything she had just discussed about the WESP opening, while Doug listened intently.

"You're going to take the job, aren't you?" he asked.

"I'm certainly giving it very serious consideration. In a perfect world, I'd have the same job I have here, and be living close to you and my family. But this isn't a perfect world, is it?"

"Are you going to tell your family about the offer?"

"Certainly. But I don't want to say anything to Mom yet until I sort this out in my mind."

"Vickie, if you don't take this job, we'll never be together. I hope that still means as much to you as it does to me."

"It does, honey. It's just that it would be such a huge change for me to pick up and move back to Eden Springs after living here for the past five years."

Doug's closing comment troubled Vickie afterward: "Personally, I don't think that you have such a difficult decision to make. Either you want for us to spend the rest of our lives together, or you don't. It's that simple."

CHAPTER 33

Dominic answered his office phone on Friday morning, hearing the angry, accusatory voice of Carmine Nardelli on the other end. "Dom, what do you know about someone torching Angelo's new Continental out in front of his building last week?"

"I don't have a clue what the hell you're talking about," Dom responded, truly puzzled.

"I'll bet you don't," Carmine replied. "Someone lit off the queen mother of Molotov cocktails under his back bumper last Wednesday night around midnight. Angie was inside with one of his girlfriends when it happened, and he came running outside naked as a jay-bird with a big fire extinguisher trying to save the building. He had to call in favors a lot of people owed him to keep everything out of the papers."

"That's the first I've heard about it, and I sure don't know nothing about who might have been behind it," Dom said, while mentally matching up the dates of the fire-bombing to Vinnie's three day vacation to visit his ailing relatives. "Why are you so upset? Your dog ain't in that fight."

"Like hell it isn't. Angie thinks I had something to do with it." Carmine grew a little calmer and explained, "There was a problem on our production run the week before. We always

144

trickle each batch of whiskey through a charcoal filter to knock the edge off after it comes out of the still, since we're not about to waste time ageing it. Some idiot who works for me part-time loaded the charcoal into a barrel holding a sack of warfarin Rat Nots that we were using to kill rats. I don't know how bad it would be if someone drank any of that particular run, but I sure don't want to chance any of those city boys enjoying our hootch in a bar, and then bleeding like stuck pigs in the men's crapper. It would definitely be bad advertising for our product."

"Why are you telling me all of this bullshit, Carmine? Why should I care?"

"I'll get right to the point. I had three of my men working in Angie's Newark warehouse trying to locate and dump out all of that batch of rodent-ade just two days before his car got burned up. Now he thinks I had something to do with his auto problem."

"I don't have any more time to waste talking to you about this, Carmine. Angie needs to shake it off and just get over it. I gotta go now."

After he put down the phone, Dom called out, "Vinnie, where the hell are you? Get in here! I wanna talk to you right now!"

Vinnie didn't reply. Having overheard the first part of the conversation, he was now driving off of company property for a day of unplanned vacation.

*****

Over the mountain and down the road from Hinton, on the south side of Abner Gap, Sheriff Earl Daniels also wanted to talk to a man right now. He was standing on the edge of the Mountain Ventures landfill near Stony Creek, signaling for the operator to shut down his D-4 bulldozer and come over to see him. Sam Barry, Ed, and Doug stood beside the sheriff as the bearded man in faded denim jeans, a sweat-stained t-shirt, and work boots approached, calling, "What do you need?"

Earl took over. "A friend of mine drove by this landfill one night a couple of weeks ago and saw a crew of men unloading two flatbed trucks. I'm checking to find out what's been going on out here."

"Must be some mistake, Sheriff. Nothing's been hauled out here and unloaded in this landfill but regular garbage and trash since I started work. You might find a little construction scrap material, but not very much. I get a look at everything that gets compacted and buried, and I can tell you that it's all stuff that Mountain Ventures collects and brings out here from town in their garbage trucks."

"I've got a young man standing beside me with 20-20 eyesight and an engineering degree who says you're not telling the truth," Earl continued, gazing at the dozer operator with steely eyes. "He watched a crew working under lights unloading flatbed trucks and putting something into a pit right here beside Stony Creek."

"Then I guess it's my word against his. Exactly where did this young man see all this mystery material going into the landfill?" the man asked, talking directly to the sheriff while ignoring Doug.

"Back over there where you've just covered your trash pit with fresh fill," Doug interjected, returning the operator's stare, which was suddenly redirected from the sheriff to him. "I was over a quarter mile away, but I can still show you where I saw something being unloaded, and it wasn't trash off of a garbage truck."

"Then point out where this stuff is buried, boy, and let's take a look. I'll excavate where you tell me to. I want you to show me what you're talking about."

Doug pointed out the location, using a large rock beside the creek for mental reference. The operator returned to his bulldozer, started it up, and then graded off the fill dirt covering the trash pit, pushing the overburden to one side. To Doug's surprise, all that could be seen was an accumulation of household refuse and very ripe garbage. "Show me where you want me to dig next, son," the operator said, grinning sarcastically.

Doug studied the layout of the pit for a couple of minutes before responding. "Skim off that layer of trash back toward the creek until you just get down to the original undisturbed soil."

The operator carefully followed his instructions, using the dozer blade to scrape off the trash, exposing the packed clay underneath, still covered in places by a small accumulation of flattened cardboard cartons and newspaper.

"Stop right there," Doug commanded.

Doug disregarded the mix of loose dirt and garbage covering his new shoes as he walked into the pit and began to lift the pieces of paper and cardboard covering the hard, damp clay. While the others stood and watched, he carefully examined the ground around his feet, searching for any telltale marks that he hoped would be still be there somewhere underfoot.

Finally, he lifted a flat piece from a cardboard carton, and was relieved to see beneath it exactly what he was hoping to find. The packed clay clearly showed a pattern of grooves imprinted by the end of some heavy container. And although the container was now gone, its tracks remained behind, like the footprints of an extinct reptile left lying in the mud of an ancient river bank, waiting for discovery.

"Sheriff, come down here a minute. I've found something I want to show you." When Earl joined him, Doug said quietly, "Here's where something big was unloaded off the truck the other night. The crew working here must have hauled it away to another location after they discovered that I'd been spying on them."

Earl agreed. "I think you're dead right, son, but there's not nearly enough evidence to file a complaint, based on what we're looking at. However, I'm going to start keeping a closer eye on what goes on out here."

After Doug and Earl climbed out of the pit, Earl turned to the bulldozer operator and said, "We're through here for the day, and you can get back to work now. But you be sure to tell those Mountain Venture people you work for that I want to know about it before hand if they plan to put in any more night shifts out here."

CHAPTER 34

"When I last spoke with you, we talked about Bradford, Houseman, and Jannsen, and some plans for us to balance the books with them, so to speak," Robert Barker drawled. "We're back together this morning so I can see exactly how much progress you're making."

Robert had convened the meeting in a back room on the second floor of the run-down Ambassador Hotel in Beckley. The room still held pleasant memories for him from earlier days, and he often used it both as a personal retreat for relaxation and for private business meetings. But this morning his chronic gout was acting up again, causing him a world of pain, and putting him in a foul mood.

Sitting across the table, his son and William Thorpe both squirmed a bit in their chairs under Robert's steady gaze, then Travis spoke up. "I'll tell you where we are now, Pa. We haven't been able to finish up some things that we hoped would be done by now, but we're working on 'em as hard as we can.

"We thought we had Bradford, taken care of. He was the one who prosecuted Darnell Robbins over in Mullins for murder, and got him sentenced to fifteen years in Moundsville. Darnell threatened to get even when he got out. We paid off several members of the parole board to get Robbins an early release, and the first thing he did he was to head back this way looking for Bradford. But the state police pulled him over for speeding, caught him carrying a concealed weapon, and now he's back in the pen to finish serving his time. We're still hunting for a way to get at the DA."

"Things are going better in our dealings with Jannsen," William Thorpe chimed in, hoping to control the growing displeasure of his hot-tempered boss before it boiled all over the stove. "We've got everything lined up to take Jannsen to trial in a malpractice suit. A conviction will ruin his reputation and wreck his career."

Travis tried to build on the success story presented by his older partner. "We've had some success in dealing with Housman. We helped to put him up in the middle of a Mafia family feud, and a couple of punks deliberately ran him down with a car. He got banged up pretty good, but not as bad as we hoped. We're not through with him yet."

"That's all you two have gotten done in the past six months?" Robert growled, leaning forward across the table, unable to shake off the intense pain in his foot. "I expected a helluva lot more from you by this time."

"We've done more," William exclaimed, jumping back in. "We've taken that abandoned farmland you bought in '52 for a coal mining operation and converted it into a profitable landfill, using our Mountain Ventures subsidiary to exploit trash disposal in this region the same as the Mafia's done for years in New York and New Jersey. We bury the kind of waste that other localities don't want dumped in their own backyards, as long as they're willing to pay our price."

Robert finally broke into a faint smile, showing some degree of pleasure with the new business initiative. "Sounds like you've picked up some good ideas from our friends to the north, and may have us a winner here, William. I like the idea of making money on trash. It's one commodity which will never grow scarce. And I like the idea of a landfill right on the doorstep of Eden Springs. Sounds like a piece down the road, people will wake up and discover they've got a rather nasty compost pile lying beneath the floor of their beautiful green valley. They may end up wishing they had nothing more to worry about than some rows of spoil and a few ponds left behind by a coal mining operation."

The pleasant interlude ended when Robert shifted in his chair, triggering severe pain in his foot, returning him to the surly mood he had been in earlier. He looked at the younger men, speaking again in his badgering voice, "You two have still haven't given me your new plans to retaliate against Bradford and Housman."

William glanced at his watch, which showed the time approaching 11:00. He considered whether to launch off and tell his boss of other plans already in progress to expand the landfill operation. The ones involving night deliveries of hazardous industrial waste to be buried at premium cost to customers, under the light of the stars, away from all prying eyes.

But he was saved by the bell. The fire alarm in the hallway suddenly began to sound, abruptly ending the meeting, and the three men quickly walked from the building out into the street.

Robert's gout was causing excruciating discomfort as he hobbled toward his car, growling, "Just go on and get the hell out of here, both of you. I'll get back to you later when I'm not hurting this bad."

Travis turned to William in relief, exclaiming, "Talk about luck. We must have horseshoes up our butts! Who'd have figured that the fire alarm would go off just in time to save us from another chewing by the old man."

"Yeah, we were lucky," William agreed with a wink, returning to the hotel to slip the bellboy another ten bucks for triggering the alarm exactly on the hour.

*****

Outside of Keystone, one of the principals in the Mafia family feud discussed by the Barkers was not feeling nearly as lucky. Carmine Nardelli surveyed the smoking remains of the detached four car garage he had built a few years earlier. The huge recreation room upstairs had contained every amenity a working man could want, including overstuffed sofas, refrigerator, chilled beer keg, and color TV. Now all that remained on top of the cracked concrete garage floor was a collection of rubble that looked like something dragged out of a coke oven. Carmine stood shaking his head, and spat out, "Angelo Vinciano, you bastard!" Then trying to find a bright spot in an otherwise black sky, he added, "Well, at least the old lady's convertible and my new truck were parked outside."

Carmine walked across the yard to take a seat on the bench where his wife, Christina, liked to sit in the shade with her French poodle, Monsieur Nuzzles. He knew in his Sicilian heart that there had to be payback but pondered just where to start. After all, Dom was the one who had gotten the feud started by threatening a lawsuit over a crummy ten grand debt. Still, Angie was the one who had just gored his prize ox by burning to the ground the only sanctuary where he could escape from a sharp-tongued wife. "Eeny, meeny, miny, mo," he said aloud, pointing back and forth between two nearby poodle deposits, which in his mind now represented his business associates.

When his finger stopped at the larger pile, the decision was made. Time for a vacation trip back to the Garden State, he thought to himself. I can drop off Cristina over at Coney Island, and she can spend the day lying on the beach getting a tan with her sister, while I pay a call on Universal Restaurant Supply Company. "Angie, Joe Louis had it right," he muttered. "You can run, but you can't hide."

Carmine got up and went inside, calling to his wife, who was camped out in the master bathroom, reading a paperback romance novel while immersed up to the neck in a tub of hot water. The bathtub was topped with a head of foam, somewhat like a good draft beer, from the big scoop of aromatic bubble bath salts she had tossed in earlier. "Cristina! Honey, how'd you like to go visit your sister next week? You can take her for a ride on the octopus at Coney. My treat." Carmine watched a big smile cross Christina's plump face, as she blew him a kiss.

*****

A little further north in the Garden State, there was less sweetness and light. Angie's ears may have subconsciously burned from Carmine's outburst about the legitimacy of his birth, but it did not distract him from his coaching session with two of his finest. "Let me get this straight. You say you torched Carmine's garage? The one with the big rumpus room upstairs? His favorite hangout with the sofas and beer cooler? Why didn't you just shoot his wife and burn his house while you were about it?

"You guys ever been around his old lady, Cristina? That woman has a voice that could crack a bank vault, and she doesn't ever shut up from morning 'til night. The only way Carmine's kept from going nuts all these years is by hiding out up in his loft. She's got a bad leg and can't get up the steps to him. I just wanted you two to do something a little less drastic in order to teach him a lesson, like torching his new truck.

"But since you guys obviously don't know jack about how to even things up, tit for tat, and have stirred up something really big, we're going to have to drag out some of those old mattresses from the back room. For the next few weeks, you two and the rest of the crew will be taking turns pulling sentry duty down here at night, waiting for a West Virginia visitor to show up. And he will be here, rest assured. I know Carmine, and it ain't a matter of if he's coming, it's when."

CHAPTER 35

"**Can I give anyone a** refill?" Richard inquired, holding up a pitcher, as the Hardy family stretch limo carrying his weekend guests continued up the road from New York City toward Fairfield. "I guess you could call these drinks virgin red-eyes, since I only mixed tomato juice with beer and left out the vodka." Sharing the luxurious rear compartment of the limo with him were his apartment neighbors, Jonathon and Jeremy Goldstein, Karen Billings, Janice Gilmore, and Vickie.

After everyone declined, he continued, "Looks like a perfect day for boating on Long Island Sound this afternoon. I thought we'd go out for a sail after you all get settled in at the house. We can have a picnic lunch on board."

Vickie had felt a little uncomfortable about accepting Richard's invitation for a weekend vacation at his folk's waterfront home in Fairfield, but he had assured her it was nothing more than a summer outing with five of his best friends. Besides, she had discussed the over-nighter with Doug beforehand, and he had told her that he didn't mind as long as she was sharing a room with Janice and Karen. But the fact that Richard had squeezed into the seat beside her made Vickie a little guarded in her small talk with him during the drive, and she concentrated on involving everyone in the conversation along the way.

When the driver wheeled the limo up a circular brick driveway and stopped in front of the Hardy home, Vickie knew that she was looking at old money. The magnificent two-story home appeared to have been built in the earlier part of the twentieth century but maintained in mint condition since day one. Brick steps led to a wide front porch, which ran the length of the house and wrapped around both ends. A dozen or so white wrought iron chairs with plush cushions invited visitors to sit and enjoy the view across the spacious, well manicured grounds toward the waters of Long Island Sound.

The chauffeur carried the luggage up the steps to the house, where Richard's mother and father were waiting to greet their weekend guests. Richard quickly made the round of introductions, with Vickie the last of the visitors to meet his folks. "Mother, Daddy, this is my friend, Vickie Vicelli."

The Hardy parents both gave her welcoming smiles and their undivided attention. His father took her hand and said, "So you're Vickie. Richie's been telling us so much about you. We've really been looking forward to getting to know you."

His mother added, "Richie's been wanting for weeks to have you come here for a visit, so that we could meet you. Welcome to our home, Fairview."

If Vickie had felt a little uncomfortable earlier about accepting Richard's invitation, she felt even more so now. Why in the world would he talk about me to his parents, she asked herself, while almost certain that she already knew the answer. "Nice to meet both of you, Mr. and Mrs. Hardy," she replied. Then, trying to set the record straight about her casual friendship with their son, she added, "Thanks for inviting all of us to spend the weekend here in your beautiful home."

Plans for a picnic on the boat were changed when it turned out that Mrs. Hardy had already instructed the cook to serve lunch in the solarium. Vickie was seated between Richard's parents, and they engaged her in conversation throughout the meal. "I hope that you'll call us Evelyn and Bernard, and that we can call you Vickie," Bernard remarked pleasantly. "Richie tells us that you're a very capable young lady, and a fast learner. He hopes to give you a sailing lesson while you're here. Richie's been handling the helm of a boat since he was twelve-years old, and he's a much better sailor than either his older brother or I."

Later that day, after the six friends had boarded the boat and set sail on Long Island Sound, Richard invited Vickie to take the helm, while he stood directly behind her, reaching around her from time to time to trim the boat's heading in the gusty wind. "You're a born sailor," he complimented her, as the craft knifed through the choppy water. "I thought you'd take to a sailboat like a duck to water, and you have. How do you like it out here"

"I don't think I've ever had more fun," Vickie replied truthfully, unaware that Richard smiled upon hearing her answer.

"I think you'll find sailing a two man Cape Cod catboat is even more fun than this forty-two footer," Richard remarked. "The next time you're here for an overnight visit, we'll take mine out. It's the one I learned to sail when I was ten-years old."

Later in the day, the wind died, and the party had to return to port under power. Vickie watched the Hardy home appear in the distance as they got closer to land and knew that she was briefly experiencing the good life of society's elite.

Back at the house, drinks were served on the porch, before everyone entered the dining room for a sumptuous dinner. Afterward, Richard and his guests strolled through the neighborhood of spectacular old homes, and he told them the history of each, as it had been related to him by his grandfather.

"I could get used to living here very quickly," Karen commented, looking at Richard with a smile. "The neighborhood where I grew up looked a little different. Not many of the people on our street had yachts tied up at their dock, or employed a chauffeur, maid, and cook."

Janice joined in. "Vickie and I both grew up in nice homes

in Eden Springs, but around here, our houses would look like maid's quarters."

"But, still, all three of you all ended up graduating from an Ivy League university with honors," Richard observed. "I don't think you were deprived of much that was really important. Besides, you'll probably lead happier lives than a lot of the big shots in this country who are obsessed with piling up all the money they can." Richard started to slip his arm around Vickie's waist, but before he could do so, she dropped back to walk beside Janice, commenting on one of the houses.

The rest of the weekend was equally enjoyable: a rowdy poker game in the library that evening fueled by drinks and snacks; an early morning breakfast on the front porch to watch the spectacular red and orange sunrise across Long Island Sound; and an early lunch with sunlight flooding the solarium where they sat surrounded by huge potted plants.

As Richard and his friends walked toward the limousine after the mid-day meal, Bernard and Evelyn Hardy accompanied them, inviting all to return. Evelyn singled Vickie out, murmuring, "I thought Richard might have exaggerated a bit when he told us about you, but his dad and I agree that, as usual, he's been entirely truthful. Please come back to visit us soon."

Back in New York, Richard took Vickie aside. "My folks were really impressed by you. They want me to bring you back again next week. Will you go with me?"

Vickie held out her hand to him and replied gently, "I don't think I've ever enjoyed a weekend more in my entire life. Your folks are wonderful people, and they made me feel so welcome in their home. Richard, nothing has changed between us. You're one of my dearest friends, and always will be. But please understand that I'm still in love with Doug. Thank your parents for their kind invitation, but this time, I'll have to decline."

Vickie saw Richard's face darken. He picked up his bag from the sidewalk and turned to walk up the street toward his apartment building. She called out apologetically, "We can still be friends, can't we?"

Richard stiffened as he heard her plea, but he continued, disappearing into the crowd of strangers.

When Vickie got home, Janice was in her bedroom, unpacking her bag and listening to pop music on the radio. Looking through her purse, she dug out the home phone number Charlie Goins had given her earlier and picked up the telephone to make a call. She had just made one life-changing decision moments earlier and was now preparing to make the second.

When Vickie heard Charlie answer, she spoke. "Charlie, this is Vickie. After a lot of deliberation and soul-searching, I've come to a decision, and I'd like to accept your offer to come to work at WESP as a news anchor. I plan to mail you my acceptance letter in the morning and give my two week resignation notice to my boss at NBC immediately afterward."

The delight in Charlie's voice was evident as she heard him confirm that she had made the right decision for everyone involved, including herself. "You've got a bright future ahead of you right here in your home town," he reassured her. "Your boyfriend and your family must be overjoyed right now." Vickie told him that those were the next two phone calls she was about to make.

As soon as Doug answered the phone, Vickie rushed to share her news. "Honey, I have a surprise. I've just taken the job at WESP!" It took her a few minutes to convince him that she had indeed said yes to Charlie, and that she would be handing in her written resignation to her boss at NBC.

Doug was almost speechless. "You're definitely coming back home?" he asked her several times, as if the news were literally unbelievable. "I was beginning to think that you'd never come back! Do you have any idea how I feel right now? I'm bouncing off the ceiling. This is the best day of my life. Wait until I tell Mom and Dad and all of our friends. When you get back home, we're going to have the biggest party this town has ever seen. I'll be counting the days until you get here. I love you more than you'll ever know."

Afterward, Vickie went into Janice's bedroom to break the news, staying for a good cry as the long-time friends and roommates realized that they would now be going their separate ways.

When she called home, her family's reaction was as ecstatic as Doug's. Ingrid was unable to contain her excitement. "Honey, this is what I've been praying to hear. Why don't you live with us when you get back to town? I've kept everything in your bedroom exactly the way it was when you left for college."

"You're welcome to my Plymouth," Tony added. "I'll put some new seat covers in it so you don't mess up your nice clothes." It was one of the few times Vickie could recall her dad at a loss for words.

"I'm glad you're coming back, sis," TJ chimed in. "We can't wait to see you. But you might want to look around for a car when you get here. When I take Dad's rattletrap down to the Texaco, I tell Old Man Perkins to fill it up with oil and check the gas."

After the last call, Vickie felt emotionally drained. But she also felt an enormous relief that the biggest decision of her life was now behind her. And she knew in her heart that she had made the right choice, both for her own happiness and that of those she loved most.

CHAPTER 36

Saturday morning, Ed and Sam Barry stood side by side with Buddy and Beau Preston near the foot of cemetery hill on the Buchanan farm. Before them was assembled the group of eighty-two Eden Spring friends and neighbors who had volunteered for duty as reenactors, all wearing t-shirts dyed either deep blue or gray. This was to be the first full scale practice on site, with an early start time chosen to avoid the sweltering summer heat which would soon follow as the sun climbed higher in the sky. Weapons had been left back at the "armory," the locked Boy Scout storage room in the basement of the Methodist church.

Across the field, near the crest of the knoll, stood Roseanna, which would provide part of the authentic backdrop for the battle reenactment. Mayor Cline's plans for the Cen Plus Ten celebration in September (developed with heavy input from the real architect of the event, his wife Edna) called for spectators in period costumes to be seated in folding chairs along the road, close to the house.

The reenactors had gotten into the spirit of things surprisingly quickly after Ed and Sam chose sides. Beards began to spring up everywhere. Yanks and Rebs bonded with their comrades in arms and turned against their adversaries to a degree that no one had expected. Almost overnight, the Blue and Gray soldiers began to give enemy troops a hard time whenever they encountered them around town.

Peg and Jerry Altice had mounted a pole flying the Confederate flag beside the road leading up to their farm house and posted a sign on the gate proclaiming that it was now open season on all Yankees. Ollie Johnson's six grown sons, three enlisted with the north and the other three with the south, had gotten so rambunctious that their mother, Olivia, had quit inviting them over for Sunday dinners until after the armistice.

It seemed as though the town were reliving the Civil War, which had turned brother against brother, and father against son. Someone suggested that double striped lines be painted down the middle of Main Street, blue facing north and gray facing south. That might have worked, except that Yank and Reb families were interspersed from house to house within the neighborhoods on either side.

Ed lifted his bullhorn and announced, "All you Johnny Rebs in the gray t-shirts, listen up. E Company's going to assemble a quarter of a mile down at the south end of the field. When Sam gives us the signal that he's ready, we'll march back up here in formation near the foot of the hill where the Yanks will have set up their ambush. Then we'll break ranks, form a skirmish line, charge up the hill, and reenact the combat scene exactly the way we scripted it. Anyone have any questions? If not, follow me."

Sam then came in on a second bullhorn to instruct his troops. "All Yanks wearing the blue of the Union Army, fall in up here on the side of the hill, and we'll start assigning you to your positions for the ambush. You'll be out in the open today, but we'll bring in logs and brush for concealment before the performance in September. Buddy's going to be assisting us Yanks, and Beau will be working with the Rebs. We're all going to be flying by the seat of our pants this morning, so just bear with us."

Sam remembered one other piece of information and added, "No reenactors will be positioned on top of the hill by the cemetery next to the big oak tree. That area will be considered off limits. You've probably heard by now that we're trying to get WESP Channel 8 out here for the reenactment, and we're hoping they'll have a camera crew stationed up there to telecast the event."

A short time later, E Company had fallen-in and was standing at parade rest, with Ed in front, and Sam Bradford beside him holding a furled red and white bath towel to simulate a battle flag. Maybe Ed was distracted, but he failed to notice something going on in the ranks behind him. The three Johnson boys had somehow managed to smuggle in several burlap sacks filled with fresh, wet road apples collected at a nearby horse farm the previous day. Bart Johnson whispered a command, "Lock and load," as the sacks of ammunition passed through the ranks, and the soldiers filled both hands with globular horse dung.

Finally, Ed heard Sam Barry start the action by keying his bullhorn and shouting out a sing-song taunt, "We're here waiting on you. All you little Rebs, come and get it!"

Ed gave the command, "Forward march," and E company moved smartly north across the field toward cemetery hill, most of the men and boys more or less in step and roughly aligned by rank and file, every single one armed with softball size ordnance in each hand.

When they neared the foot of the hill where forty-two of their friends and neighbors were kneeling or lying prone in ambush positions, Sam called out, "Open fire!"

Ed quickly countered with, "Break ranks! Form a skirmish line! Move up the hill to engage the enemy!"

The next ten minutes were pure bedlam. Some of the event organizers had worried that the volatile mixture of adrenaline and testosterone produced by eighty-two men thrown together in mock combat might generate more action than was called for by the script. However, none of them had anticipated that the troops in gray would charge up the hill, pelting the men in blue with softball sized lumps of wet horse manure.

The Yanks fell back from the onslaught but quickly regrouped and counter-attacked from the high ground, hurling the same equine cannon balls that had just been directed at them back into the faces of their gray enemies below. In a short time, there was no one on the battlefield who was not marked with deep brown stains by multiple hits to the head and body.

The six Johnson boys were going at it hardest, seemingly in mortal combat in one big pile of blue and gray, rolling around on the ground. Buddy and Beau watched, grinning ear to ear, offering friendly encouragement and helpful advice. "Bite his ear! Gouge his eyes! Kick him in the groin!"

Ed and Sam finally disengaged themselves from the other combatants, found their bullhorns, and called off their warriors. Buddy and Beau offered their assessment. "Helluva of a good first practice!" Buddy exclaimed, clearing a small piece of horse shrapnel from between his teeth. "By September, the spectators will think you guys really are trying to kill each other!"

Beau added, "But we'll have to cut out the horseplay when we break out the muskets at the next rehearsal and get down to serious work on safely conducting the shooting action during the battle. Y'all need to start selecting who will go down as the dead and wounded victims. What do you say we get together back here in three weeks for the next battle rehearsal?"

Sam Bradford knocked the dirt and horse dung off his face and arms, observing with a laugh, "There's going to be a big run on liniment and pain killers at the drug store tonight. I'm going by there first thing when I get back to town, to be sure I get my supply before they sell out."

Ed and Sam dismissed the reenactors, thanking Buddy and Beau for driving up for the weekend to act as consultants. On the drive home, Ed asked Doug, "Heard any more from Vickie?"

"Yeah, I talked to her last night. "She'll be flying home on the Fourth of July weekend, and she'll have a week off before starting to work. Her mom's planning a surprise welcome home party when she gets in."

"It's going to be a big adjustment for her coming back here to live," Ed commented. "Sometimes picking up where you left off is very difficult. People and places change a lot over the period of five years that she's been away."

"I know that. All I can hope is that she enjoys the new job, and that it really challenges her. Maybe she'll be so busy trying to get her arms around TV broadcast work that she doesn't have time to stop and think about all the things she's given up for good in New York."

As they passed the Mountain Ventures property, Ed glanced over at the entrance. "Looks like the people operating the landfill have put a locked gate across their road since we drove in there with Sheriff Daniels. I'm sure that having you sneak up on them at night is the reason the gate's been installed."

"That Mountain Ventures guy with the beard acted pretty cocky when we came out here," Doug replied. "He knew that whatever I saw being unloaded over by Stony Creek had been hauled back out long before we arrived. He seemed to enjoy giving me a bad time. Sheriff Daniels told me that he's going to start keeping a closer eye on what's going on out here. So am I."

CHAPTER 37

"**I can't believe I'm actually** coming back home to live," Vickie exclaimed, as she and Doug departed the Charleston airport.

"I hope you mean that in the sense of 'it's just too good to be true,' and not 'I must have been out of my mind to do something like this,'" Doug joked. "Truthfully, I had begun to doubt that this day would ever come."

"In one way, it was an easy decision, and in another, it was about the hardest one I've ever made," Vickie confided. "The people at NBC gave me a big going away party, and then Janice, Karen, and Richard took me out to dinner. I shed a few tears before I left New York. Guess I'm one of those people who tend to cry when they have to say goodbye, either coming or going."

Doug reached over to give her hand a sympathetic squeeze.

As they approached the Vicelli home, Doug saw that there were no cars parked on the street in front or in the driveway. But he spotted Mike's and Freddie's cars a half block away, and knew that everyone was already inside, waiting for her to appear. Vickie walked through the front door and was greeted by a cacophony of voices shouting "Surprise!" She was overwhelmed to find the house decorated with banners and balloons and to find all of her family and many of her old high school friends waiting to greet her, including Sandra, home from Radford College for the summer. It quickly became apparent that Vickie not only cried when saying goodbye, but also, sometimes, upon saying hello.

Doug stepped aside to watch the reunion unfold. After greeting Vickie, Ingrid and Sandra came over to join him, and he slipped his arms around both. "She's home now, Doug," Ingrid whispered in his ear. "She came back because of you." He pulled Mama V a little closer.

The party soon moved out into the back yard where a picnic had been spread. A record player was cranked up, playing all of the current hits, but the music was almost drowned out by the number of conversations being carried on simultaneously. Freddie took Marilyn around the yard and proudly introduced her to all of his friends. Everyone was having a great time, and no one seemed to be in any hurry to leave, so the party continued on until 11:00, with only Tony and Ingrid bowing out early.

Doug and Vickie settled in together on the sofa after the last guests left. "Quite a good start for your first day back home, wouldn't you say?" Doug inquired. Vickie replied by putting both arms around his neck and pulling his face down to hers When the two finally said goodnight, and Doug walked to his car, he noticed that the light in Tony's bedroom was still on.

Vickie spent the following week getting settled back in her old home town. Freddie showed her a number of apartments for rent, helping her select a one-bedroom efficiency down the street from Doug. She found time to go by the Fresh Harvest Supermarket, working a check-out counter for several hours. Many of the store customers recognized her, including Arnella Umberger, her eighty-year old first grade teacher, who walked over to give her a big hug.

Doug called on Friday to suggest that they triple-date that evening with Mike, Ginny, Freddie, and Marilyn, to go dancing at Brookside, a popular nightspot just a few miles south of town. "I'll be ready at 8:00," she told him. "Just be sure to come to the door and get me- don't blow the horn out front." She heard Doug laugh and knew he was also remembering her dad's reaction to a former boyfriend who had done just that when she was a high school sophomore

Freddie volunteered to drive, picking up everyone in his Olds hardtop that evening. The parking lot at Brookside was almost full when they arrived, but once inside the dimly lit, low-ceilinged room, they found a vacant table close to the small dance floor, far enough away from the juke box that they could talk.

The waitress came by to deliver their mugs of Bud draft at the same time Paul Anka was crooning his sentimental hit, *Put Your Head on My Shoulder*. Vickie sang along in a surprisingly good voice, looking at Doug as she stressed the lyric, "Whisper in my ear, ba-by!"

"Here's to good friends and good times," Mike said, proposing a toast, the others reaching out to touch their mugs to his. "Here's to Ginny, the best wife and mother in the whole wide world; to Vickie, the prodigal daughter who's finally come home; and to Marilyn, our new friend and the best damn vet in West Virginia." The three couples jitterbugged to the fast numbers, and slow danced to the love songs. It was a magical evening that none of them ever wanted to end.

The group was so engrossed in sharing stories and laughing that, at first, they didn't notice two men approaching their table. The larger of the two, holding a long-neck beer bottle in his hand, stood in front of them and exclaimed, "Look who's here tonight! It's my old girl friend!" He paused to look over the group seated at the table, and then loudly slurred, "Vickie Vicelli! You look just as good now as you did when I used to take you out in high school. Maybe even better. Where in the world have you been all of these years? I just got in town from Bluefield and was asking people whatever happened to you. Let me grab a chair and sit down. It'll be like old times."

Doug looked up into the bloodshot eyes of Len Hacker. He had not set seen him in seven years, but though Len appeared to have lost some hair in front, and gained some weight around the middle, he was still unmistakably the same person Doug remembered from their violent encounter in high school. He glanced across at Vickie, reading the obvious look of dismay and alarm that flashed across her face, along with a silent appeal for help. She had not been in Len's presence since he had made a drunken pass at her in his car when she was sixteen, and she was totally disconcerted by his unexpected appearance tonight.

Doug whispered, "Do you want Len coming over here?" She shook her head vehemently. He rose to his feet and told Len, "Vickie doesn't want to talk to you."

"Who the hell asked you what she wants?" Len rasped, turning to face Doug. "Butt out- I'm talking to my old girl friend here."

"I said she doesn't want to talk to you," Doug repeated, now in an eye to eye stare down with Len. "You and your friend shove off."

Len pushed the beer bottle down into the back pocket of his pants, then grabbed the front of Doug's shirt with both hands. Doug quickly knocked his hands away, giving Len a hard shove backward. The burly bouncer, who had been watching the altercation develop from behind the bar, came running over to put a stop to it before it went any further. "If you two got some kind of disagreement, take it outside. There ain't going to be any fighting in here tonight."

"Come on outside with me, Dougie," Len muttered. "We'll finish talking about this in the parking lot."

Later, it was hard to remember exactly who said what in the minutes that followed. Vickie pleaded with Doug not to go outside. Mike and Freddie wanted to stand up with Doug and make it three against two in the parking lot. Doug finally got his way, insisting that it was between him and Len.

Doug followed Len out the door and away from the building, trying to control the butterflies that had come to life in his stomach and the apprehension that was now threatening to overwhelm him. When Len suddenly wheeled around to face him, Doug heard Mike shout a warning, "Dawg! Watch out!

He's got a beer bottle in his hand!" At that instant the adrenalin kicked in, and the butterflies quieted.

Doug had not had much to drink that evening, and Len had been going at it hard for several hours, which made a difference in their reaction times. Without hesitation, Doug brought his right fist up in a short, powerful upper-cut that caught Len squarely on the left side of his jaw, snapping his head to the right. The impact of the blow knocked Len backward, and he was already unconscious from the concussion before his legs folded under him, and he crumpled to the ground.

Doug looked at the stranger who had been with Len, and said tersely, his voice quivering with emotion, "Better take care of your friend. If he has any thoughts about reporting this to the sheriff, remind him that there are two witnesses here that saw him try to come at me with a beer bottle before I hit him." As Mike and Freddie drew closer, Doug urged, "Let's go inside and get the girls, and get the hell out of here. Thanks for backing me up tonight. If that other guy had waded in on me, it would have been bad news. It feels like I may have broken my hand when I hit Len."

The six friends quickly piled into Freddie's car and took off. When Freddie stopped at Vickie's house, Doug walked her to the front door. She was still shaking as he held her for a few minutes, promising, "Don't worry, I believe we've seen the last of Len Hacker. I may have busted my hand, but I think he might have a broken jaw."

Walking toward the car after Vickie had gone inside, Doug glanced back and noticed Tony Vicelli's bedroom light. Somehow, despite all the emotional turmoil he was feeling, it helped to reassure him that everything was still OK in their world.

CHAPTER 38

"**How did your first day** on the new job go?" Doug asked, as he reached over to open the car door for Vickie, after patiently waiting for her in the parking lot of the station for half an hour. "There must be a lot of activity in there. I've been watching a bunch of people coming and going while I've been here."

"It's been pretty hectic, but everything seems to be coming together on schedule," she replied, as she slid across the seat, close to him. "We'll be putting out a test pattern in a few days, and Charlie still expects us to begin broadcasting in August."

Doug smiled at her use of the words "we" and "us," noticing how quickly she'd begun to personally identify with the station. "What will you be doing until the station goes on the air?"

"Charlie's assigned me to work with the sales department. I'll be calling on businesses to drum up advertising contracts. His plan is to start in this vicinity before moving out further in our broadcast coverage area, so I'll be calling on people in town for the next few weeks. But enough about that; how's your hand?"

"The x-ray didn't show any fractured bones. All that they did at the hospital was to wrap it with an elastic bandage and some adhesive tape. The doctor did tell me to stay out of the ring for six months," Doug added wryly. He glanced at his watch, adding, "Mom's expecting us for dinner, so I guess we'd better be on our way."

When they walked through the front door, Laura, Ed, Lizzie, and JR were all waiting to greet them. Doug and Vickie had been an item for seven years, and despite Vickie's five year sabbatical in New York, she was still a member of the family to all four. "How's our news anchor doing today?" Laura inquired.

"I'm afraid that the news anchor job is still just a gleam in my eye," Vickie replied. "If you ask me how the TV advertising saleswoman is doing, I can probably give you a better answer."

Over a table loaded with Laura's fried chicken, potato salad, green beans, and lemon pie, Vickie turned to Ed and asked, "Granddaddy's trial is still set to begin next Monday, isn't it?"

"That's right. All of the pre-trial procedures have been completed. I've already deposed the plaintiffs. The next step is jury selection. Opening statements will begin immediately afterward."

Laura asked curiously, "Do you expect to have any problem selecting an impartial jury?"

"I think that's going to be a much bigger problem for the plaintiffs' attorney than for me. I've seen a jury list, and most of them have lived around here for quite a while. I suspect that some of the prospective jurors or a family member have been treated by Dr. Jannsen at one time or another."

Ed glanced at Vickie, adding, "There used to be an old radio program called *Dr. Christian* that everyone enjoyed when I was growing up. The main character was a wise, kind-hearted, salt-of-the-earth family doctor that everyone in town thought could walk on water. I think that's the same kind of affection that most of the folks around here have for your grandfather. I don't envy Samuel Lukins in trying to seat twelve people sympathetic to the Scaggs family and their lawsuit."

Lizzie, who had been waiting patiently throughout the meal for an opportunity to get Doug's attention, suddenly interjected,

"Doug, there's a leak in our new dam. All the water's run out. The ducks don't have a place to swim."

Doug responded sympathetically, "Sounds pretty serious, Liz. Vickie, would you be willing to help me with this civil engineering project? Mom can hold the dinner dishes for us to wash when we get back."

Laura waved them off with a smile, saying, "You two get on out there with Lizzie. I'll handle the dishes if you two can take care of the leak. We don't want another Johnstown flood."

Doug and Vickie borrowed some well-worn Bermuda shorts, t-shirts, and tennis shoes from Ed and Laura, then followed Lizzie out to the branch running down the hillside a short distance from the house. When they arrived, JR and the four ducks were on already on site, as though surveying the damage.

The cause of the problem was obvious. Where Doug, Mike, and Freddie had dammed up the branch three weeks earlier using old railroad ties, the water no longer went over the spillway, but now ran out beneath the dam through a newly created hole. "Looks like some muskrats have been at work here," Doug observed, "but it's nothing we can't fix. We'll just stack rocks and sod at the base of the dam on both sides. Let's take our shoes off and get to work."

The three hauled a pile of large creek rocks and muddy clumps of sod from the stream bank above them. Doug then waded into the water to begin repairing and reinforcing the base of the dam. As soon as the hole was plugged, the water level quickly began to rise toward the spillway and was soon deep enough to soak the hems of his Bermudas.

The project was coming to a successful and peaceful conclusion, when Doug was overcome by a mischievous male impulse, totally abandoning normal common sense. Swinging his hand across the surface of the rising pool, he slung a heavy stream of muddy water in Vickie's direction, drenching her from head to foot, and immediately triggered Armageddon. Letting out an Amazonian war cry, she jumped into the muddy pool and tackled him, knocking him backward off balance, and sending him beneath the surface. When he tried to get his face above water, she jumped on top of him and shoved his head back under again. The third time he came up for air, he managed to back away from her, laughing and choking, throwing up his hands, and shouting, "Uncle! Uncle!"

Looking at the muddy water streaming down Doug's face, Vickie read him the riot act. "You're a complete idiot, Housman, you know that? This branch flows through a big dairy farm upstream, and the water down here is bound to be full of cow poop. I hope you swallowed a gallon." Then she lost control and began to laugh, recovering just long enough to repeat, "You really are a typical male idiot."

Lizzie, JR, and the four ducks had been watching the show with great interest. Finally, Lizzie chimed in with her opinion, showing that even at a very early age, she had the genes of a budding feminist. "I'm glad you beat him up, Vickie. When boys start doing things like that to us, we need to get them back. I bet Doug won't pick on you again."

The three walked back toward the house, leaving JR and his web-footed family to enjoy their newly refilled pool. On the way, Lizzie asked, "Did y'all notice that Lena and Lori are boys?"

Vickie replied, "Yep, I could tell that two are males and two are females. Is that a problem?"

"I guess so. But I don't want to change their names now, because they've gotten used to them."

"I've got a suggestion," Doug chimed in. "Around here a lot of boys have two names, like Jim-Bob or Joe-Dan. Maybe you could change the names of the two drakes to Lena-Bob and Lori-Dan. What do you think?"

"I think that's a good idea, Doug. That's exactly what I'm going to do," Lizzie replied, squeezing Doug's hand.

"Well whatta ya know!" Vickie said, pulling Doug's head to the side to kiss him on his muddy cheek. "You finally came up with a good idea. Chalk one up for my idiot."

When the three walked through the back door, Ed and Laura looked at Doug and Vickie's wet, muddy clothes without saying a word, but they glanced at each other with knowing grins. Laura collected a clean towel and wash cloth for each of them. Her only comment was directed to no one in particular, but Ed and Doug knew that it was aimed at both of them, when she said, resigned, "Like father, like son."

CHAPTER 39

"**I know that we're getting** pretty close to the wire, but I believe that I've come up with some new information that may help you with your defense strategy for the trial next week." Andrew Stover looked at Arnold and inquired, "Does the name Shelby Murray ring any bells with you?"

"Yes, it certainly does," Arnold replied, trying to recall the facts. "Shelby was a temporary employee who worked for me as a receptionist about six months ago, while one of the other ladies in my office was out having a baby. Why do you ask?"

Andrew picked up his cup of coffee, then delivered his bombshell. "Because I've discovered that she was the link between Samuel Lukins and the Scaggs family."

"I can't believe that," Arnold replied, in disbelief. "Shelby's a nice woman who's had to deal with a lot of hard luck in her life. I won't take time to go into all of the details, but I always considered her to be completely trustworthy."

"I'm afraid that we're back to the old cliché, everyone has his price," Andrew continued. "A lifelong run of bad luck can create enough desperation for some people to violate their own rules of conduct. I'm afraid Mrs. Murray falls into that category."

"Exactly how did she come to get involved?" Ed asked.

"Here's the way I see things," Andrew replied. "I'm going to give you my theory about what's gone on behind the scenes, with a pretty high degree of confidence that this old gumshoe has it right.

"You've told me that Robert Barker and others working for him have been trying to get back at both of you for something you did seven years ago. I think he wanted to attack you, Arnold, where he thought it would hurt you the worst, by damaging your reputation and standing in the community. He hired Samuel Lukins, an attorney known throughout the region as a legal pit bull, to search for any Achilles' heel that you might have. Lukins found an employee of yours, Shelby Murray, whom he could exploit. He discovered that she was financially strapped, with access to your medical files, and he paid her to find a patient who did not have a perfect outcome to his medical treatment. That's where the Scaggs family comes into the picture.

"Lukins learned that the third Scaggs boy, Harley, is mentally handicapped, and he contacted Dudley and Patsy, convincing them that he could collect a lot of money for them in a bogus malpractice suit. He told them that all they would have to do is tell a few lies in court, testifying that Dr. Jannsen injured their son during the delivery. We know that they sold out to Lukins. And in order to assure a winning verdict, Barker gave Lukins a blank check to buy some expert medical testimony from Dr. Emil Heinz to support his lawsuit, leaving us where we are today."

"I wish we'd learned this earlier, so I could depose Shelby Murray before the trial. But I'll subpoena her as a witness and make her think about whether she's ready to risk the consequences of committing perjury."

"I believe that she'll be a pretty fragile witness, Ed," Andrew agreed. "She has two young daughters to support, and the prospect of being sent away to serve time for lying under oath, leaving them alone on their own, will be terrifying."

"You'll be available to testify if I need you?" Ed inquired.

"I plan to be right there in the courtroom the whole time,"

Andrew replied. "After all of the investigative leg-work I've done, watching this go to trial will be the frosting on the cake for me."

When the meeting broke up, Ed felt confident that he had a stronger case for the defense. A little of his exhilaration evaporated the following morning when he received a call from Sheriff Daniels.

"Ed, I've been unable to serve a subpoena on Shelby Murray to appear as a witness. She's disappeared out of town without leaving an address where she can be reached. We're still working to locate her, but I'm doubtful we'll be able to serve her in time for the trial next week."

"She doesn't have a family or close friends who know her whereabouts?"

"I'm afraid not. She lives alone, and it appears that she keeps pretty much to herself. I can't find anyone who has seen her since last week. But we're still following up to see if we can develop any leads. Is she that important to you?"

"You have no idea, Earl. Please pull out all the stops and do everything you can to locate her. It seems more than a coincidence that she's disappeared just at we're trying to get her added as a post discovery witness for the trial next week."

As soon as the sheriff was off the line, Ed placed another call. "Andrew, you're going to have to wait a little longer to sample the frosting on that cake. Shelby Murray's run. Earl Daniels tried to serve a subpoena on her, and he discovered she's disappeared without a trace. Samuel Lukins must have found out that I was going to put her on the witness stand and helped her get out of town. Earl's still looking for her, but I'd like for you to start searching, too. Can you get on this right away?"

"I'm on it this minute. I'll call you back as soon as I can find out what's going on."

On Friday morning, Ed heard from Andrew. "I'm not having any more luck than the sheriff in finding Shelby Murray. One of her neighbors told me that she saw Shelby come out of her house around noon on Wednesday of last week, and that was the last time she could recall seeing her. The neighbor noticed that her car was gone from the carport on Thursday morning. I tried calling her closest relative, a sister living in Marion, Virginia, and she hasn't heard from Shelby during the past couple of weeks. For Shelby to disappear so suddenly, you have to think that someone slipped her an envelope full of cash and told her to take a vacation."

"That's pretty discouraging news, Andrew. What can you do now?"

"In investigating a crime, cherchez la femme. But in our case, we're not having much success with that, so I decided to cherchez l'homme, and look for the man. Shelby's had a boyfriend named Mick Murphy in her life off and on for several years. I tracked him down south of town where he works at Austin's Esso and talked to him. He turned out to be a gold mine of information."

"What'd he tell you?"

"I had to work on Mick for a while, swearing that we weren't going to go after Shelby or him for anything they've done. Then he started to open up. Shelby told him everything that went on between Lukens and her. He knew that Shelby steered Lukens to the Scaggs family. And Mick helped Shelby blow the money Lukens paid her. He said that the two of them took a trip to Las Vegas, hoping to win big at the craps table so that they could retire and spend the rest of their lives on easy street. They ended up blowing every dime they had within two days and had to borrow money for gas to get home."

"Is he aware that I'm going to get a subpoena served on him to appear in court next week, and that I'll be putting him on the stand as a witness for the defense?"

"I think he's resigned to that, Ed. But as far as finding Shelby, even Mick doesn't know where she's run to this time."

'Incredible work, Andrew. I think you've come up with the alternate witness we need, and just in the nick of time. Let me get a little more information from you. I plan to drive over and talk to Mick later, so I don't get any surprises when he testifies

And by the way, you can have all of the frosting on that cake now. You've earned it."

CHAPTER 40

Ed and Dr. Jannsen walked side by side into the courtroom on Monday morning, finding it was already starting to fill. Ed surveyed the crowd, recognizing a number of family members, friends, and acquaintances.

On the other side of the room, he spotted Samuel Lukens standing next to Dudley and Patsy Scaggs. Samuel was wearing an expensive custom tailored suit that would have satisfied the sartorial taste of a Wall Street banker. Dudley and Patsy both looked as if they had recently been outfitted at the bargain counter in the local Belk, and neither seemed particularly comfortable in either their new fashions or the courtroom setting. Ed observed Dr. Emil Heinz nearby, recognizing him from a photo.

This was the moment in a trial, just before proceedings began, that often gave Ed a flashback to the climatic action scene in an old Saturday matinee horse opera. He always pictured two gangs of men standing on opposite ends of a dusty Main Street in the hot sun, low-slung six-guns on their hips, starting their slow walk toward each other and their destiny. He always liked to picture himself as one of the group wearing white Stetsons, trying to size up the adversaries in dark hats, as the distance separating them continued to shrink, and all hands inched closer to leather.

Looking at Samuel Lukins and Emil Heinz, he wondered which was one was his biggest threat, the one with the fast gun.

Ed knew that the clock was now ticking down toward that time when he would find out, as he watched Betty Blankenship move toward the front of the room to take her seat as the court reporter, followed by Arlene Smith, who quietly slipped into her chair at the court clerk's table in front of the bench. He and Arnold took their places at the defendant's table, almost rubbing shoulders with Samuel Lukins and the Scaggs, as they filed by to the plaintiffs' table.

As the hands on the wall clock moved toward 9:00, everyone in the room found a seat, and promptly on the hour, the bailiff entered the courtroom. "All rise. US District Court is now in session, the honorable Judge Winston Averhart presiding."

Judge Averhart followed the bailiff into the room, moving to his place behind the bench, cutting a figure not soon to be forgotten. The shock of white hair topping his deeply creased face and his lanky frame beneath the full black robe, gave him the appearance of a senior member of the First Continental Congress. Judge Averhart's expressionless look sent a clear message that he was all business, but in Ed's previous dealings with the judge, he had found him to be open-minded and fair. Ed had learned earlier not to be deceived by the white mane. Judge Averhart still had a mind as quick as a steel trap and the ability to recall every fact contained in all of the books in the Library of Congress. He announced in a resonant baritone, "If the plaintiffs' and the defendant's counsel are ready, we'll begin with the jury selection."

Jury selection proceeded quickly through the calling of twelve jurors and voir dire questioning by the judge, followed by the opposing counsels' challenge for cause. When the process was completed at noon, the panel was made up of five men and seven women, who were sworn in by the clerk.

Samuel Lukin's opening statement quickly revealed his strategy for the trial. With a disarming smile that almost reached

his eyes, he greeted the jurors in a friendly manner, belying his
reputation as a legal pit bull.

"The trial you will decide this week is not about good people
versus bad. There are no villains in the true story I will relate
to you in the following days. Rather, this lawsuit is about a
young, innocent child who has suffered a grievous, permanent
injury, and whose life, and whose parents' lives, have been forever
damaged because of a tragic accident. An accident caused by a
kind hearted old doctor who has spent his life caring for people
in this community. But a doctor who has worked too many
hours for too many years, and whose medical skills and physical
coordination have deteriorated at his age of seventy-seven years.

"I will provide evidence and testimony proving beyond a
reasonable doubt that a moment of carelessness by this elderly
doctor only minutes after delivery left an infant with trauma to
the skull and permanent brain damage. For this lifelong affliction,
and all the hardship and suffering it entails for the child, Harley
Scaggs, and his parents, Dudley and Patsy Scaggs, there must
be compensation from the party directly at fault, Dr. Arnold
Jannsen."

Samuel laid the foundation for his case. "There comes a time
in everyone's life when he must acknowledge that his professional
skills are no longer good enough to continue in his chosen field.
With increased age, obsolescence in education and training
and diminished stamina and endurance are certain. A doctor
who graduated from medical school fifty years ago and began
to practice at the age of twenty-seven can no longer provide the
same quality of medical care as a younger physician with an up
to date education and the vigor of youth. A seventy-seven-year
old physician should know that it is in his best interest and that
of his patients to retire before his compromised ability causes an
irreversible injury."

Samuel continued, stating that Arnold Jannsen's career had
extended too long, and that fatigue and eroded medical skills on
the night of the delivery were directly responsible for his having

dropped Harley Scaggs against the metal foot of the bed. The impact had fractured the infant's skull, causing brain damage, creating a lifelong mental handicap and untold suffering and cost.

Ed's opening statement for the defense was shorter. Standing before the jurors, he spoke in a manner that a professor might use to address a classroom of students.

"You've just heard the plaintiffs' counsel describe the mental condition of the child, Harley Scaggs, and when he's brought before you in court, you will observe that his mental development appears well behind the norm for a twenty-six-month old. The claim of some sort of defect in or damage to the young boy's central nervous system, resulting in a permanent mental handicap, appears undeniable. But the plaintiff's allegation regarding the cause of the child's mental condition is totally unfounded.

"The defense will provide evidence and testimony during the coming week to completely refute the claim of an accident at birth, and to exonerate Dr. Arnold Jannsen from all wrongdoing and any connection to the child's mental problems. Furthermore, the defense will provide you with the true cause of the child's mental handicap and identify the party responsible. And, in addition, the defense will show you who started this attack on the reputation of Dr. Arnold Jannsen, one of the finest people in the medical profession to ever serve his community."

Samuel returned to the floor and called his first witness, Dudley Scaggs, who self-consciously ambled across the floor to the witness stand and was sworn in by the clerk. The attorney began his direct examination by asking Dudley a series of previously rehearsed, innocuous questions, before moving into the critical and equally well rehearsed part of his interrogation.

Samuel inquired about Dudley's phone call to Dr. Jannsen late at night on June 1, 1957, to request the doctor's assistance in the delivery of his third child. Although Dudley was having no trouble regurgitating the answers he had been force-fed earlier, he was starting to fidget uncomfortably in the witness chair, and

Ed was sure he knew why. Dudley had been dried out to prepare for the trial, and he was starting to feel the effects of going cold turkey after years of hard drinking. And the longer he was cut off from alcohol, the more difficult it was going to be for him to sit and concentrate.

Samuel's line of questions advanced to Dr. Jannsen's appearance and performance at the home that night. "Did he appear physically exhausted when he arrived late that evening?"

"Dr. Jannsen looked to me like he was completely wore out when he got there. He said he'd just gone to bed when I called him."

"Did his hands appear less steady than when he delivered the first two boys fifteen and sixteen years earlier?"

"I think he looked shakier working on Harley than when he was at the house to deliver Lonnie and Marvin."

Then Samuel went for the knockout. "What happened after Dr. Jannsen delivered the baby and finished tying and cutting the umbilical cord?"

Dudley delivered the lines that had been scripted for him. "Dr. Jannsen was just finishing up tying and cutting the umbilical cord, and I was standing right there next to him watching. He was holding Harley over near the foot of the bed, and all of a sudden, the baby slipped out of his hands and hit his head on the metal frame. Harley didn't make no sound at first, and then he started to whimper. Dr. Jannssen said he wasn't hurt bad. He finished cleaning him up, and then handed him over wrapped up in a diaper and a baby blanket for Patsy to hold."

The effects of reciting a lie under oath while seated only feet from a judge looking as sober as Moses coming down from the mountain had Dudley disconcerted. Simultaneously experiencing the discomfort of precipitous alcohol withdrawal made it ten times worse, and he nervously shifted in the chair, rubbing his hands together. He would not soon get relief, for as soon as Samuel wrapped up his questions, he handed Dudley to the defense counsel for cross-examination.

"I want to remind you that you're under oath and have sworn to tell nothing but the truth on the witness stand," Ed said, while staring Dudley in the eye. "Remember as you answer questions today that perjury is a felony, and that's a very serious offense.

"I want you to tell the court exactly what the doctor did with Harley after he delivered him."

"I'm not real sure what he did right after he took the baby up in his hands."

"Your wife's already given a statement under oath that Dr. Jannsen placed your infant son across her belly, on his back, near the center of the bed. Since you were standing right next to her watching, didn't you see that?"

Dudley shook his head, now wishing to be gone from the witness chair. "I must have looked away for a minute."

"Then why did you just tell the court that you saw Dr. Jannsen holding Harley near the foot of the bed? I remind you again that you're under oath, and I advise you that I have sworn testimony taken earlier from your wife that contradicts such a statement."

"Objection! Bullying the witness, Your Honor!" Samuel squeezed his pristine handkerchief into a knot, clearly wishing it was something else.

Judge Averhart turned a granite-hard face to the attorney, silencing him with an emotionless, "Objection overruled."

"Why would Dr. Jannsen lift the baby from the center of the bed and hold him over the foot of the bed?"

Dudley hesitated, and then admitted, flustered, "I don't know why he done that."

He squirmed in his seat as Ed asked a key question. "You've alleged that you saw the infant slip out of the doctor's hands and drop against the metal bed frame, after the doctor had cut the umbilical cord. What part of the child's head struck the foot of the bed?"

Dudley had been well coached for this question, and he quickly answered, "He hit the right side of his forehead against the bed."

Ed walked to the defendant's table and returned with a large paper bag. He reached inside, withdrew a life-size baby doll, and handed it to Dudley. "I want you to demonstrate exactly what you allege happened that night. You can stand in front of the witness chair, and use the arm of the chair facing the jury to represent the foot of the bed."

"Objection! The defense counsel is staging a stunt that has no bearing on this trial, and is intended to mislead the jury."

The jurors shifted forward in their seats to get a better look.

"Your Honor, this demonstration will validate a key assertion by the defense regarding the alleged accident. It is an essential that the jury see it in order to understand why Harley Scaggs could not have been injured in the manner alleged by the plaintiffs."

"Overruled. The defense may continue."

Dudley stood and held the doll face down out in front of him over the arm of the chair.

Ed corrected him, "You said the doctor had been attending to the umbilical cord, so you need to turn the child to face upward." Glancing to his left, Ed noticed Judge Averhart's eyes narrow as he watched the simulated accident with keen interest.

Dudley tried to spin the doll as he released it and let it fall against the arm of the chair, but the best he could achieve was enough rotation for the doll to strike the right rear of its head, not the right forehead. "Let me try it again," he interjected, droplets of perspiration beading his forehead, quickly picking up and dropping the doll a second time, and then a third. He tried to put so much spin on the doll as he dropped it on the last attempt that the staged event was ludicrous, and several of the jurors broke into smiles.

"That will do," Ed said. "I have no more questions. I think the jury has seen enough to know that Harley Scaggs could not possibly have received an injury to the front of his skull as a result of being dropped by a physician working on his umbilical cord. The defense will explain the real cause for Harley Scaggs' mental condition when further witnesses are called to testify."

As soon as Dudley stepped down, Judge Averhart intervened. "The court is now recessed until 1:00."

That afternoon, Samuel called Patsy to the stand. It was obvious from the look on her face that she was quaking in her boots as she came forward. Samuel started with a list of questions regarding Harley's slow progress, and she began to regain her composure as she fed the anticipated one-word answers back to his smiling face. "Is Harley able to do the things at twenty-six months of age that that your two older sons did? Can he stand and walk alone? Can he feed himself? Is he out of diapers?"

Each question brought the same repetitive, emotionless answer from Patsy, "No."

Then Samuel moved into another line of questions, gently leading her down the garden path into previously rehearsed perjury. "What was your state of mind following the birth of your son? Were you aware of what Dr. Jannsen was doing after the delivery?"

"No. I was still in a lot of pain after labor, and I was kind of groggy. I'm not completely clear about what Dr. Jannsen did when he first took the baby and cut the umbilical cord. I only heard some sort of commotion near the foot of the bed later, and I heard the baby crying. I remember the doctor handed the baby to me to cuddle right afterward."

"So you may have been confused when you testified earlier that he set the baby across your belly after delivery?"

"Yes. I wasn't thinking too clear if I said something like that before. I can't remember what happened." After reciting the last statement, Patsy looked to Samuel for approval, relieved that he seemed pleased with her performance.

Ed began the cross-examination on a gentle, almost tentative note, not wanting to seem bullying. "Mrs. Scaggs, we need to clear up the bout of amnesia that you seem to be experiencing this afternoon. I want to read you your sworn statement regarding the events following Harley's delivery, provided during a deposition on June 5, just seven weeks ago. At that time you were quite clear about what went on. You swore, and I quote, 'Dr. Jannsen took the baby right after I delivered him, and set him across my belly on his back. He did everything with Harley just the same as he did with Lonnie and Marvin.' Aren't those your words?"

"I suppose so, but I must not have been thinking too clear then." Patsy checked with Samuel again to see how she was doing.

"You were under oath at that time, and you seemed certain of your facts. Remember that you're under oath again today, and telling a story that's untrue would be a very serious matter.

"When you testify now that you were not thinking too clearly at the time you were deposed, aren't you really saying that you wish that you'd been more guarded? That you wish you'd not disclosed Harley was handled exactly like your other two sons and placed face up across your belly in the center of the bed after the delivery?"

Patsy was flustered by the unscripted question and also starting to feel an intense need for a drink. "I don't know. You're getting me all mixed up."

"I think you do know, Mrs. Scaggs. I think you gave an honest answer when you were deposed. And I think you also know that there never was an accident that injured Harley on the night he was born."

"Objection. Defense counsel is trying to lead the witness and also is expressing a personal opinion unsubstantiated by evidence."

"Sustained. The jury is instructed to disregard the last statement made by defense counsel."

"An old proverb tells us that truth is powerful and it prevails," Ed lectured Patsy, who was now staring down at the floor.

He could see that his final remark resonated with the jury, and knew from years of courtroom experience that the panel would not easily disregard the truth, even though instructed to do so by the judge.

Judge Averhart struck his gavel against the sound block

and pronounced, "Court is hereby adjourned until tomorrow morning at 8:00."

"How are you holding up?" Ed asked Arnold, as they walked toward his waiting family.

"It seems like we're working bankers' hours here, and I'm feeling fine," Arnold replied. "But I'd rather be tending to sick patients around the clock than sitting in this room listening to all of the lies about me. It appears to me that Mr. and Mrs. Scaggs are very pleased to be finished up with their part in all of this."

Ed looked at Arnold with the flash of a predator's intensity transforming his normal gentle demeanor. "If that's what they're thinking, I'm afraid they're in for quite an ugly surprise."

CHAPTER 41

The trial gained momentum the next morning. Samuel Lukins continued to build the plaintiffs' case by calling his expert witness, Dr. Emil Heinz, the Beckley pediatrician. Samuel quickly ran through a litany of medical education and experience credits to validate Heinz's expertise in his field. Then Heinz took the stand for direct examination.

As he was questioned about the cause of Harley Scaggs's disability, Heinz used an x-ray of the child's skull to show the jury the barely discernable hairline fracture on the right side of the forehead. "This is where all of the child's mental problems started," he expounded authoritatively. "The fracture may not look significant today due to new bone growth during the past twenty-six months, but knowing that the injury occurred immediately following birth, I'm certain that this small fracture indicates a blow to the newborn infant's skull which caused devastating trauma to his developing brain."

"Have you treated other children during your practice who suffered similar injuries from blows to the head?"

"Certainly. It's not uncommon to encounter fractured skulls in children who have been the victims of automobile or bicycle accidents."

"Have any of these children sustained permanent mental impairment as a result of such trauma?"

"I have treated a number of patients who never recovered following a severe cranial injury during childhood."

"What do you think the chances are that Harley Scaggs will ever achieve normal cognitive function?"

"Slim and none."

During cross examination, Ed challenged Heinz's assertion that the injury occurred immediately following birth. "How can you be sure that the fracture shown by the x-ray occurred at the time of birth, and not days, weeks, or even months later?"

"You can't determine from the x-ray exactly when the injury occurred," Heinz admitted reluctantly.

"You testified that you've treated a number of patients who never recovered following a severe childhood cranial injury. Is the hairline fracture shown by this x-ray typical of the trauma sustained by such children suffering permanent brain damage?"

Knowing that the defense had another pediatric expert in the courtroom, Heinz answered grudgingly, "Some of the patients might have exhibited more severe fractures."

Later, Ed launched the case for the defense with a statement to the jury. "You'll now hear an accurate and complete account of what happened the night of June 1, 1957, from the family doctor, Dr. Arnold Jannsen, who's provided free medical care to the Scaggs family for many years." He emphasized the word "free," noticing that it registered with the panel.

He then called Arnold Jannsen to the stand for direct examination. After being sworn in, Arnold shared his account of the events that unfolded from the time that his wife took the phone call from Dudley Scaggs, at 11:00 PM on June 1, 1957, and he drove out to the Scaggs's trailer.

"Dr. Jannsen, did you observe anything unusual when you arrived at the house and Dudley came out to meet you?"

"I detected the strong smell of liquor on Mr. Scaggs when he walked up. And when I went inside to examine Mrs. Scaggs, I could smell alcohol on her breath, too."

Samuel immediately interrupted. "Objection. This line of questioning is irrelevant and only intended to bias the jury against my clients."

Ed countered, "Your Honor, this question goes to establish causation of Harley Scaggs' condition as the court will see when the defense continues."

"Overruled. The defense may proceed," the judge said flatly.

"Dr. Jannsen, please continue with your account of the delivery," Ed encouraged the older man.

"It was a routine birth, if there is such a thing. Labor wasn't difficult for Mrs. Scaggs, since this was her third child, and he was smaller than either of her two older sons. The child was born less than an hour after I arrived. I received the child from the mother, gave him a light slap on the butt to start him breathing, and laid him gently on Mrs. Scaggs' abdomen, on his back, the way I always do. I tied off the umbilical cord and then snipped it. I cleaned up the baby with a sterile piece of linen, wrapped him in a clean diaper and baby blanket, and handed him to Mrs. Scaggs to hold. I stayed around for an hour afterward to make sure that there were no complications before leaving."

"Was there any sort of incident or accident associated with the delivery? Did the baby drop or fall at any time?"

"Nothing like that ever happened. Any allegation that it did is untrue. The child came so easily that I didn't even have to use forceps."

"So the baby appeared normal to you then?"

"As far as I could tell, he was a perfectly normal child when I left him in his mother's arms."

"What happened afterward, as you were preparing to leave and Mr. Scaggs walked with you to the door?"

"He thanked me for coming out to take care of his wife. As I recall, he said, 'Patsy and I really appreciate what you did for us tonight, Doc.'"

Samuel's cross examination consisted of questioning how long Arnold had worked earlier that day, speculating as to how tired and deprived of sleep he was upon arrival.

With a condescending smile, he spoke slowly and loudly to Arnold.

"At the age of seventy-seven, how could you work a ten-hour day and then go back out at midnight to deliver a baby without fatigue interfering with your performance? How could you be alert enough to provide competent medical care under those conditions?"

Arnold's answer did not help Samuel. "It was just another long work day for me, the same as many others. Doctors learn how to keep going on a few hours of sleep in medical school and residency. If you require a lot of sleep, medicine's the wrong field for you."

"Do you really expect the jury to believe that your hands were as steady at midnight when you were working on the Scaggs child as they were the previous morning when you first begin your day?"

"I see one or two jurors that might be able to tell you how steady my hands are after a long day. One of them had this tired old doctor performing an appendectomy on his mother at midnight, and another had him delivering a friend's baby by C-section at 2:00 in the morning. I believe both patients are alive and well at this time."

Samuel could see that his cross examination was going in the wrong direction. He shook his head to indicate his skepticism of Dr. Jannsen's truthfulness, closing with, "No further questions."

Ed addressed the jury before calling his expert witness. "I told you in my opening statement that there was no accident the night the Scaggs child was delivered, and Dr. Arnold Jannsen's testimony has now borne that out. Nothing went wrong on

January 1, 1957, at the Scaggs home when Harley was born. Absolutely nothing.

"The witness that you will now hear, Dr. Eugene Rosenthal, will explain typical childhood accidents which might account for the mild fracture of the child's skull shown in the x-ray. He will also give you his expert opinion as to whether such a fracture would be likely to cause permanent brain damage. And following that, he will explain to you the real cause of the abnormal mental development of this young boy."

Dr. Eugene Rosenthal was called to the stand, and Ed reviewed the doctor's professional resume, including his present position as Professor Emeritus of Pediatric Medicine at the University of Virginia. He then began leading Rosenthal to the crux of his case.

"Can you recall during your medical practice a single incident where a baby was dropped during delivery, sustaining a fractured skull?"

"Not one."

"Have you seen hairline skull fractures in young children similar to that shown on the x-ray we're looking at today, and if so, what have you found to be the most common causes of such injuries? "

"Yes, I have. Except in the case of something such as an automobile accident, a skull fracture in a young child usually occurs after the child begins to walk and falls head-first into a hard, unyielding object. I've also seen fractures result from head-first falls down steps."

Rosenthal displayed a number of x-rays showing minor skull fractures similar in nature to the one incurred by Harley Scaggs. He elaborated on the cause for each one, stating that none of the children sustained permanent brain damage.

Ed then started the most critical line of questioning. "Dr. Rosenthal, you've testified that you've never encountered a single incident where a child was dropped by the attending physician during delivery. You've also provided an expert opinion that the mild fracture to the Scaggs child's skull, from whatever cause, at whatever time, would be unlikely to result in permanent brain damage. Now, I want you move forward to tell this court what's really behind Harley Scaggs' impairment.

"Dr. Rosenthal, do you see anything in the x-ray of Harley Scaggs' skull, other than the hairline fracture, that appears abnormal? From looking at this picture through an expert's eye, can you detect what's really wrong with this twenty-six-month child?"

At that moment, Ed observed the jurors coming awake, leaning forward in their seats. Judge Everhart clasped his hands together, staring down intently from his perch, the courtroom now quiet enough for a dropped pin to be heard.

"Yes. Take a close look at this x-ray of Harley Scaggs' skull. Don't focus on the hairline fracture. We've moved on now. I want you to look at the overall bone structure, because it shows what's wrong with the child, and explains why he's not developing normally.

"Look at the eye openings in the skull. You can see that they are abnormally small. Then look at the cheekbones. In normal children, they aren't nearly so flat. I'm going to show you x-rays of three other children with similar skeletal deformity." Rosenthal held up the x-rays, allowing time for the jurors to carefully view each one.

"Dr. Rosenthal, what's the common element shared by all of these children with these abnormal skeletal features?"

"They all were born to mothers who consumed excessive amounts of alcohol during their pregnancies."

"Was there any short or long term impact on the mental development of these other children with the same abnormal skeletal features, who were exposed to alcohol through their mother's bloodstream?"

"Yes. The children whose x-rays I've shown you today have permanent mental impairment. I believe the prognosis is the same for Harley Scaggs."

Ed saw the surprised looks that came across the faces of the jurors.

Samuel was rattled, but he quickly rallied to attack Rosenthal's conclusion in his cross examination. "How many articles have been published in the Journal of the American Medical Association about the damaging effect of alcohol on an unborn fetus?"

"None have been published to date, but papers have been written by medical researchers such as myself and my colleagues that document this finding. These studies will appear in JAMA in the future."

"You're asking this jury to accept your speculation that a woman's consumption of alcohol during pregnancy presents a risk to her unborn child? Everyone knows that women have been drinking alcoholic beverages during pregnancy since biblical times."

"There are obviously no records to show the number of children who have been neurologically damaged in the fetal stage by alcoholic mothers, but we have evidence today that proves alcohol consumption during pregnancy presents a very high risk to the normal development of the unborn child."

Samuel shook his head from side to side in theatrical disbelief, trying to convince the jury that Rosenthal's testimony was ludicrous. "Dr. Rosenthal, if mothers' consumption of alcohol during pregnancy damaged their babies' minds, the prophets of the Old Testament would have all been mentally handicapped," he added sarcastically.

Ed called Patsy Scaggs back to the witness stand. "Did you drink alcoholic while you were pregnant with Harley?"

Realizing for the first time that she was responsible for the condition of her third child, Patsy answered, "Yes. I didn't know I could do my baby harm by drinking while I was carrying him." She added, her eyes starting to fill with tears, "If I had known it might do something bad to him, I never would have touched a drop."

"You admit that you did continue to drink throughout your pregnancy?"

"Yes, sir. But I wouldn't have done nothing in the world like that if I had thought it might hurt Harley." Tears were streaming down Patsy's cheeks by the time Ed wrapped up his questions. He didn't bother to call Patsy's neighbors to testify about her drinking problem. It was already out in the open and on the record.

Mick Murphy was Ed's last witness for the defense. An unimpressive man in an ill-fitting suit, Murphy's eyes shifted nervously as he took the stand, but he still managed to exude an air of self assurance as Ed began his questioning.

"Do you have an acquaintance with a woman named Shelby Murray who worked for Dr. Jannsen as a temporary receptionist during the past year?"

"Shelby's my girlfriend. We've gone together off and on for years"

"Did Shelby ever tell you about a contact with the plaintiff's attorney, Mr. Lukins, during that period?"

"Yes. She told me Mr. Lukins came to see her and offered her money to give him information about the Scaggs family. She told him about Harley's condition and the problems he was having, and she ended up collecting five-hundred dollars in cash from Mr. Lukins. We spent the money he gave her on a trip to Las Vegas."

Samuel was on his feet before the words were out of Mick's mouth. "Objection. Your Honor, this man's lying. Shelby Murray's not in the courtroom today. If she were here, she'd tell the court that there's not a word of truth in what he's saying. There's nothing to corroborate his allegations. His testimony should be stricken from the record."

Judge Averhart stared at Lukins with narrowed eyes and replied, "Sustained."

In his closing argument, a very nervous Samuel Lukins restated his original claim. "When Dr. Jannsen dropped

Harley Scaggs after the delivery, it was an accident caused by an overworked, elderly physician. However, the brain damage sustained by this child is irreversible. He will never be able to lead a normal life, and he will always be a burden to his parents. That's why your deliberation as jurors is so important. You can make this doctor consider whether it is time for him to join his medical school classmates in retirement, assuring that there will never be a recurrence of this tragic accident. You can assure that the Scaggs family is awarded funds to pay for the care that Harley Scaggs will always require. You can weigh the evidence, follow your conscience, and do what you know is right. And when you do so, there is only one verdict that you can render: 'Guilty.'"

Ed's closing argument was also brief and to the point. "The allegation of a delivery related injury to Harley Scaggs resulting in permanent brain damage is a complete fabrication. There was no accident that night, as you're now aware from testimony presented in this courtroom. We will probably never know what caused the minor skull fracture that Harley experienced at some point in time, but we do know that it was not the cause of neurological damage and slow development. Harley's disability was caused by exposure to alcohol in his mother's bloodstream.

"One question that has not been answered is the motive behind a malicious, fraudulent law suit against one of the finest citizens to ever serve this community, Dr. Arnold Jannsen. I hope that some day we will have an answer to that question. Your duty today as jurors is to weigh everything you have learned during this trial and render a fair and just verdict. When you do so, I am confident it will be 'not guilty.'"

Judge Averhart gave the jury their instructions on Wednesday morning, and they retired for deliberations. Two hours later, the foreman informed the bailiff that a verdict had been reached, and the bailiff led the jurors back into the courtroom. After the judge reviewed the written verdict carefully, he handed it to the clerk.

Arlene Smith read in a loud, clear voice, "We, the members

of the jury, hereby find the defendant, Arnold Jannsen, not guilty of all charges."

The courtroom was silent for a moment, then it erupted in an outburst of excited voices. Arnold gave Ed a spontaneous, emotional bear hug of thanks before the two filed out into the hallway, where Arnold's wife, Greta, ran over to throw her arms around him, tears streaming down her cheeks. Laura wrapped her arms around Ed and held on, as if she never intended to let him go.

Tony Vicelli hosted a dinner at the Stafford Steakhouse for Arnold and Greta that evening. The Housmans and Andrew Stover were there to share in the celebration. Tony offered a toast, "Here's to Arnold Jannsen, the most capable doctor and the finest man I've ever known. And here's to my friend Ed Housman, the best trial lawyer in West Virginia."

But further to the north, there was no joy in Beckley. Samuel Lukins and Emil Heinz were apprehensively contemplating what now lay ahead for them. And William Thorpe and Travis Barker were trying to figure out how in the world they were going to break the news of Arnold Jannsen's acquittal to their explosive boss.

CHAPTER 42

"**How do we tell my** old man that Jannsen was acquitted?" Travis Barker asked, staring down into his drink at the Beckley Regency bar. "When he hears Lukins lost the courtroom battle to Housman after all of the money he stuffed down a rat hole, he's going to go completely apeshit."

William Thorpe, slumping dejectedly on the barstool beside him, didn't even bother to look up. "Damned if I know," he said disconsolately. "Robert's definitely going to go through the roof when he learns what happened. We've got to convince your pa that Jannsen's acquittal was only a minor setback, not an unmitigated disaster, and that we've got other plans in the works that will give him his revenge against Housman and Bradford."

"Actually, the trial did turn into a disaster," Travis commented. "You know that Housman's going to file a complaint, charging that Lukins initiated a malicious lawsuit over a fake injury. I'll bet you every penny I've got that there's going to be a criminal investigation coming up soon. But I'm pretty sure that even if Lukins and Heinz are indicted, they'll be afraid to link Barker Mining with the conspiracy."

"Do you want to be the one to tell him the news?" William

asked. "He'll take it better from blood kin than from an employee like me."

"Let's go in together and lay it on him. I'll start off doing the talking, but I want someone else standing there when he blows up. I still recall how he'd lose his temper back when I was a kid and beat my butt black and blue with his belt. No one ever dared cross him all the time I lived under his roof, including my ma. But we'd better break it to him soon. It'd be even worse for us if he got blindsided by reading about it in the newspaper."

*****

What Travis and William didn't know was that Robert had already been blindsided that morning, when he'd picked up the Beckley paper and read about the acquittal of Arnold Jannsen on page three. After throwing his coffee mug against the wall, watching ceramic shards land all over the room, he'd decided it was time to take matters into his own hands. "If you want something done right, you got to do it yourself," he screamed at his English bulldog, Moe. Moe was smart enough to look up at him from the other side of the room, keeping his distance. He'd felt Robert's size twelve brogans up against his butt more than a few times before.

Robert wheeled his late model Buick onto the highway, heading toward Keystone. It wasn't a long a drive, but he knew that the shortest route took him on stretches of winding two lane mountain road, where you could get tied up behind a slow moving coal truck for miles. Carmine wouldn't be expecting him until the afternoon, so he was in no hurry. All he had to do was shake off the anger and disappointment he was still feeling toward his son and Thorpe. "Both of them must have been standing behind the door when they handed out the brains," he exclaimed aloud to Moe, who was stretched out in the back seat, panting heavily, drooling all over the upholstery.

Robert turned off the state highway at Dooley's Texaco and proceeded south for another mile, following a narrow road cut into the hillside of a steep ridge rising high above a deep hollow filled with rhododendron. He drove very carefully, observing the precipitous vertical drop-off just beyond the narrow shoulder of the road and lack of any guard rails to stop him if he went off of the pavement.

The countryside opened up before him at the head of the hollow into a secluded industrial site surrounded on all sides by a chain link fence topped with barbed wire. He could make out the rusty metal sign on the fence as he drove closer, *Keystone Bottling Company.* Just inside the gate was a manned guardhouse, and beyond that a large flat-roofed, two-story concrete block building, now painted a faded tan. Bleeding through the paint on the front of the structure was the name of the original business housed there twenty years earlier, *Northfork Meatpacking Company.*

"I'm Robert Barker, here to see Carmine Nardelli," he called out to the guard.

The guard, wearing a holstered pistol on his hip over his faded blue jeans, walked across to open the gate and let him pass, then locked the gate behind him. "He's in his office through the front door on the right, waiting for you."

Carmine was standing at the front window watching for him, and he came out to greet Robert. The two walked to Carmine's office, which still contained the original furniture left behind by the meatpacking operation. On the walls looking down on them through unblinking glass eyes were the mounted heads of four bucks with very impressive racks.

"What did you want to talk to me about today?" Carmine asked, offering Robert a small glass filled with the Keystone Bottling Company product from yesterday's run. "You don't get over this way often."

"It's about a business proposition that has some attractive features for both of us," Robert replied, enjoyably sipping the corn whiskey after his long, hot drive. "How would you like to expand the business you operate down in Cinder Bottom to a new location on the outskirts of Bluefield?"

"What business would that be, Robert?" Carmine said guardedly. "You know that my associates in New Jersey would not want to find out that I'm involved in anything down here that would distract my attention from their beverage business. It's their big money-maker."

"Are we going to talk openly, or are you going to play some bullshit game today? If you are, I'm out of here right now," Robert replied, not bothering to conceal the irritation he was beginning to feel.

"Settle down, Robert. We can talk in confidence here. I just want you to know how important it is to me that nothing we say goes outside this room. What did you have in mind?"

"I'm talking about the chance for you to expand the red-light operation you're running here in Keystone down in Cinder Bottom to a second, even better business location. Right now, you draw customers from all over the West Virginia coal fields to Keystone. But in Bluefield, you could bring in a lot of Saturday night business from Virginia, too. I can put you in touch with the right people, and facilitate the right payoffs, to keep the law off your back. You could probably double or triple what you're making now."

"What's in this for you? Why are you making this pitch to me?"

"One hand washes the other, Carmine, and I do have an agenda of my own. Let's say that there are two people who have been thorns in my side for seven years, and I want both thorns removed, so that I can start to heal. One's a district attorney, and the other's a lawyer in private practice. If I were to help you get set up in business outside of Bluefield, I would expect to see both of my problems disappear permanently. I guess that we might refer to such a transaction as 'quid pro quo.'"

"How tough is my 'quid' part of this deal? Getting to a DA could be a difficult proposition."

"If we agree to do business here today, I don't plan to tell you how, when, or where to take care of your part of the agreement. But I will make one suggestion. The DA happens to have his pilot's license, and he keeps a small airplane at a private landing strip in Madison County outside of Eden Springs. Occasionally, the lawyer goes up with him on Sunday afternoons for sightseeing trips around the area. If that plane were to have engine trouble, there aren't a lot of good places to set it down. And if he crashed during an emergency landing, that might be the end of both of my thorns. Just a thought."

"And if I opened a branch operation outside of Bluefield, a couple of houses wouldn't get a lot of attention from the local law enforcement people?"

"Not with my connections and the right payments. After all, it's a victimless crime, and everyone knows that it's the world's oldest profession."

"You've got a deal," Carmine said, extending his hand.

"It's going to be a pleasure doing business with you," Robert replied, pushing back his chair. He observed agreeably as he set his empty glass back on the table, "This stuff you're distilling here isn't half bad." As an after-thought, he interjected, "I believe I forgot to tell you that the DA is Jack Bradford, and the attorney is Edward Housman."

"I never heard of the DA, but that name, Housman, sure rings a bell," Carmine replied. "Let me go to work on my end of the deal, and I'll get back in touch with you as soon as I have a plan." As if the two had just shared Sunday dinner after church, Carmine added pleasantly, "Have a safe trip back to Beckley."

Winding his way along the treacherous serpentine road down the mountain Robert felt his mood improving. "Time to head back home now, boy," he called out to Moe, who was curled up in the back seat, trying to sink his teeth into the hungry flea that had been gnawing on his rump.

CHAPTER 43

Freddie picked up the phone in his room early Sunday morning, hearing his new lady friend from Georgia inquire in her soft drawl, "Freddie can you help me out this morning?"

The question required no time to consider, and Freddie automatically answered, "Sure," even before he knew whether "helping me out" meant something pleasant like driving her to the store, or something considerably less enjoyable, such as shoveling out the dog pens at the animal hospital. Marilyn now owned him lock, stock, and barrel only two months after they had met, and whatever she asked for she was going to get, assuming it was within his power to provide.

"I just got a call from Gertrude Buchanan out at Roseanna telling me that her husband and his brother have a cow that's down and in critical condition trying to deliver a calf. The large animal vet in town is out for the weekend, so they called our hospital looking for help. I told them I'd come out and try to lend a hand, since I had some training with livestock in vet school. I'd like to have you go along with me, in case I need another set of hands. Be sure to wear some old clothes and a pair work shoes."

Marilyn picked up Freddie a half-hour later, and the two rode out to Roseanna in her Ford pickup. Daniel met them when they arrived, and after introducing himself to Marilyn, he climbed into the bed of the truck to direct them down a hard-packed dirt road to an outlying barn. Marilyn parked the truck in front of the rustic gray building, and she and Freddie climbed out to follow Daniel through the open door. "I'm back with the vet," she heard him call out encouragingly to someone inside."

Marilyn walked into the dimly lit barn, where she saw the other twin, kneeling beside a young cow, which was down on its side, lying on a bed of fresh straw. The animal's wide-eyed look of fear reflected the intense stress of the long, hard labor. "I'm Jonah," the man said, looking up at her. "Thanks for coming out, Doc. She's not going to be able to have the calf on her own. Before you got here, I was afraid we were going to have to put her down to get her out of her suffering."

"As near as we can tell, the calf's in a normal birth position, with both feet forward and its head between them," Dan added. "It just looks like the calf's too big for her to have on her own. Do you think you can do anything to help?"

"Bring the lantern over a little closer, while I get ready to examine her," Marilyn replied. She went out to the bed of the truck, returning with a cardboard box filled to the top with an assortment of articles left from her vet school days. After rolling her right sleeve up to the shoulder, she put on a long rubber glove extending the length of her arm and applied lubricant over the entire surface. "You two try to calm her down and hold her so she can't move. Freddie, how about you coming back here beside me? I expect I'll need some help in a little while."

Freddie had been taking in everything with the awe of a barnyard virgin, unfamiliar with the indescribable sights, sounds, and smells threatening to overwhelm him. Although starting to look a little green around the gills, he came over as Marilyn requested and dropped on one knee beside her. Then he almost lost his breath, as she slowly inserted her right arm deep within the cow's dilated pelvic opening and began her examination. A minute later, she retracted her arm. "The calf's in a normal birth position, just as you thought. But it seems to be an awfully large calf for such a small cow. We're going to have to pull it."

Marilyn rose and went back to her box again to dig out a pair of obstetrical chains. Making two loops around her gloved arm with the first OB chain, she inserted it inside the cow's birth canal and attached both loops of the chain to the right foreleg of the calf. Then she repeated the procedure with a second chain and attached it to the calf's left foreleg in exactly the same manner. Things were beginning to swim in front of Freddie's eyes as he watched the incredible performance from his front row seat, struggling against his chronically weak stomach, which was now orchestrating an overwhelming urge for him to throw up.

"Here's where I need your help, Mr. Palmer," Marilyn said, enjoying his obvious distress despite the tense situation. "We're going to try to "walk" this youngster out by alternately pulling on the right and left front legs. I hope you ate your Wheaties this morning, because we're going to be doing some hard tugging."

If it had been anyone other than the new love of his life asking him to do such a thing, Freddie would have run screaming from the barn all the way back to town. But he knew that Marilyn was counting on him, and he was determined not to let her down.

What followed was an intense experience for the cow, calf, and four people trying to help. It took all of Daniel and Jonah's strength to restrain the terrified cow during the painful assisted delivery, and much of the muscle power of both Marilyn and Freddie to pull the calf through the pelvic opening. But they did it successfully, delivering a healthy young calf. With Daniel and Jonah's assistance, the cow was soon able to get back on her feet, and nature took over the rest.

"We can't thank you enough, Doc," Jonah said to Marilyn after everything was under control. "Neither our cow or her new calf would have made it through the day if you hadn't come out and taken charge. You've saved two lives this morning."

The four walked to the house to clean up, after stowing Marilyn's box of veterinary tools back in the truck. Gertrude had a Sunday brunch spread out on the dining room table for them, including country ham sandwiches, potato salad, and large glasses of her personal specialty, sweet tea.

"I can't thank you enough for coming out today," Gertrude said to Marilyn. "How did a pretty young lady like you happen to go into such hard, demanding business?"

"You have to really love working with animals," Marilyn replied, smiling. "I don't get much practice these days on large livestock, so this has been a good opportunity today to knock the rust off some things I learned in vet school." She then glanced across at Freddie, joking, "I think my friend, Mr. Palmer, has taken a real liking to veterinary medicine this morning and may be thinking about giving up the real estate business and going to vet school himself."

Freddie's stomach had just settled enough for him to contemplate eating the plate of food sitting on the table in front of him. He looked around at the others and replied wryly, "Yeah! That's exactly what I'm planning to do. Just as soon as hell freezes over."

Gertrude asked about Marilyn's bill after they had finished the meal, but Marilyn replied, "Just show us around this beautiful old house, and we'll call everything even."

Gertrude took Freddie aside during the home tour, commenting, "You remember when you and Mrs. Housman were out here before, and we were talking about how unfriendly the new owners of the Simpson and Henderson properties were acting? I think something strange is going on over at that new landfill. Dan and Joe see trucks coming and going at night, and the drivers are unloading at the dump site without using any lights. It isn't natural for people to work in the dark like that."

"I'll pass on what you just told me to the Housmans when I get back to town," Freddie replied. "Call me and let me know if you see or learn anything else."

Freddie did not try to hide how much Marilyn had impressed him with her medical skill as they drove home. "You pulled off an amazing piece of work to save that cow and calf. I've never been involved in anything like that before." Then thinking a bit longer, he added, "And I sure as hell hope that I never will be again."

"But it was worth going through everything, just to be kneeling on the floor of the barn working side by side with the lady vet, wasn't it?" Marilyn teased him.

"I'll have to give that a little more thought," Freddie countered, concealing a grin. "Yeah, I admit that it was. But only because I'm going to marry that lady vet some day, and have her beside me for the rest of my life."

Marilyn swerved off the right side of the road and killed the engine. Turning toward Freddie, she hugged him, leaning in for a kiss. Freddie's arm hit the truck horn, but they let it continue to blow, almost unaware of the sound, as the world narrowed to hold only the two of them.

CHAPTER 44

Vickie drove into the parking lot of WESP on Monday morning, noticing all of the bright red, white, and blue banners tied to the side of the building and the colorful helium balloon flying high overhead, bobbing about in the summer breeze on a long tether rope like a giant beach ball. Today was the kick-off celebration for broadcasting local and NBC network programming from Eden Springs, and General Manager Charlie Goins was determined to make it the kind of spectacular event that would have even Cecil B. DeMille eating his heart out.

He had passed on a quote from the renowned movie director to Vickie and her co-anchor, Vince Carlton, tongue in cheek, "Remember you're a star. Never go across the alley even to dump garbage unless you are dressed to the teeth." But both heard the message Charlie was sending. They were expected to be two attractive personalities who would be the faces of WESP to viewers across West Virginia and beyond. The number of people tuning in, and station's subsequent advertising revenue, would depend to some degree on how well liked they would become during the weeks ahead.

Vickie realized that the entire day would be a dog and pony show. Free hot dogs, soft drinks, and ice cream would be handed

210

out at noon, followed by a welcoming speech by Charlie, and his introduction of the WESP staff. Then there would be a congratulatory speech by Mayor Preston Cline, appearances by the reigning Miss West Virginia and the WVU Mountaineer mascot, and a short concert by the Eden Springs High School band. She waved to the friendly receptionist in the front room and walked back to her small office. A cut-glass vase containing a dozen red roses was sitting on her desk, with a scrawled handwritten message on a small card reading, "Vickie, break a leg! I love you- Doug."

Vince and Vickie met with Charlie and the rest of his staff to review individual assignments for the day. The two then broke away to go over the local six o'clock news program with their immediate manager, news director Bob Slater.

Vickie realized that she had been dealt a good hand when she was first introduced to Vince. He was a young looking thirty-year-old with a crew cut, who looked more like the new quarterback at Marshall than an experienced TV newsroom anchor. But he had five years under his belt at a station in Pittsburgh, and Vickie knew that he was the real deal. And with an attractive wife and two young children, he was definitely not just another good-looking young man on the make, the kind that she had so often encountered around NBC headquarters in New York.

All of the WESP employees, including Vickie, gathered at noon with Charlie on the makeshift stage in the station parking lot, and the TV cameras started to roll. Vickie looked out over the large gathering of townspeople, spotting her family, the Housmans, Doug, Freddie, Mike and Ginny, and many more of her old home town friends, waving to her, and trying to get her attention. It suddenly occurred to her what it really meant to be a big fish in a small pond. She had never received this kind of affectionate reception before, and it made her feel good to realize that she was not just another face in the crowd, as she had been in New York.

Doug worked his way over to her as the opening ceremonies

were wrapping up, asking, "Are members of the audience allowed to hug TV celebrities?"

"No station rules against that. Thanks for the beautiful red roses. I was really surprised to find them when I came to work this morning."

"Are you nervous thinking about your first newscast tonight?" Doug inquired, handing her a paper plate holding a mustard-covered hot dog on a bun and a Dixie cup of chocolate ice cream with a small wooden paddle on top.

She shook her head, trying to take the first bite without dropping mustard all over her dress. "Nope, it's too late for a case of nerves now. If you'd like, come on back just before we go on the air at 6:00, and watch the show live through the window in the studio. Bob Slater told me that it would be OK for me to invite you."

The high school band suddenly opened with _Stars and Stripes Forever_, making further conversation almost impossible, but Doug was able to flash her a thumbs-up to accept the invitation.

Freddie caught up with Doug shortly after Vickie had gone back inside. "Since we've both got the afternoon to kill, why don't we go on a reconn mission out to Stony Creek this afternoon? Gertrude Buchanan told me her husband and his brother are seeing some work going on at the landfill after dark."

"Let's do it. I'll follow you back home, so you can drop off your car and grab your binoculars. Then you can ride out with me."

The two were driving up the hard-packed dirt road running along the foot of Pine Ridge a half hour later, gravel pinging against the undersides of the fenders. Looking to the east a quarter mile away, they could see a bulldozer working at the landfill on the opposite side of the creek a half mile away. "Park on the top of the hill just ahead," Freddie suggested. "Let's see what we can make out through a good pair of 10 x 50's."

The two climbed out of the car, and Freddie studied the landfill activity for a few minutes before passing the binoculars to Doug. "It looks like Mountain Ventures has built a new gravel road extending along the creek past the main landfill area. Can you tell what that's all about?"

Doug continued to scope the area, resting his hands on the top of the car to steady the powerful lens. "It looks like there's now another pit that's been opened further down the creek. I can tell by the color of the ground where they've removed the top soil. But there's no way to tell why that second pit was excavated, or what they're burying there."

Freddie took the binoculars back for a final look. "It appears that the dozer operator has spotted the sunlight reflecting off of our windshield and sees us up here watching him. He's stopped work and is staring over this way trying to figure out who we are. I'd give him the finger, but he probably wouldn't be able to make it out."

"Yeah, that would be a waste of energy," Doug replied with a grin. "You need to be in close range for something like that." Freddie was laughing when they got back in the car, and headed toward town.

Doug made it to the TV station a few minutes before 6:00, in time to join Bob Slater at the studio window overlooking the news room just as the WESP Channel 8 Evening News went on the air.

Vickie looked striking, with impeccably styled hair and makeup, seated beside Vince at the news desk. She was completely at ease under the bright lights as the TV cameras rolled, whether because of her Columbia journalism classes, her stint at NBC in New York, or the inherent self assurance she had shown since Doug had first caught sight of her in the tenth grade. She and Vince introduced themselves, then took turns delivering the news, with easy, comfortable teamwork. Some of the lines that Bob had scripted for them were deliberately intended to create tension-easing laughs between the two.

Thirty minutes flew by quickly, and then it was over. Vickie looked up at Doug, whose eyes were fixed on her through the glass window, and gave him a big smile. Charlie Goins entered the news room to congratulate Vince with a friendly handshake and a pat on the back, and Vickie with a warm hug. "Great job!" he told both of them, with obvious sincerity. "Vickie, I was half expecting you to sign off with that line you delivered at the end of your test shoot, 'th-th-th-that's all folks!'"

"I wasn't sure that you or the station owners were ready for any of my Porky Pig imitations today," she laughed. Then she turned to Vince. "Thanks for helping me through a stressful first night on the job."

"If you were feeling any stress, no one could see it. I thought you looked as cool as a cucumber. It's going to be a pleasure working with you."

Doug and Vickie left the building shortly afterwards, climbing into his car to go home. "I thought you looked like a real pro in front of the camera, although I'll have to admit I'm a little biased when it comes to judging newscasters," he told her. "By the way, do you think that would it be OK with WESP if your number one fan were to mess up that million dollar makeup job by laying one on you?"

Vickie slid closer to him to put her arms around his neck, closed her eyes, and answered, "Why don't you just take a chance."

CHAPTER 45

Ed, Arnold, and Andrew were seated at the conference table in Jack Bradford's office enjoying coffee and doughnuts on Friday morning. "I want to go over this malpractice lawsuit conspiracy with all of you one more time to be absolutely sure I'm clear on what role each of the principals on the plaintiffs' team played. Ed, how about walking us through what went on?"

"It's pretty easy to summarize," Ed replied. "The motive behind this seems to be retaliation by Robert Barker against Arnold for his part in helping the Buchanans recover their farm back in 1952. You and I were also involved, and I suspect we're on his list of enemies as well. It appears that this conspiracy was orchestrated out of Beckley, as you'll see.

"Barker's top lieutenant, William Thorpe, apparently hired a Beckley attorney, Samuel Lukins, as the mastermind. Lukins enlisted Emil Heinz, a local pediatrician, to advise him, then used Shelby Murray, one of Arnold's employees, to locate the pseudo-victims Dudley and Patsy Scaggs, living outside of Eden Springs. Each one of these people is guilty of criminal fraud, and obstruction of justice. The Scaggs are also guilty of perjury.

"I'd start at the bottom of this big pile of manure if I were walking in your gum boots, and shovel my way to the top. The

215

Scaggs will want to deal for a plea bargain beyond the shadow of a doubt, which will implicate Lukins and Heinz. Making the connection from Lukins to Thorpe and Barker at the top will be more difficult. Barker seems to have everyone in the region completely intimidated.

"I'm planning to follow your criminal prosecution with civil lawsuits for damages against the top tier in this conspiracy. I've promised Arnold to collect enough money for him to endow a couple of scholarships at UVA."

Jack followed his three visitors into the hallway, raising a new subject with Ed. "Tomorrow after we Rebs finish our muzzle-loader training with Buddy and Beau, how would you like to go up and look over the reenactment battlefield from the air? I haven't had the chance to take my plane up for a month now, and I'm looking for a good excuse to get in some flying time."

Ed quickly accepted the invitation.

Jack added, "I'm off to pick up the gas. See you tomorrow."

*****

Bud Duncan was also thinking about putting gas in the plane, as he approached the outskirts of Eden Springs and turned east toward the Madison County Airfield. It would be a long day for him by the time he wrapped up the assignment given him by boss, Carmine Nardelli, and drove back home to Keystone. Still, there was a bright side. The job should not take long, and if he pushed the speed limit on the return trip, he would probably have time to make a brief stop in Cinder Bottom for some R & R, before he went home to the little lady and his six kids.

As he approached the airfield, he could see that there was only one hangar, resembling an enormous shed. It was constructed of white-painted concrete block walls on three sides and was open on the front side facing the runway, which was located some fifty yards away. The flat roof was supported by metal trusses and steel posts. Inside the structure, he could see a dozen private aircraft parked in orderly rows. At the side of the building, a canvas windsock on a tall metal pole flapped in the gentle breeze.

Bud pulled up beside the building, and observing that no one was in sight, slipped inside. He walked toward the rear, looking over a number of Cessna and Piper single engine, high-wing aircraft, until he spotted a Cessna 170 that was tied down next to a post with an attached small sign reading "J. Bradford." Time to fill 'er up, he thought, as he went back to the trunk of his car, slipped on a pair of gloves, took out a two gallon can, and returned to the plane. It took only a minute for him to remove the gas filler cap and pour the contents of his can into the plane's tank, listening to the splashing sound of the liquid as it ran down inside.

Bud quickly replaced the filler cap when he had finished and carried the empty can back to his car. He was careful to drive away slowly, not wanting to draw attention if anyone should be watching.

I wonder how that plane will run on gas that's been sitting in my '48 Farmall out in the field behind the barn for three years, he wondered. There must have been a cup of condensed water lying in the bottom of the can. I doubt that old gas would ignite if you held a match to it. The tractor never fired a single time when I cranked it last summer. Well, anyway, "Happy Motoring" to you, J. Bradford.

Then his mind turned to more agreeable matters as he headed back toward Keystone. Maybe Wanda's working tonight, he thought with pleasant anticipation.

*****

Jack Bradford was also filled with happy thoughts when he woke up on Saturday morning and thought about what the day held in store for him. Forty recruits from Housman's Confederate Company E were to show up at a field outside of town for training by Buddy and Beau Preston, including instruction on how to load, fire, and clean the borrowed CS Richmond .58 caliber muskets that would be used during the reenactment. Later, he and Ed would go up for a little aerial sightseeing around the region in his plane. It was definitely a pleasant change of pace from the prosecution of habitual criminals for unpleasant and nasty offenses, and the threats directed at him afterwards.

Later that morning, Buddy and Beau spent an hour going over reenactment procedures with the group, focusing on the safe handling and discharging of firearms. By the time they were finished, everyone was aware that a musket loaded only with black powder and patch could still blind, deafen, or even kill if discharged with the muzzle pointing in the wrong direction. Then, one by one, each of the recruits was given the opportunity to load and fire a muzzle loading rifle, experiencing the noise, black smoke, and acrid smell produced by a lethal Civil War infantry weapon.

After the training exercise Ed followed Jack on the short drive to the airfield. "How about grabbing a couple of these gas cans out of the back," Jack requested, while releasing the rope that had secured his trunk lid in a partially open position for ventilation. Together, they carried fuel to the plane, adding twenty gallons of high octane gas to the tank.

"I feel comfortable going up as your passenger again today," Ed commented, as they removed the chocks from the wheels, and untied the plane. "You flew a fighter jet for the Air Force during the Korean War, didn't you?" he asked, having already heard a mutual friend's stories about the district attorney's exploits as a USAF pilot.

Jack waited until they were out onto the old cracked concrete runway before replying, "I flew quite a few missions in an F-86 Saber Jet over North Korea, Ed. I don't think the Korean affair was ever officially upgraded from a 'police action' to a 'war,' but when you were in the middle of a dogfight with MIG-15's barreling at you out of China south of the Yalu River, it seemed like a war to all of us that were there. I'm a lot happier these days flying this little '52 Cessna 170."

Jack checked to see which way the wind was blowing, then taxied the plane to the downwind end of the concrete strip. "Here we go," he exclaimed, after setting the flaps to the take off position, as he smoothly opened the throttle, and the plane gained speed. It lifted off cleanly after using less than three quarters of the runway, and he eased back on the yoke to begin a smooth climb toward the cruising altitude for a sight-seeing excursion. "The plane feels a tad sluggish today for some reason," he commented, turning to glance at Ed. "Maybe it's because I'm used to flying alone and usually don't have an extra one-ninety pound load sitting beside me."

They continued north over Abner Gap at seventy-five hundred feet, watching the green valley between Pine Ridge and Chestnut Ridge disappear below, replaced by wooded terrain and mountains starting to reach upward toward them. Jack continued to point out landmarks as they cruised northward for twenty miles, then he began to turn the plane around. "I promised to fly you over the Buchanan farm so we could study the battlefield for our reenactment. When we get out of the mountains and back over the valley, I'll take the plane down to a lower altitude and give you a good look around."

He had been speaking in a loud voice to be heard over the noise of the one-forty-five horsepower engine, but in an instant, he could have dropped his voice to a whisper and still have been understood clearly. With only a staccato sputtering lasting a few seconds, the engine suddenly quit, the propeller stopped, and the only noise to be heard inside the cockpit was the sound of wind passing over the aircraft. Jack let out an expression uncommon for his controlled demeanor, "What in the hell?" He tried to restart the engine, but despite repeated cranking, it refused to fire.

"Ed, the engine's not going to restart," he said, calmly stating the obvious before getting on the radio. "Charleston Tower, this is November Juliet Bravo One Two Two… lost engine power… location one mile due south Abner Gap…altitude seven five zero

zero… will attempt dead-stick landing on highway two one nine seven miles south Abner Gap. Do you copy?"

"November Juliet Bravo One Two Two, repeat location and altitude."

"One mile south Abner Gap...altitude seven five zero zero. Do you copy?"

"We copy. How many on board?"

"Two. Pilot and passenger."

"Copy that. State Police notified. Emergency vehicles will be standing by on highway two one nine seven miles south Abner Gap. Highway will be blocked for emergency landing. Good luck."

Jack turned to Ed as soon as he was off the radio with the Charleston Tower, informing him, "We're one mile above ground level ahead. We've got seven miles to find a straight stretch of road."

"I'll sit back unless you ask for help. You'll get us down safely."

"I'll try. At least there's no MIG-15s."

Ed watched the mountain ridge tops, studded with rocky cliffs and tall bull pines, coming closer as the small aircraft continued to glide downward through the air. Jack was demonstrating remarkable self control, and Ed tried to follow his example, despite thoughts of Laura, Lizzie, and Doug waiting for him back home. When the pilot glanced over at him, asking, "Know *Amazing Grace*?" Ed nodded, but showed no interest in singing.

The USAF had invested a lot of money in developing Jack Bradford's flying skills, and he demonstrated that it had been money well spent. He adjusted the aircraft heading to line up with the general course of the winding two lane highway that now appeared between two ridges up ahead, stretching out into the distance below them. Looking further forward, it appeared to him that there was a straight stretch of the road running through a mountain meadow, but he realized that keeping the plane in the air long enough to reach it would be touch and go. He trimmed the nose of the aircraft downward slightly to maintain the airflow over his wings, and maximize the distance he could cover before the plane would run out of sky. The mountain ridges he had seen earlier beneath the aircraft were now visible through the windows on both sides and starting to tower above him.

Jack made a final correction to the heading of the Cessna to point it directly toward the straight sector of roadway rapidly coming up to meet them and trimmed the noise up in final preparation for touch down. He rechecked the ignition switch to be sure it was off, then began to coax the little plane onward as though it could understand and respond to his coaching. "Come on, girl! You can do it!" Then he called out to Ed, "Brace for impact."

Ed saw that there were State Police cruisers with flashing lights stationed near both ends of the straight stretch of highway. He also noted a fire truck and an ambulance with flashers parked up ahead well off of the roadway.

Holding the aircraft in alignment with the highway, Jack pulled the nose up before meeting the onrushing ground, narrowly clearing a drainage ditch running beside the road. Both front wheels of the little Cessna straddled the median, and the rear wheel smoked a black mark in the white paint stripe as all three simultaneously contacted the pavement, and the aircraft sped forward on the smooth surface, continuing to decelerate as it rolled up the highway.

The straight stretch of roadway was too short for the plane to be brought to a stop, and it careened off the shoulder at the first curve, continuing across a cleared field. Providence stepped in at that moment, and as the plane ran over a downed barbed wire fence, strands of wire snagged the tail wheel. Rotten fence posts snapped off at the ground and dragged behind as the plane pulled the wire forward, creating a braking effect which helped to bring the plane to a stop within a couple of hundred feet.

Jack bowed his head in gratitude and exhaled softly, "Thank

you, Lord. That was like landing a plane on an aircraft carrier using a tail hook and restraining cable."

Ed responded, "Incredible performance, Jack. I knew you'd get us down safely."

By the time they had unfastened their seat belts and climbed out of the plane, a State Police cruiser, fire truck, and ambulance had pulled in beside them. The emergency rescue team was as impressed as Ed with Jack's flying skill in getting the plane down in one piece on a short stretch of highway.

The young trooper commented, "I've always heard that any landing you can walk away from's a good landing, but what you just pulled off was one helluva of a piece of work. Driving over here a few minutes ago, I wasn't expecting anyone to come out of this alive. I thought that there'd be pieces of your airplane strewn around in trees all over the place. But you hardly put a scratch on the plane, except for some damage to the landing gear."

Ed called Laura, and as soon as she could grab her handbag and Lizzie, she raced down the highway to see for herself that they were safe. With relieved tears spilling over, Laura poured out her gratitude to the modest middle-aged lawyer who had saved her husband's life. "We're not planning to have any more kids," she said, giving him a big hug, "but if we slip up, we're going to name him Jack."

Two days later certified aircraft mechanic Ralph Byrd came out to work on the plane. He identified landing gear damage, and the parts that would need to be replaced. But when he began a tear-down of the aircraft engine, he was astounded at what he found wrong with the fuel system. He called Jack Bradford, exclaiming, "You need to come out here right away and look at what I've discovered. I've never seen the kind of crud that I'm finding in your gas tank, fuel lines, carburetor, and on your plugs. Your plane's engine didn't shut down because of some kind of electrical or mechanical failure, it was because of contaminated fuel. It looks to me like someone deliberately sabotaged your plane before you took it up."

By mid-week, the state police, the sheriff's department, and the FAA had investigated the emergency landing. Each report concluded that the engine shut-down was the result of deliberate sabotage to the plane's fuel supply. But none of the investigative work pointed to any particular suspect, or suggested a specific motive for the crime. All three reports noted that the DA had undoubtedly made enemies during his career as a prosecutor, and contained recommendations that he move his plane to a secure location as soon as possible.

The aircraft emergency landing incident was reported on the WESP evening news, with a Vickie Vicelli interview of Jack Bradford, who related the harrowing experience of landing a crippled plane on a mountainous highway.

Robert Barker happened to be watching the evening news broadcast in his Beckley home. Realizing that Jack and Ed had walked away from that quiet mountain meadow unscathed, he picked up a heavy glass ashtray and hurled it toward the brightly lit picture tube. An explosive crash followed, and fragments of glass covered the room, but it was definitely not the crash that he and Carmine had planned.

CHAPTER 46

Fredo Mengarelli drove up the winding mountain road, checked in with the guard, and pulled over in front of the Keystone Bottling Company building, breathing a sigh of relief to have made it safely. Several times on the way, he had made the mistake of glancing to the side, observing that only a couple of feet of soft shoulder stood between him and a roller coaster ride hundreds of feet down the ridge to the rocky creek bed below. He had been afraid of heights since he was a child, and although he had driven up to call on Carmine on several occasions before, the road never ceased to terrify him. The thought had crossed his mind along the way that he wasn't getting enough money to put up with this kind of dangerous assignment.

Carmine was expecting him, walking out to shake hands after Fredo got out of his car. Without waiting to exchange pleasantries, Fredo quickly launched off with some unsolicited opinions that were fresh on his mind. "You ought to do something about your road, Carmine. It's like a death trap, and it scares the hell out of me. I don't like having to drive up here, wondering every time I come if I'm going to make it alive. Why don't you put in a guard rail, or at least lay a row of big logs alongside the road, to keep people from going over the side and down into that gorge?"

"That's the reason we don't put in a guard rail. It scares the hell out of the people in town, too, and the word's gotten around, so we don't have a lot of uninvited guests driving up here to sightsee and check out our business operation. Looks like you made it OK. If you'll come on inside, I'll give you some refreshments from yesterday's run to settle your nerves."

Fredo followed Carmine inside the building to his office, still completely out of sorts after his nerve-wracking experience. Glancing around the office, he continued to vent his irritation. "Why don't you go down to the local thrift store and buy yourself some office furniture? This stuff smells like old sausage from the meatpacking plant they used to run here. And why don't you throw away those crappy, moth-eaten deer heads staring down at us? They give me the creeps."

Carmine handed Fredo a glass he had cleaned earlier by spitting on an old undershirt and wiping off both inside and out with a couple of quick swipes. He poured three fingers of Keystone Bottling Company's latest run into the tumbler and said in his friendliest voice, "Here, this'll calm you down. By the way, what brings you here today all the way from Jersey?" Actually it was somewhat of a rhetorical question, since he already had a pretty good idea as to why Fredo had shown up on his doorstep.

Freudo looked him over carefully to gauge whether the inquiry was remotely sincere, quickly confirming his original opinion that honesty was not Carmine's strong suit, and then replied with equal deceit. "Nothing special, really. Don wanted me get a first hand look at how your production operation's doing these days. Some of the family businesses are down, and we can't afford any falloff in our beverage sales." He continued, with all the finesse of an old boar starting to put the move on a young sow. "Did you think there might be another reason for me calling on you today?"

Carmine hesitated a moment before he replied, studying the position of Fredo's chess pieces on the board now in play between them. Obviously, Fredo was in the area today trying to find out why two of the Jersey family's soldiers had gone MIA after an intelligence gathering mission to Keystone a week earlier. The best gambit seemed to be getting Fredo to show how much he knew. Carmine decided to play dumb, replying pleasantly, "I thought you might have come down to enjoy the beautiful scenery and fresh air here in the West Virginia coalfields."

"That's just a side benefit to the trip. Keystone's a lovely place to visit this time of year, but remember, I'm from Elizabeth up in the Garden State, which also has lovely natural scenery and clean air." Fredo, realizing that he was in a standoff, decided to lay everything out on the table. "Let's cut the chit-chat, Carmine. I'm here looking for a couple of family employees who were down your way a week ago, DT and Frankie Picarelli. I want to know if you've run into them, and can tell me their whereabouts right now?"

Carmine was taken back by Fredo's candor. Angelo Vinciano had called him earlier from Newark to tip him off that DT and Frankie were on their way to West Virginia to find out what business Carmine was suspected of covertly running on the side. It had not taken them long after arrival to discover the attractions of Cinder Bottom, and determine who was the new proprietor of that red light district.

While Carmine had not run into them, one of his security people had, at about forty miles an hour while sitting behind the wheel of a dump truck. As to where they were now, he pretty much knew, give or take a couple of hundred feet within the landfill. But Carmine was not ready to be nearly as direct as Fredo, and he replied, "No, I haven't run into them, and as to where they are now, who knows?" He rationalized that he was not being totally untruthful. Although he knew the approximate location of their remains, he figured that their souls could be in either heaven or hell, with odds of nine to one on the second.

Fredo stared straight into Carmine's eyes, trying to read his mind. His intuition told him that Carmine was lying through his teeth, but Carmine was so cool with his replies that he could not be certain. "You sure you don't know anything about where they are?"

"No, but I'll tell my boys to be on the lookout. DT's tall, has a crooked nose, and two missing front teeth, and Frankie's going bald and has a beer gut, right? We'll keep our eyes open, and if we spot them, we'll tell them to call home." Carmine noted a flicker of a smile pass across Fredo's face when he spoke about them phoning home. Both were aware that the only home the Picarelli brothers had known in recent years was a federal penitentiary.

Fredo pushed his chair back and prepared to depart, his mission unaccomplished. In the back of his mind, he had the feeling that DT and Frankie would not be returning to Jersey now, soon, or ever. He was almost certain that Carmine knew a lot more than he was letting on. He was equally certain that he would never be able to get the truth out of Carmine without beating it out of him, and that was not an option today. And he still had to drive down that treacherous West Virginia mountain road before he could get back onto a safe federal highway going north.

Carmine reached out to shake hands, speaking in his most hospitable tone, "I sure wish you could stay longer, Fredo, but I guess you probably don't like driving around in these hills after dark. Before you get out of here, how about me pouring you one more drink for the road?"

"Yeah, that's exactly what I need before getting on your death road going back down the mountain," Fredo replied. Then he took charge again, resuming the family underboss-capo relationship between him and Carmine. "By the way, when I get back to Elizabeth, I'll tell Donatello about his two soldiers MIA down here. He'll probably want to personally talk to you some more about it, one on one."

Fredo climbed back into his car, tried to steady his nerves for what was coming up, and started back down the winding road, keeping his eyes focused on the center of the pavement in front of him. He was careful not to cut his eyes to the side until he reached the bottom.

As soon as he was off the property, Carmine dialed up Angelo Vinciano. "Angie, I owe you one. Fredo was just down here looking for two of his boys that were snooping around town last week. They learned too much, and I had to deal with the situation."

He paused to listen for a couple of minutes to the excited voice on the other end, then continued, "No, I don't think Donatello is going to lose too much sleep over either of them. We're talking about street punks here, DT and Frankie Picarelli. He can recruit a couple of more just like them in any bar in town."

Then he listened again for a minute, replying, "Yeah, I'll watch my step. I don't want trouble with the boss any more than you do. Call me if you learn anything else."

CHAPTER 47

Laura and Margaret Barry walked into the Crystal Ballroom of the Eden Springs Resort on Saturday morning, where they saw Edna Cline sitting alone at a table, waving for them to come and join her. They crossed the room, noting that Edna had already spread out her notebook and several poster boards on the table top, ready for their meeting to begin. Neither of them was surprised to find Edna to be the early bird. Her only daughter was grown and gone, and she did not hold a paying job; therefore, all of her boundless energy and careful attention was directed toward helping her husband the mayor run the town of Eden Springs, and she was obviously already open for business this morning.

"We've got a lot of planning to do for the Cen Plus Ten Ball," Edna proclaimed, after giving the two new arrivals a warm greeting. "The men seem to be so far ahead of us in their preparation for the celebration. I'm starting to see a lot of new beards on faces everywhere I go. And remember, we have to be ready a day earlier, since the ball is to be held on Friday night, and the battle reenactment won't take place until the following afternoon."

Laura and Margaret sat back, watched, and listened as Edna

presented her elaborate plans for the event. Both had mixed emotions about their roles, glad to know that Edna would not be making extensive demands for their help, but also wondering if the only reason Edna had invited them to join her committee was to rubber stamp her ideas.

"Everyone must be in antebellum costume for the ball, with the ladies wearing gowns. The men will, of course, be wearing their Confederate or Union military uniforms. That's one reason I was so adamant with Preston about holding the ball before the battle reenactment. I'm sure that the men will get their clothing soiled and sweaty during the battle, and that would certainly spoil the whole effect of elegant grandeur that we want to create."

Edna continued to roll out her ideas, and it was apparent that she hadn't overlooked many details. "The Huntington String Trio will be in town to provide music in keeping with the Civil War era, and I've obtained permission for them to perform *Tara's Theme*. Since we will have some high school age young people participating, we will serve Baptist Punch and cake, both made from authentic old recipes. We'll need to set up tables to accommodate a crowd of well over a hundred people, and have folding chairs arranged around the perimeter of the room to seat additional guests if the turnout should be larger. And for the crowning touch, the new TV station in town has promised to film the event for broadcast on the evening news. Have I missed anything?"

"Not that I can see, Edna," Laura replied, genuinely impressed. "You've done an amazing job of making plans for the ball, and I think it will be a big success. It looks like all that Margaret and I need to do is get over to Thimbles and Thread, and put our gowns on order with the Garrett sisters."

"I give you the same high marks as Laura," Margaret added. "But this may be the last time we're allowed to agree on anything, since Ed will be commanding the Rebs on that weekend, and my Sam will be leading the Yanks."

Laura and Margaret were as good as their word, and after

wrapping up their planning committee meeting with Edna, they drove over to Thimbles and Thread, where Abagail Garrett took their measurements and helped them select patterns and fabrics for their ballroom gowns. "Do you both want the petticoats with the hoops?" Abagail inquired. "Most of the ladies will be wearing them. And what about the pantaloons?"

"Definitely the hooped petticoat, but I'm going to have to think for a few minutes about the pantaloons," Margaret answered. "Well, maybe I'd better go ahead and get the pantaloons, too, while I'm about it. I've got to ride over to the Eden Springs Resort that night in the front seat of our Chevy, and I'm afraid that I might give some of the men in town quite an eyeful if those hoops flipped up on the way." The other two Garrett sisters, Agnes and Anne, always the perfect audience, could be heard laughing in the next room.

"Oh, our southern gentlemen would be far too chivalrous to glance at a lady's exposed ankle," Abigail smiled. "I'm sure they would politely cover their eyes with the brims of their hats and avert their gazes."

"You've got to be kidding me," Margaret interjected. "I've taught a lot of those Southern gentlemen at Tyler High over the years, and I can assure you, they wouldn't be averting their gaze; they'd all be reaching for their binoculars.

Laura drove over to the realty office after she and Margaret split up. Freddie's car was the only vehicle in sight, and inside, she could see him through an open door, at work in his small office. "Haven't you got something better to do on a pretty Saturday morning than come in here to work?" she joked, taking a seat across from him.

"Not really," Freddie replied in his usual good-natured way. "Marilyn's working at the animal hospital today, so I took the morning to show some houses to a new family moving into town. They seemed to like the vacant Adams' home over on Fourth Street, and I think they may want to make an offer on it next week. What exciting things have you been up to this morning?"

"I'm not sure you could call it exciting. I've spent most of the morning in a planning committee meeting with Edna Cline and your old high school math teacher, Margaret Barry, going over Edna's ideas for the big Eden Springs anniversary dog and pony show coming up in September. And speaking of dogs and ponies, how are things going between you and the new lady vet? I don't know when I've laughed as hard as when you told me about that lab class she gave you three weeks ago in Assisted Calf Delivery 101."

"We're getting along great, except that after working as her vet assistant on that pregnant cow, I'll probably never be able to eat red meat again." He stopped to pat his stomach, adding, "But I don't think I'm losing so much weight that I'm in any danger of the wind blowing me away."

Freddie hesitated for a minute, then asked a question that showed just how highly he regarded Laura, both as his boss and as a trusted friend. "Can I ask you something about a personal matter? How long do you think a couple who are in their mid-twenties should go together before they're ready to consider getting married?"

"Wow! Tough question! Obviously we're talking about you and Marilyn, right?"

"Yes. I've never met anyone like her. I think about her constantly when we're apart, and want to be with her all of the time. I realize that we've only known each other for three and a half months, and that's not very long, but I already feel like I'm ready to commit to her for a lifetime. You and Ed didn't go together for long before you got married, and things have worked out great for you two, haven't they?"

"That's true. We were both older, and had each been in a happy marriage before. We already knew all the give and take that a successful marriage involves, and all of the joy and heartache. We both felt a strong, loving attraction and connection almost from the time we met, and when he proposed, I was ready to accept.

"You and Marilyn are younger, and this would be a first marriage for two people who have grown accustomed to living independent lives up until now, making all of your own decisions. Once you're married, there'll be two different personalities under one roof. You need to be sure that both of you are willing to be flexible and share not only your love, but also all of the responsibilities of marriage for a lifetime ahead. That includes the good times and bad, ups and downs, financial difficulties, medical problems, and countless other challenges, 'til death you do part.' Do you think you two are at that point yet?"

"I shouldn't speak for Marilyn, but I can tell you that I am. Independent living and doing exactly what you please whenever you want sound great on the surface, but living in a boarding house can be lonely. I've never wanted to be the chief in the teepee and have everything my way. Yes, I think I'm ready now to commit to her, and share everything with her, good and bad."

"It sounds to me like you're ready. I think it's time for you to have a serious conversation with Marilyn and find out how she feels about getting married. If she's looking for a special person to share her life, it may be a good time to pop the question."

Laura rose from her chair, speaking quietly, "You're a sweet young man, Freddie. Now that she's gotten to know you, I bet Marilyn feels the same way about you. I have a feeling that she'll be happy to discuss marriage, and when you propose, I'm betting that her answer will be 'yes.'"

Freddie walked over and wrapped his big arms around Laura. "Thanks for giving me your advice. The next time I talk to Marilyn, I'm going to steer the conversation around to marriage and try to find out whether she sees a future for the two of us. If she gives me a cue that that she'd like for me to be part of her life for the long haul, I'll start checking out engagement rings."

"I'll be holding the good thought, hoping things work out

for you. One other thing, while we're having this heart to heart talk. I think it's now time for us to start working on the plan we discussed earlier, promoting you to partner in our real estate business."

CHAPTER 48

"**DT and Frankie Picarelli aren't** coming back," Fredo commented to his two brothers in the back room of the Old Italy Restaurant. "Carmine Nardelli knows what happened to them, but he's not about to talk. My guess is that DT and Frankie found out about that profitable red-light entertainment business Carmine's running in Keystone, and he didn't want them to spill their guts to us."

It was the first time that the three Mengarelli brothers had assembled in a family meeting since Fredo returned from West Virginia, and Donatello, the oldest and the top boss within the family, had been waiting impatiently for his report. "How'd you find out about it?" Donatello inquired. "You didn't stick around in West Virginia on your trip but a couple of days."

"That was long enough to learn a lot of things. Cash talks, and in that town a little money goes a long way. I ran into a couple of locals in a bar, and the first thing you know, I'm starting to buy their beer. They thought that I had some money burning a hole in my pocket, and before very long, they were suggesting that we all go over and check out the frisky ladies working in the houses over in Cinder Bottom. I acted like I was interested, and started trying to find out from them who would think about starting an indoor recreation business in such a backwater town.

"After about the fifth round of drinks, one of them told me that there was some wealthy Italian named Nardelli who owned all the property. He said that the guy had a management staff that handled all of the day to day business, including the muscle to crack a few heads on Saturday night when some drunks out of the coal fields start getting too rowdy. According to those two, it's standing room only on weekends. They'd even heard rumors that Nardelli was doing so well he was making plans with a big shot in the coal mining business to open another operation outside of Bluefield."

"Who's he partnering up with?" Donatello asked, now having difficulty controlling his increasing displeasure and well-known short fuse.

"The two didn't want to talk about it, Don. One of them dropped the name Barker, and then tried to cover it up. Apparently he's some mining company big shot who has the reputation all around those parts for coming down hard on people who cross him, and my two beer drinking buddies seemed to be afraid to say anything that might get back to him."

"What do you think we ought to do?" Don asked, as though open to suggestions, but unable to conceal a look that showed he had already made his own hard-line decision.

"We could just let it go," Fredo offered. "Carmine's doing OK running the production end of the family beverage business. The only thing he's done that's way out of line is chiseling us out of our cut from his new red-light entertainment operation."

"The hell it is!" Donatello cut in. "We sent two of our soldiers to Keystone to check on what he was up to, and apparently he took both of them out, then lied to you about it. It doesn't matter that DT and Frankie were both low level punks who can be replaced without the family business missing a step. What matters is that Carmine lied to you, and the disrespect he's shown to the family. If we let him get away with this, the word will get around, and we'll lose the respect and control of everyone we have to deal with. Something has to be done."

"I think we need to get rid of our problem, and put a new man in Keystone to run the production operation," Giacomo suddenly chimed in, trying to show that despite being the youngest of the three brothers, he was just as tough as the older two. Maybe Giacomo would have been wiser to have just sat back and listened, keeping his head down and his recommendations for retribution to himself. But he had piped up now, and he was about to bear the consequences.

"I agree, Giac," Donatello replied, announcing the final decision. "I want you to take charge of this whole deal. I'm giving you Nic and Ricco Costa to work with you, and they're the two best soldiers in the family. I expect you to find out who this Barker person is, and what he's been up to with Carmine. I want you to start figuring out what we need to do to fold the Cinder Bottom red-light operation into our family's businesses.

"You need to get down to West Virginia and spend a couple of weeks working with Carmine at the Keystone Bottling Company, taking a crash course in bootleg whiskey production and learning how to run the distilling and bottling plant, so you can step right in and keep things going."

Giacomo had a sick feeling in the pit of his stomach. He never dreamed that when he spoke up with his one and only recommendation, Don would immediately seize it and then dump the whole can of worms right in his lap. He knew that once Don spoke, the command might as well be graven on a stone tablet, and no protest would be tolerated. As bad as it seemed, it got worse when the eldest brother spoke again.

"After you get all that done, I expect you, Nic, and Ricco to take care of Carmine, and anyone else who might create a problem for us, including that mining big shot, Barker, whoever he is. That means these people should disappear without a trace, just the same way that DT and Frankie did." Donatello unexpectedly broke into a smile, adding, "Giac, just pretend you're a famous magician like The Great Blackstone, and poof, you make them all go away in a puff of smoke."

Brothers usually stick together, but in some families like the Mengarellis, they also stick it to each other. With all the heavy lifting now assigned, Fredo jumped back in with his two cents. "Good plan, Don. Giac, send me a postcard from Keystone. And enjoy driving that scenic road from town up to the Keystone Bottling Company every morning. It's really spectacular, particularly after a good rain, when there's lots of water running in the creek down in the bottom of the gorge."

Giacomo sprinted for the lavatory just as soon as Donatello signaled that the meeting was over. Sitting on the cold seat, he pounded his fist against the plaster wall again and again, wishing he could turn back the clock, and somehow return the short straw he had just drawn. Later, he settled down to a numb state of acceptance regarding his new assignment, and unlocked the door, still rubbing the severely bruised knuckles on his right hand.

Giacomo did not bother saying goodbye to his brothers as he left from the back room and continued out of the building and down the street. He stopped at a neighborhood hangout called Royce's Bar and Grill and ordered a boilermaker. It went down so easy that he decided to have seconds, before continuing on another block to a dark brick building and taking the stairs up three floors. Down the hallway, he could see a glass door marked Billiards, and hear the staccato clicking of pool balls coming sharply together on a number of tables in play.

He stepped through the door without any of the dozen pool shooters seeming to pay any attention to the newcomer who had just entered. After all, no hustler with reasonable smarts was going to lose his concentration on the table when there was serious money riding on a game of eight ball. Not unless someone yelled "Raid," and a group of uniformed officers came through the door.

At a table in the back, Giacomo spotted a dark-haired,

heavy-set man with the thick arms of a weight lifter and the crooked nose of a street fighter now in the process of running the table. Leaning against the wall watching the action was a tough looking, wiry man with a shaved head and tattoos on both arms. He waited until the powerfully built man had just driven the eight ball halfway through the corner pocket, and was collecting his winnings before he approached, and commented with an approving smile, "Good shot, Nic." He nodded to the spectator standing nearby, and joked, "Got a job holding up the wall, Ricco?"

Both men walked over to extend their hands to their under boss, like two dogs in a pack paying homage to the alpha male. "I need for you two to follow me over in the corner where we can talk privately," Giacomo commanded. "We've got some business to take care of in a couple of weeks, and I need to tell you what's going down. This is coming straight from the boss, so you need to give me your full attention."

Nic racked up his cue stick, and he and Ricco fell into line, following behind Giacomo until the three were standing alone in the corner, well out of earshot of the other men in the room. Both Nic and Ricco were alert and paying full attention, pleased to be part of some important family business undertaking and to be taking orders directly from an under boss. They might have felt a little less enjoyment if they could have anticipated all that the new assignment entailed.

CHAPTER 49

Doug had no more than walked through the front door of Epstein's Jewelry Store on Friday when he was approached by Mrs. Marcus, a matronly sales lady wearing a wide smile. "Douglas, it turned out beautifully. I think you're going to be very pleased when you see the ring. Wait just a moment 'til I can go in the back room and get it." When she returned, she handed a small box to Doug and stood back without saying another word, carefully watching his reaction.

Doug opened the box and looked at the sparkling diamond engagement ring inside, a one-third carat stone with a striking white gold setting. "Mrs. Marcus, it's even more spectacular than I'd hoped." Closing the lid, he gave her a warm hug.

"Douglas, you're one of my favorite customers, the kind that makes me love my job so much. I knew you'd like it. Does that special lady have any idea that you're about to present her with an engagement ring?"

"No, ma'am, she doesn't know about it yet. But Vickie and I have been going together for almost seven years, so I don't believe she'll think that I'm exactly rushing into things when she sees it."

"I watch her on the evening news, Douglas, and I think

you're about to become engaged to the prettiest young lady in these parts. And just between you and me, I think she's about to get the finest young man in Eden Springs for her fiancée."

"You just did wonders for my self confidence, Mrs. Marcus," Doug replied, giving her another hug. "I'll tell Vickie how much you helped me with the ring."

Doug went by Ed and Laura's house after work to show his family the new purchase. Laura examined it carefully, and gave her approval. "I think your ring will take Vickie's breath away." She passed the solitaire to Ed, commenting, "We can't wait to hear how she reacts when you give it to her."

Ed checked out the ring, and agreed, "It's a beauty. Tell Vickie that we said welcome to the family. We're claiming her from the time you slip this on her finger."

Lizzie clinched it when she added, "I like Vickie. She treats me like a big sister, and she shows me how girls should stand up to boys. She really got you back good after you threw that muddy water on her."

Doug had to move quickly in order to get dressed and pick up Vickie after the newscast. The evening he had planned for her involved a trip back in time, and he wanted to make the experience authentic. Part of his preparation involved digging out a bottle of Old Spice from the back of his dresser drawer and splashing a generous amount on his face after showering and shaving.

Vickie breezed out of the station door, finding Doug waiting in the parking lot. She slipped into the front sear beside him, giving him a quick kiss. "What's on for this mysterious evening you've cooked up that you won't tell me anything about?" She sniffed his cheek and asked, "Are you wearing Old Spice? I didn't know they still sold that stuff." Then she ran her hands through his short red hair, adding, "If you're still using that aftershave, maybe you ought to start wearing a flattop again."

Doug ignored her comments. "Just hang onto your hat, sunshine. You remember the movie we took in last week at the

Lyric, *Have Rocket, Will Travel*, where the Three Stooges took that trip to Venus? Well, you ain't seen nothing yet." The Four Aces' harmonic rendition of *Tell Me Why* played on the radio as they continued across town and back in time.

As they started up the gentle hill approaching Tyler High, Vickie asked, "Hey, honey- You're not taking me back to high school, are you? Remember, we graduated five years ago." She poked him in the ribs, giggling, "No one thought you'd make it, including Principal Stoner, but you fooled them."

"We're taking a trip back to 1952 tonight," he said, walking with her hand in hand to the front door and unlocking it with the key that Principal Barry had loaned him that morning.

The building was eerily quiet as they entered, and Doug switched on the lights in the hallway. Each footstep sounded on the worn wooden floor, and the echoes bounced and rebounded up and down the empty corridors. "Is there anyone in the building with us?" Vickie asked in a low voice.

"Not unless you consider 'anyone' to be the ghosts of all the students and teachers who've passed through these hallways since Tyler High was opened in 1902," Doug replied. "Does it bring back a lot of memories standing here and looking around at the rows of lockers? Mine was 97, and yours was 109, back in '54 when we were seniors."

"I don't know how you can remember trivia like that," Vickie commented, standing close to him. "But I will have to say, being here in this deserted building really takes me back. It's almost spooky."

"Give me your hand, and we'll take a walk," Doug suggested. The only sound other than their footsteps was the accompanying quiet creaking of loose floor boards as they continued, stopping in front of the door marked 104.

"Do you remember this room?" Doug asked.

"Yes. This was Mrs. Wilson's classroom. She taught Latin and English, and she also had us for homeroom.

Doug opened the door and switched on the light, then

stepped back for Vickie to enter. "Do you remember anything else about this room? Do you recall where you sat on the second week of school when you were a sophomore?"

"Good grief, no. Do you think I have the memory of an elephant? Tell me, do you believe that anyone in our class could remember anything about being in this classroom way back then?"

"I can remember exactly where I was at that time, and I can also remember where you were, too. You were sitting on the front row by the window. Would you take a seat at that desk before we go on?"

Vickie took her place, then Doug continued, "You were wearing a red plaid dress, with your hair up in a pony tail tied with a red ribbon. It was my first day at Tyler High, and Principal Stoner had just walked me up to Room 104 to meet my new classmates. I was doggone nervous about being the new kid coming in, feeling like a bug under a microscope standing in front of the room with everyone checking me out. But the thing I remember most clearly was seeing you, and thinking that you were the prettiest girl I had ever seen. The first time I looked at you, I thought, someday, she's going to be my girlfriend."

"I'm amazed that you can remember all of that. A few things are starting to come back to me. A week before you got here, Principal Stoner announced that a city boy from Charleston would be coming to Tyler. All of us girls started to talk about how he would be as handsome and hip as Troy Donahue. By the time you got here, no one could have lived up to the advance billing. When Mrs. Wilson introduced you to the class, you looked more like a bashful kid than a heartthrob movie star."

"Mike told me all of that right after I started school. I know that I didn't make much of an impression on you right away, but somehow things worked out after you broke up with Len Hacker, and we started going together. By the time we began going steady, I knew you were the only girl I would ever want to marry."

Vickie started to stand, when Doug murmured, "Please don't get up yet." He pulled the ring from his pocket, dropping to one knee on the floor in front of her. "Victoria Marie Vicelli, will you marry me?"

Vickie was speechless at first, nodding her assent, as Doug slipped the engagement ring onto her finger. She held up her hand, watching the diamond refract the soft overhead light into a rainbow of colors. Then they both came to their feet, and she whispered in his ear as they embraced. "You knew that I meant yes, didn't you?"

"I knew," he replied, holding her close for a long kiss.

Vickie continued to admire the ring, as Doug explained, "The diamond is from Mother's ring. She gave it to me a month before she died, and she made me promise that I'd only give it to someone I would cherish for the rest of my life. The gold is from her ring, and one of Mom's. She said it represents the love that brought us together."

"Can we stay here for a few more minutes?" Vickie asked, holding on to Doug, tears streaming down her cheeks. "I don't want to go outside still crying like this."

A loud fluttering noise from outside suddenly caught their attention, causing both to stop and listen.

"What was that?" Vickie asked.

"I think it was a flock of pigeons flying out from under the eaves," Doug replied. "Then again, it could have been the spirits of old Tyler High students giving us their congratulations."

Doug and Vickie left the building and the Ghost of High School Past behind, locking the doors on their way out for the last time, driving to the Eden Springs Regency Room for dinner. Late that evening, as the two held each other close and danced to the pianist's beautiful rendition of *I Only Have Eyes For You*, Vickie told him the things he wanted most to hear. "I love you, Doug. I'm glad I finally came back to you."

CHAPTER 50

Nic and Ricco walked into the Keystone Diner early Friday morning, joining Giacomo in a booth near the back. It had been over two weeks since their boss had called them together in the corner of the poolroom in Elizabeth to give them their marching orders, just after Nic had finished hustling a local boy out of two big ones.

"Glad you two could make it," Giacomo said sarcastically. "I've been here drinking coffee for an hour waiting on you. I think the old woman working behind the counter brews this crap with army surplus coffee beans and water out of the North Fork "

"Sorry, Boss," Nic replied. "We were a little late getting to sleep last night."

"Save the bullshit," Giacomo said, cutting him off. "I don't need to hear about your midnight romances this morning. I've been hanging out down here in this one-horse town since the last time I saw you, sleeping in a flea bag motel and driving that nightmare of a road up to the bottling plant every day. I want to finish everything we talked about before the day's over. Let's get out of here now and on the way to Beckley. You brought along everything I told you to, didn't you?"

"Yeah, Giac," Ricco fired back quickly. "We've got everything we'll need to take care of business. And I put the stolen tags on the truck this morning. You sure Barker will be at his place?"

"You let me worry about Barker being there. Just make sure that your late night escapades don't interfere with your job performance today," he added ominously, throwing down a dollar on the counter. Then the three were out the door and into the panel truck, off on the winding road to Beckley.

*****

Carmine Nardelli was also on the road at that moment, but heading for a sunnier and happier destination. He had gotten a call from Angelo Vinciano the night before, telling him it would be in his best interest to take early retirement and quickly relocate to a southern climate for reasons of health. He had taken only enough time for Christina to pack up the silverware and her jewelry collection, and for him to throw three suitcases of his own into the trunk of the Buick, a small one containing sunglasses, a straw hat, warm weather clothing, and a shaving kit, and two very large ones stuffed to the top with carefully bundled US currency in large denominations.

"Are you looking forward to living in Miami?" he murmured to his bride of twenty-five years, glancing over to watch Christina gently stroking her French poodle, Monsieur Nuzzles.

"You're driving too damn fast," she replied sharply. "And I don't know why we had to get out of the house so quickly. I left my mink stole behind. Then her demeanor quickly changed, and she inquired in a cajoling, sweet voice, "Honey, would you be willing to turn around and go back home so I can pick it up?"

Carmine deliberated for a moment about reaching across the front seat to open the passenger side door, and shoving his beloved and Monsieur Nuzzles out of the speeding car onto the shoulder of US 301. Then he reverted to his usual loving and tolerant manner, acquired over a quarter century of surviving life with Christina, and replied, "I don't think that would be for the best, sweetcakes. Monsieur Nuzzles might get car sick if we went back. I'll just buy you a new fur when we get there."

*****

Giacomo, Nic, and Ricco were also about to get there, but not the sunny place in south Florida. "We'll drive straight on over to Barker's house on Front Street," Giacomo commented as they approached the city limits of Beckley. "It's a big old Victorian pile of bricks set way back off the road almost out of sight in a grove of trees. I've found out that the old man lives alone with his pet bulldog, and he takes a nap after lunch every day at 2:00 sharp. He's got the reputation of being meaner than a badger with a toothache and for going after anyone who crosses him. I understand that no one has the guts to set foot on his property and that he doesn't even bother keeping a security guard."

Nic turned north onto Kanawha Street and followed it across town. He finally located Front Street, but not before making a number of wrong turns, and receiving some hurtful opinions from his boss about his intelligence and driving skills. The three finally managed to locate the driveway leading to their destination by checking for the numbers on adjacent houses. Giacomo tersely rasped out as they approached, "I'm sure that's the one. Turn in here."

The pot-holed asphalt drive led from the street across a long, overgrown expanse of weeds that had probably once been a lawn, toward a home barely visible through the trees. "Just drive on up toward the house like we own it," Giacomo commanded. "Pull in beside the place and find a place to park behind some shrubbery where we'll be out of sight."

Nic wheeled the panel truck up the long driveway and behind the house, parking it a short distance away from the back door behind some overgrown wisteria vines.

"Showtime," Giacomo said quietly as he opened the door of the truck, trying to conceal behind a weak smile the apprehension he always felt before this kind of family business. He checked his wrist watch again, observing that it was 2:15, then commented in a low voice. "We're right on time. Barker should be dead to the world by now. Just watch out for his dog."

All three were outfitted with leather gloves and rubber soled shoes for their mission. Giacomo patted the outside of his pocket, feeling the reassuring bulk of the snub-nosed S&W .357 Magnum causing his pants to droop on the right side. Ricco was carrying a shortened ball bat drilled out and loaded with lead on the business end. Nic toted an oversized canvas duffel bag, and a plumber's friend with a cheese cloth bag containing a pound of finely ground red pepper duct-taped to the rubber suction cup.

It took Ricco only a few minutes to pick both of the deadbolt locks on the back door and lead the way into the dimly lit interior, with the other two right on his heels. They silently checked out the downstairs of the old house room by room. Not a creature was stirring, except for one fat old gray cat, which furtively scurried away when it caught sight of them. The three intruders were startled when a grandfather clock ticking slowly in the parlor unexpectedly gonged the half hour but quickly regained their composure as the sound echoed through the hallway and died.

Ricco led the way as they ascended the winding staircase to the second floor and began their search of five upstairs bedrooms. Their pulse rates jumped each time they quietly cracked open a door to peek inside and look for signs of life. The first four rooms were empty, and their reaction was the same each time, a brief wave of relief followed by increased apprehensive suspense, knowing the probability of finding someone inside was quickly growing larger. When they cracked the door to peer into the fifth bedroom at the end of the hallway, they spotted a burly old man on the bed.

Robert Barker was lying on his back, snoring like a freight train, still dressed in his street clothes and his sturdy black leather shoes, with his cane beside him. What they were unable to see was Moe, sleeping peacefully on a rug near the far side of the bed, just out of sight. Nic eased open the door, and as the three men silently entered the room, all hell broke loose.

Moe instantly transitioned from REM sleep to full attack mode. He came out from behind the bed like an angry wolverine, springing on Ricco and locking his fangs into his thigh before Ricco even realized what was happening. Robert heard the commotion and woke out of a sound sleep, completely confused about what was going on around him. Nic took a swing at Moe with his pepper stick but missed, since Ricco was spinning around wildly trying to dislodge the fifty-pound bulldog gripping his leg. Giacomo stood back in consternation, watching the action but not sure where to jump in.

Robert came to his senses, quickly validating the legends of his toughness and his ability to swing a club. Grabbing his stout hickory cane, he delivered a hard blow to the side of Nic's head, causing him to stagger backward in a daze with a new cauliflower ear. His second blow landed directly on Giacomo's collar bone, causing him to back away yelping in pain. But that was the point where the battle began to turn.

Ricco stood still long enough for Nic to hit Moe squarely across the muzzle with his plunger several times, and as the dog's huge head turned red with hot pepper, Moe released his grip. All of the fight went out of the bulldog, as he rolled on the floor, pepper in his eyes, nose, and throat, burning and suffocating him. Robert retreated to a corner of the room, still fighting off the intruders with his cane. All three members of the Mafia family would later agree that you had to give the devil his due for guts, remembering that Robert had called out to them, "Leave the dog alone. This is between you and me."

Still fighting like a wounded old cape buffalo trapped by three young lions, Robert gave a good account of himself, never asking for quarter, still swinging his cane, until Ricco's club finally clipped him across the head and knocked him senseless to the floor. At that moment, the old man's heart gave out. Robert Barker had lived by the sword, and by biblical injunction, he also died by the sword. But it was all in keeping with his twisted code of honor. He was a supreme gladiator until the very end, beaten but never bested in the violent arena of his life.

With blood still running down his leg into his shoe from Moe's bite, Ricco took a bucket of water drawn from the spigot in the bathroom and poured it across the dog's head to wash off the pepper. Moe sat on the floor, looking up at him in gratitude, one warrior paying silent respect to another, after a hard fought and honorable hand-to-hand battle.

Nic and Ricco carried Robert out in the large duffel bag and loaded him in the back of the panel truck. They carefully cleaned up the blood spots from the floor and walls with bleach and swept the pepper from the floor. By the time they had finished, the fifth bedroom looked little different than the other four. Giacomo picked up Robert's sturdy cane, ordering, "Throw this in the bag with the old man's body, and bury it with him. I've never seen an old guy that tough. He deserves respect. And when you put his body in a drum to go to the landfill, make sure it's a nice, clean one with a tight lid."

It was late evening by the time the three men stuffed Robert's body into a shiny new cylindrical coffin and tapped on the cover. It took all of them to muscle the steel barrel up into the back of the panel truck, which would carry him, together with a half dozen similar but rustier metal drums, to his final earthly abode. Giacomo provided a short benediction after they finished, bowing his head, crossing himself, and repeating, "Rest in peace, old man. You were one helluva fighter."

Giacomo later checked his room phone at the North Fork Motel, finding there had been a call that he needed to return. He recognized the number as that of a pay phone in Elizabeth where he could talk privately with Donatello. Giacomo made the call, and after the phone rang for a couple of minutes he heard his older brother answer. "Don, we're finished with the miner. Now we're going after the bootlegger."

He was surprised to hear Don tersely reply, "Don't bother

trying to look him up. Someone must have tipped him off, and he's flown the coop. Just be sure you've got a good man in charge who knows what he's doing, running things up on the hill and down in the bottom, before you pull out and come home. Apparently our friend Carmine salted away a lot of cash for a rainy day. I doubt we'll ever be able to find him and his old lady."

CHAPTER 51

"I wasn't sure that you'd ever want to fly with me again," Jack Bradford laughed, as Ed joined him at the airfield on Friday afternoon. "I guess you're using the same rule that you did when you were a kid learning to ride a bike. When you fall off, you've got to get right back on, or you'll be scared to do it for the rest of your life."

"Actually, I'm more comfortable flying with you today than I was before that emergency landing. I don't think there are many private or even commercial pilots who could have pulled off that maneuver you did without cracking up. I'm positive that you're all alone in the record books for using a barbed wire fence and a tail wheel to stop a rolling plane. That was brilliant."

"That was more luck than brains, Ed, if we want to be perfectly honest with each other. I think Saint Peter wasn't ready for either of us to show up at the Pearly Gates that day." Jack dropped the tail gate of his truck and invited Ed to have a seat beside him. "I wanted to fill you in on a couple of things while it's quiet out here, before we get in the plane and fire up the engine."

Ed boosted himself up on the tailgate and listened as Jack continued. "This conversation today is off the record, but I think you deserve an update on what's happened since you, Arnold

Jannsen, and I met following the doctor's acquittal. After all, you're the one who exposed the conspiracy against him and identified the culprits and their motives.

"Dudley and Patsy Scaggs have agreed to a plea bargain and will testify against Samuel Lukins if I'll go easy on them with the charges of criminal fraud and perjury. They don't have any money to hire legal counsel, and their former lawyer is the very one they'll be testifying against. I've never seen two people more frightened of being separated from their family and serving time behind bars.

"Samuel Lukins is representing himself in the criminal fraud case. He's contacted me, suggesting that he'll implicate the people who bankrolled him in exchange for my dropping some of the charges against him. He's hoping to avoid a felony conviction, having to serve time, and being disbarred. But he won't provide any names until we strike a deal. You've already discovered a link between Lukins and William Thorpe, indirectly implicating Robert Barker, but it's a bit tenuous. Barker Mining could claim that any payments from Thorpe to Lukins were for legal services associated with their mining business. What do you think about letting Lukins off easy in order to nail Thorpe and Barker?"

"Jack, you can go as easy on the Scaggs as you like. They're such miserable human beings that I don't want to add to their troubles. But I would really like to see you find a way to hammer Lukins as well as Thorpe and Barker. Lukins is a slimy embarrassment to the legal profession. Thorpe and Barker have managed to run over decent citizens of this state for too long, and it's time to hold them accountable for all the trouble that they've caused. For the record, I'm going to go after them in a civil suit after you're finished in criminal court, just like I promised. Arnold and I have agreed that any money collected over and above our expenses is going toward endowed scholarships at the University of Virginia School of Medicine. Neither of us is looking to make a dime."

"Your position's about what I expected, Ed. I'll see if I can build a case against Thorpe and also against Barker without giving Lukins a pass." Jack slipped down from the tailgate, adding, "Something else you should know. I'm not sure what's going on, but when I tried to contact Thorpe this morning to bring him in for questioning, I got the word from his secretary that he hasn't been at work for a couple of weeks. After that I checked on Barker's whereabouts and was told that he hasn't been at his office lately, either. If they're both still out of touch on Monday, I'll get the Beckley Police involved in trying to find them."

"Something's wrong, Jack. Those two aren't likely to go off together on a two week fishing trip with a few cases of beer. I'll be interested to hear what you find out."

"I'll get back to you on that Monday. Anyway, we need to hold the discussion for now and take the plane up right away if we're going to fly today. There's a weather report of a tropical storm coming up from the Gulf that'll be moving into West Virginia tonight. Flying in a driving rain would be a lot more excitement than either of us old timers needs."

*****

The weather man got it right. The sun disappeared later, and the southwestern sky began to darken to a non- threatening shade of dishrag gray, followed by a sporadic sprinkle of rain. But within an hour, low hanging, ominously dark clouds charged with electrical energy moved in overhead, spewing lightning to the ground, with each flash of light followed by the loud crash of thunder. The rain fell in sheets, as if a cosmic water line had ruptured. It overran the gutters on houses, flooded streets, and ran into poorly drained basements, in a monsoon-like downpour that the locals called a "frog drowner." The storm clouds seemed to be in no hurry to pass through the area, hanging around throughout the night, still cascading down their reservoir of water with undiminished intensity into the morning.

Electrical power lines were out, but the telephones were still working when Doug tried to dial Vickie on Saturday morning.

There was no answer at her apartment, so he took a chance and dialed the number for the TV station. It took a dozen tries to get through the overloaded phone circuits and reach the station, but when he finally got a connection, he heard a tired voice answer, "WESP Channel 8."

Doug was able to tie up the TV station phone line long enough to briefly speak with Vickie. "Are you OK?"

"I'm fine, honey, but the weekend broadcast crew won't be able to get to the station, so I'll have to stay here and work. We're running on emergency generators, broadcasting weather related news continuously to anyone out there who's still got electrical power."

"I'm glad you're safe. The power is out here in my apartment building. I've talked to Dad and Mom, and your mother, too. Everybody's OK, and all of us are just riding it out. I've been listening to my battery powered radio, and I've heard that many of the streets in town are blocked off by water. The police and sheriff's department are asking people to stay where they are and not go out unless it's an emergency."

"Thanks for letting me know our families are OK. I'd better not tie up the station phone any longer. Bye, sweetheart. I love you. Stay dry."

*****

Staying dry was not an option for Sheriff Earl Daniels and his deputies, as they patrolled throughout the night and into the morning, looking for anyone who might have been trapped in their automobiles or homes by the rising waters. "I know we need the rain," Earl commented to his youngest deputy, Billy Nichols, as the patrol car wipers ran at top speed trying to clear the windshield. "But I sure wish we wouldn't get a six month supply dumped on us in just twelve hours."

By late morning, the leaden gray clouds accompanying the tropical depression began to move out of Virginia and West Virginia, advancing up the east coast. But the streams in West

Virginia still overflowed from the heavy rainfall, and as water spilled down the hillsides and spouted from wet-weather underground springs, Earl was aware that they would not peak for hours to come.

Chapter 52

Earl and Billy continued their patrol on Saturday morning, slowly driving from town on a now deserted highway north toward Abner Gap, with water spraying out from beneath their wheels, loudly drumming against the car.

Billy was to the first to notice that Stony Creek was completely out of its banks, carrying a rapidly flowing river of clay-colored water which spanned the valley from the foot of Pine ridge several hundred feet back toward the highway. "The Mountain Ventures Landfill is completely flooded," he said excitedly. "I bet that flood water's doing a job over near the creek where most of the recent work's been going on. There's no trees or sod to hold the dirt, and the water will carve out a big gulley right down through the field."

"We need to get a little closer to see how bad it is," Earl replied, as he turned left at the posted signs and started down the unpaved access road that led to the landfill. The higher elevation of the roadway permitted the two to move in for a good look, and the sight was worse than either had expected.

"I told the board of supervisors that Mountain Ventures shouldn't be allowed to use that low-lying flood plain next to the creek for a landfill," Earl said, exasperated. "This isn't the first time that area's flooded, and it won't be the last. After the creek returns to its banks, the ground will be swampy over there for weeks."

"Hey! I see some junk sticking up out of the water near the creek," Billy exclaimed. "Earl, look over toward the creek bank in line with those big rocks. There's a whole bunch of metal drums all over the place. Where do you think they came from?"

"What in the hell!" Earl exclaimed. "There's not supposed to be any metal drums in this landfill. I'm damn positive that those things aren't part of the trash that the town chartered Mountain Ventures to bury out here. You can see a bunch of them now, and when the water drops, we'll probably find even more. I'm going to grab a camera and get a few pictures."

"You think the landfill people have been breaking the law out here?"

"I'd bet my bird dog on it, Billy. I'm afraid you've just tumbled onto something that's going to give us a lot of investigative work to do. It looks like we've got an ugly mess on our hands here. As of right now, I think some Mountain Ventures people are in a heap of trouble."

"I'll go along with the ugly part," Billy commented. "I remember how pretty this stretch of bottom land used to be. I always heard the bobwhites calling out here during the mating season. I've caught a bunch of trout in this section of Stony Creek over the years since I was a kid."

"Me, too, son. I think that Stony Creek is sick about what's been dumped along its banks, and finally decided it's had enough and vomited up the whole mess."

Trying to determine just what had been churned up had to wait for three more days until Stony Creek pulled back within its banks, and the landfill drained enough for the sheriff's department personnel to walk across the ground without sinking up to their hips in mud. On Tuesday morning, two of the deputies, wearing high boots and their oldest clothes, waded their way over to the closest of the drums and pushed a dozen of them into upright positions. Wearing gloves and goggles, and working with a crowbar, they began to work the tops off of the drums. "Don't splash any of that stuff on you," Earl warned. "The Lord only knows what's in those barrels."

"Looks like some king of industrial waste material," one of the deputies surmised, as the first lid came off. "I've seen stuff like this where I worked before I joined the department. It could be the residue left over from a paint manufacturing process." Other drums contained the same dark, viscous liquid.

"We won't know for sure what we're up against until the State Police get their investigators out here and follow up with some lab testing," Earl observed. "I'll get on the radio in a few minutes and call them to join us." He fell silent as he spotted a drum that stood out from the others due to patches of shiny metal showing through a covering of black silt. "Open up that one over there before we quit, boys," he instructed.

Billy Nichols happened to be standing closest to that container, and he quickly gripped the crowbar and went to work. For the rest of his life, Billy would think twice about being the gung-ho deputy who jumped in first when the boss gave an order. He managed to pry the top off the tightly sealed drum and discovered a canvas sack emitting a stench so foul that it made him turn away to retch as his gag reflex kicked in.

Earl dryly called out helpful advice, "Move upwind, son, and take a few deep breaths. No need to lose your lunch over something like that." Then he added, "Don't go any further, boys! I'm afraid there's a body in that can. I think we'd better secure this area as a crime scene and hold up until we get the State Police here to work with us."

Shortly afterward, uniformed troopers swarmed in. They quickly set to work cordoning off the area and dividing it into grids. A police photographer recorded the overall site, and then the contents of each grid. By now, the creek had receded enough to expose the tops of more drums. Each one was tagged, and a sample of the contents was taken for laboratory analysis. The foul smelling barrel holding the canvas bag was tarped and moved by four mud-covered law enforcement officers into the back of a panel truck, then dispatched to the State Police Forensic Lab in Charleston.

Major Norman Harless took Sheriff Daniels aside, advising him, "I'm almost certain we have toxic material dumped out here. This landfill needs to be closed until we find out what we're up against. If this turns out to be hazardous material as we suspect, and any of these containers was brought here from out of state, we'll call in the FBI."

"This dump's going to be closed forever if I have any say," Earl replied. "I'll see that a locked gate goes up today. The town of Eden Springs will have to go back to using the old town landfill until they come up with something better. You and I both know that the Stony Creek flood plane should have never been used for this purpose. Dumber than hell, if you ask me."

"As soon as the lab people finish their analysis, and we all know what we're up against, I'll talk to you about moving the containers to an impound site," Norman commented. "After that, someone higher up the chain of command will have to decide how we're going to dispose of them."

The next afternoon, Harless called Earl. "Sheriff, I've got the reports back from the lab. First and foremost, that drum with the canvas bag did contain a corpse. It's the body of a very influential coal mining magnate who's lived in Beckley for many years, Robert Copperfield Barker. He's been reported as missing for the last few weeks. The cause of his death was ruled to be heart failure, apparently precipitated by trauma from a blunt force blow to the head. He's the owner of Barker Mining and a subsidiary called Copperfield Enterprises. It appears that he also owns Mountain Ventures, the company operating the landfill. Seems sort of ironic that he developed his own graveyard."

"I've had bad dealings with Barker and his people going back seven years," Earl replied. "It's going to take some work to figure out everything that's been going on around here. What about the contents of those drums? What's in them?"

"It looks like there's a mix. Some of it seems to have come from a lead paint manufacturing plant. Other materials appear to be the residual chemicals from chromium and zinc electroplating lines. Everything the lab tested would be rejected at a legally operated landfill. We're definitely going to have to impound and quarantine all of it. It's the type of stuff nobody wants left sitting in their backyard. And someone smarter than me's going to have to decide what to do with it for the long haul."

"I think that some pretty smart people are going to be working for a long time trying to sort this whole thing out," Earl replied. "But I'm not going to shed any tears over the death of Robert Barker. Let me know when that information will be available for publication. I have friends in town who'll want to know."

"You won't have to wait long, Earl. This story's too big to sit on. I think the discovery of Robert Barker's body will be announced by State Police officials in Charleston later today, and I'm sure that not long after that, it'll be on the news all over the state. Is there anyone in particular you need to bring into our confidence right now?"

"Yeah, if it's OK with you, I'm going to make a call to an attorney here named Ed Housman. He's been battling Barker and his crew head to head since 1952, trying to protect the town and our people, and he deserves to hear what's going on from me before he learns about it on the news."

CHAPTER 53

"**Mrs. Housman, I mean, Laura,** could I talk to you for a few minutes?" Freddie asked, when Laura came into the office on Thursday.

"Sure, Freddie, come on in and have a seat in my hang-out. You're in at work early again today."

Freddie plopped down in a chair across from Laura, and began to speak sincerely. "I wanted you to know how much I appreciate everything you've done for me, sort of taking me under your wing. When I dropped out of Marshall and came back home without any prospects for a job, you hired me and worked with me until I was able to get my real estate license. You've been a mentor and a great boss. And when I came to work this morning and saw that new sign, "*Housman and Palmer Real Estate Sales*," I couldn't believe it. I can't begin to tell you what it means to have you bring me in as your business partner."

He would have continued if Laura hadn't impulsively hugged him. "Freddie, if I've done anything for you, you've repaid me in spades, and I'm not just talking about your sales. You bring a lot of sunshine into this office every day. I'm fortunate to have you working with me."

"Laura, remember when I talked to you the middle of last

month about proposing to Marilyn? You told me that I'd be able to tell whether she was serious about me, and I'd know the right time.

"We've been together three or four nights every week, and we always hang out together on weekends when we're not working. She has me going to church with her. Now days she's as likely to phone me in the evening to talk as I am to call her. She's told her folks back home in Georgia how much time we're spending together, and said that they want to meet me."

"Good Lord, Freddie! What are you waiting for? Are you expecting to catch sight of her trying on wedding gowns downtown? I've never heard of a girl sending stronger signals that she's serious about a man."

"That's exactly what I'd hoped you'd say," Freddie replied. "I've never connected with any girl the way I have with Marilyn. Not even Shirley Martin, during all of those years we went steady. With Mike and Ginny married, and Doug and Vickie engaged, I don't feel like I'm moving too fast. I was thinking about popping the question tomorrow before we go to the centennial celebration party. I'd like for her to be wearing my ring when we go out on the dance floor at the ball."

"Sounds like perfect timing, Freddie. This time, I bet Rhett Butler and Scarlet O'Hara will have a wonderful life together."

"Thanks for taking the time to talk with me, Laura. In all the time I've been asking for your advice, you've never steered me wrong. You always seem to have the right answer."

Those words were still on Laura's mind when she joined Ed, Preston and Edna Cline, and Sam and Margaret Barry for lunch at the Cricket Diner, knowing what decision now needed to be made about the upcoming Eden Springs birthday party.

"It looks like the ship's hit the sand, if I may paraphrase a common expression that seems appropriate right now," Pres commented wryly, as the six sat around a table near the back of the room. "The Mountain Ventures landfill got washed out in the flood a few days ago, and it sounds like everything turned up but

Noah's Arc. I understand the entire area is gated and locked off as a crime site."

"I'm afraid that you still haven't heard how bad the situation really is," Ed interjected. "Vickie called me from the TV station just before I left the office. A news bulletin has just been received from the West Virginia State Police reporting that a large number of metal drums filled with hazardous chemicals have been found.

"She told me that the lead story on the evening news tonight will be the discovery of a body in one of the drums. The State Police are absolutely certain it's Robert Barker. I had a confidential briefing about this yesterday but wasn't at liberty to tell anyone until the news was officially released. I understand more of those steel barrels are still showing up as the creek level drops, and the Lord only knows what else the law enforcement people will find."

"Ed, why didn't you tell me the news about Robert Barker's body being discovered when you first learned about it?" Laura asked. "How could you keep me in the dark on something so important after all we've gone through together dealing with that man?"

"I wasn't permitted to talk, honey. Sheriff Daniels told me the news yesterday in strictest confidence, and I couldn't breathe a word until the State Police made it public just a short time ago."

Pres interjected, "I know that this is a huge development, and we would all like to talk more about it, but first, we need to decide whether we want to go ahead with the Cen Plus Ten celebration this weekend, or pull the plug. What do you all think we should do? "

Edna was the first to speak, and it was in a loud and emotional voice with strong language that none of the others had ever heard the devout Baptist lady use before. "Pres, I've worked my fingers to the bone preparing for this town's one-hundred tenth anniversary celebration, and if you'll pardon my French, I'll be damned if some dead thug is going to ruin it no matter how powerful he is, or was. I say that the show should go on, and will go on, and to hell with Robert Barker."

Edna carried the day with her forceful speech. When Pres asked for a show of hands supporting the recommendation to proceed, six arms shot up.

"Then I'll get the word out that there's to be no change in plans," Pres stated emphatically. "I'm glad the rest of you agreed with Edna. We have a broken spring in our sofa, and I wasn't looking forward to sleeping on it."

Laura turned to Ed and said only half-jokingly, "What else do you know about the Mountain Ventures landfill and Robert Barker debacle that you haven't bothered to tell me, honey?" Then she added in a saccharine sweet yet vaguely threatening voice that only thoroughly annoyed women can project, "Our living room sofa is as uncomfortable as Edna's."

CHAPTER 54

"Vickie, got a minute?" Doug asked by phone early Friday morning. "Is it OK with you if I pick you up at the TV station tonight and we meet Mike and Ginny at the Regency Room for dinner? Afterwards, we could walk over to the ballroom, and meet up with Freddie and Marilyn. Do you have any problems with that?"

"You, Mike, and Freddie will be wearing your reenactment uniforms, and Ginny and Marilyn will be in costume, right?" Vickie laughed. "When I come out the door at WESP wearing an antebellum gown with a hoop skirt, I want to be sure everyone else is looking just as conspicuous."

"Frankly, my dear, you won't stand out because of the dress," Doug replied in his most engaging Rhett Butler imitation. "It will be because you are the most beautiful and alluring belle in the South."

"Then I'll be ready when y'all come by to pick up little ol' me." Vickie replied. "I'm really looking forward to attending this little ol' centennial extravaganza with y'all."

"Yeah, me too," Doug agreed. "By the way, magnolia blossom, you might want to start working on that accent. You still sound an awful lot like a New York City girl. Maybe you could get a few lessons on southern elocution from Marilyn. She has it down pat."

Marilyn did indeed have her southern elocution down pat when she answered the door that afternoon and saw Freddie before her with his usual grin. She gave him a quick kiss, saying, "I wore some comfortable hiking shoes like you told me to, and I'm carrying a sweater in case it cools down later. Are you sure that you have everything we'll need?"

"Mrs. Owens packed us a picnic basket, and she wouldn't even let me pay for it. I threw in a few cold drinks. Yep, I think I'm carrying along everything we'll need."

The clear blue sky and bright sunshine made it seem more like late summer than early fall as they drove out to the Buchanan farm and turned right onto the gravel road leading up to the old mansion on the knoll. "Roseanna would fit right in where I hail from in Georgia," Marilyn commented. "I love this old house."

Gertrude, Daniel, and Jonah were striding down the front steps to greet them by the time Freddie had pulled in and parked out front. The Buchanan twins were again wearing salt and pepper beards, grown especially for the town's anniversary celebration. Somehow, they appeared more authentic as Civil War era folks than anyone in town, with their burly physiques and ruddy complexions.

Gertrude spoke up with a warm smile, "We're so glad to have you all stop by before you go on your hike today. Dr. Nelson, that little cow has done beautifully since you came out here and got her safely through that hard calving experience. We still talk about how you saved both of them, and then refused to bill us."

Freddie and Marilyn were soon off on the trail leading across the fields and up the side of Chestnut Ridge beside Stony Creek, continuing on along the spine of the ridge toward Chimney Rock. Wild flowers bloomed in random clusters everywhere, creating splashes of bright color across the green landscape. "You lead the way, and I'll try to keep up," Freddie commented, laughing.

Freddie had been smitten since the day he had first encountered the lovely young Dr. Nelson, and he could not take his eyes off of her trim, athletic figure as he followed her up the ridge toward the cliffs above. In fact, he would have been at a loss to report on any of the natural scenery that they encountered along the way.

Freddie reclaimed his old high school class clown title, asking repeatedly during the climb, "Are we there yet?" They were indeed there, right at the tip top of Chimney Rock the last time he chimed that persistent, annoying question.

Marilyn finally had it, uttering something like, "Aarrrgghh," as she turned around and threw herself at him, causing Freddie to fall backward. He tried to recover his balance by grabbing her, and they both tumbled to the ground, landing in a bed of dried leaves, with food parcels from the picnic basket spilling out on the ground all around. "If you say that one more time I'm going to strangle you," she said, unable to keep from laughing.

Maybe it was the sight of Marilyn's face only inches from his, or the fragrance of her cologne, but some sixth sense told Freddie that this was exactly the moment he had been waiting for. Reaching into his pocket, he pulled out a tiny box, took out the ring, and pleaded in an emotional voice, "Marilyn, will you marry me?"

Marilyn was totally surprised to find herself lying on the ground beside Freddie, surrounded by spectacular rock formations, with a blue sky overhead, hearing a proposal of marriage. She extended her left hand for him to slip the ring on her finger, replying, "Yes, sweetheart, I'll marry you." She moved closer and lifted her head to exchange a kiss. Then she added, "But there's one condition. You have to promise me that you'll never ask me that idiotic question again as long as we live."

Freddie had concealed a bottle of champagne at the bottom of the basket. The wine was no longer chilled, and it had been thoroughly shaken during their hike up the ridge, so when he popped the cork, much of it bubbled out onto the ground. But there was still enough to fill two small paper cups to toast their future together.

"When can we plan to get married?" Freddie asked. "Would you want to have the wedding in your home town, or here in Eden Springs?"

"I haven't given any thought to either right up until this moment," Marilyn confessed. "Maybe it would be nice to have a late fall wedding. I've been away from home for so long that there aren't a lot people back there any more I feel close to. I'd want for Dad and Mom, and my kid sister Sarah to attend, and my college suitemates, Betty Wilson and Becky Harper. What would you think about a Thanksgiving wedding right here in Eden Springs?"

"That would be fine with me. I'd be happy getting married to you on Christmas Day at the North Pole if that's what you want. I've only got a small family and a few close friends, so it wouldn't have to be huge event from my end. But I'll be happy to go along with any wedding plans you make."

Time got away from Freddie and Marilyn as they continued to plan the start of their new life together, sitting side by side on top of the world in their own private skybox, staring off into the distance. Only the sight of the sun dipping low in the sky finally made them aware of the time, and they hurriedly gathered their belongings before starting hand in hand on the trail back to Roseanna.

CHAPTER 55

Friday night, something unexpected happened at the Eden Springs spa, something even Edna Cline hadn't anticipated, when she had almost single-handedly planned the Cen Plus Ten anniversary celebration. Maybe it was triggered by mists rising above the springs, where settlers had taken the healing waters since the Revolution. Maybe it was caused by the large assembly of lovely ladies in hoop-skirted ball gowns, and their escorts, wearing Yankee blue and Rebel gray. But for whatever reason, the surroundings seemed to revert to an earlier era.

The lighting was subdued both inside the resort and on the grounds outside when Doug, Vickie, Mike and Jenny arrived and pulled into the parking lot. The four were greeted at the door by the resort staff, all dressed in costumes that public house attendants would have worn during an earlier period. A harpsichordist played Brahms in the Regency Room. The classical music combined with the flickering candlelight to create the illusion of stepping through a door into another place and time.

Vickie was wearing a spectacular blue gown, with a neckline exposing enough cleavage to give Doug trouble keeping his eyes on the road during the drive across town. Ginny sparkled in a bright red dress that suited her vivacious personality, turning her into a saucy Southern belle. Doug and Mike were wearing their custom made one-hundred percent virgin wool Confederate uniforms that both felt must have come from Thimbles and Thread with a liberal amount of itching powder sprinkled into the lining by the Garrett sisters.

"Where are we?" Ginny wondered. "I feel as though we've wandered into the antebellum south."

"What if we can't find our way home to 1959?" Vickie added. "I'll be out of work. I don't think there were many openings for TV news anchors back then."

Doug destroyed the mood by chiming in, "They had jobs you probably could have qualified for back then, Miss Scarlett. It took a lot of stout workers to plow the fields behind a mule and clean out the stalls in the barns."

It wasn't long before they spotted Freddie's imposing gray-uniformed figure following Marilyn through the door. She looked striking in her crimson gown that stood out even in the dimly lit ballroom, as they walked across the room to join their friends. "We were starting to wonder when you would get here," Doug commented, as Freddie pulled back a chair for Marilyn, and she carefully arranged the hoop skirt to take a seat. "Where have y'all been this evening?"

Marilyn answered with a pretty smile, "Freddie took me for a picnic hike up to the top of Chimney Rock this afternoon, and the time got away from us. We've been on a dead run ever since, trying to get here to join you. Thanks for saving us a place."

She might have gone on about their afternoon excursion, but suddenly Ginny saw something that took the conversation in an entirely new direction. "Marilyn, when did you get that beautiful ring? What's going on?"

Freddie couldn't keep still any longer, answering for her, "I proposed to her this afternoon up on top of Chimney Rock, and she accepted. Marilyn and I are engaged."

Mike proposed a toast, "Here's to the new couple, Marilyn and Freddie. May they have a long and happy life together."

Doug followed with a second toast, in a more light-hearted vein. "Here's to Freddie, who like Mike and me, has somehow latched on to a lady who is far better than he deserves." Ginny, Vickie, and Marilyn touched their glasses together in full agreement.

Marilyn told them what had happened during the hike, with Freddie's surprise proposal. "We've talked about having a small wedding this fall right here in town, maybe around Thanksgiving."

"Your plans sound a lot like Doug's and mine," Vickie mentioned. "It seems like a coincidence that the four of us seem to be going down the same path at the same time."

Ginny interjected, "Y'all remind me of two couples in my favorite novel, *Pride and Prejudice.* You could pass for Mr. Darcy and Mr. Bingley getting engaged to Lizzie and Jane Bennett. That story ended up in a double wedding."

"But they were sisters, weren't they?" Mike inquired. "It seems like I remember you reading half of that book aloud to me."

"They were not only sisters but also best friends," Ginny continued. "The six of us have all been so close since Doug moved here during high school, and Marilyn came here to live last year, that we're almost like a family. The thought crossed my mind that a double wedding would be really special. But whatever plans y'all make, I hope I'll get to be a bridesmaid." Vickie and Marilyn smiled at one another, and Ginny could see that the seed had been planted.

"Let's take the ladies out on the floor and dance," Mike suggested, pulling back Ginny's chair for her to stand. "This may be the only evening we get in our entire lifetimes to waltz with beautiful southern belles."

Later, Marilyn excused herself, returning a short time later. "I just ran into the nicest gentleman, who may be someone you know, Doug. He's dressed in a Union army uniform, and he told me his name's Trent Barlow. He said he's known your dad and Jack Bradford for years. I showed him where they were sitting, so he could stop by their table and say hello."

Doug looked puzzled. "I don't recall ever hearing that name before. If you see him again, please point him out to me. I'm curious to know who he is."

Marilyn did not catch another glimpse of Trent Barlow. The party finally broke up at midnight, when the three couples decided that it was time to call it a day. Tomorrow was the grand finale for the Cen Plus Ten celebration, the long-awaited reenactment of the Battle of Eden Springs.

CHAPTER 56

Saturday morning dawned sunny but quite cool in Eden Springs, probably due to the fervent prayers offered up by eighty-two townsmen who would soon be transformed into soldiers in hot wool uniforms.

"Ed, or should I say, Captain Jason Taylor Early, you better get a move on," Laura called down the hallway to the far bedroom. "Lizzie, shake a leg and slip on that dress I made for you and get in here to breakfast. We'll all need to be out at the Buchanan farm by 10:30 if we want to find a parking place. Your dad should be out in the field with his company, standing in formation at 11:00, and the time's sneaking up on all of us."

"Laura, what'd you do with that saber I borrowed?" Ed called out, as he stepped from the bedroom in full uniform. "Wait a minute. I found it here in the closet where I put it last week."

Laura was wearing the same dress she had worn the night before, as she set a light breakfast on the dinette table. "I didn't think any of us needs a big meal, since I'm taking a full picnic lunch for us to eat on the lawn after the reenactment."

Vickie was also wearing the same dress she had worn to the ball, as she scurried around her apartment, eating a honey bun on the fly. Charlie Goins had asked that she and Vince be at the studio in costume by 10:00 to go over plans for the telecast. Charlie was hoping that a segment would be picked up by NBC and broadcast on national TV that evening, and he wanted it to be good.

The phone rang, and when she answered, she found that it was Doug, telling her he would meet her at Roseanna after the reenactment. "I've got to run now, honey," she called out to him before hanging up, lifting her skirt and dashing out the door to her car, then speeding off to the studio.

When Ed, Laura, and Lizzie arrived at the top of the knoll near the old mansion, good parking places were becoming as scarce as hen's teeth. Edna Goins was in the middle of the action, trying to handle everything from directing traffic to showing the movers just where she wanted all of the folding chairs to be placed. Volunteers had been busy all morning, hauling them to Roseanna from every church in town in the backs of their pickup trucks.

"We need to move along quickly," she kept saying nervously to no one in particular. "It's getting close to time for the men to take the field."

Finally, two trucks and a Jeep Wagoneer marked WESP Channel 8 arrived, and the TV crew began hauling camera equipment toward the crest of cemetery hill, overlooking the reenactment site.

Vickie and Vince rode with Charlie Goins in the four-wheel drive vehicle to the top, where they sat quietly talking, watching all of the hustle and bustle taking place while waiting to go on camera. Only Vickie took time for a quick glance at a tall, husky man wearing the long blue overcoat of a Union Army officer, who was standing a short distance away from the graveyard, almost out of sight behind the trunk of the huge oak tree.

At precisely 10:45, an American Legion VFW bugler sounded the assembly call, signaling the men to pick up their arms and move to their positions for the start of the reenactment. Beau and Buddy were waiting at an improvised armory kiosk beside the roadway to issue the .58 caliber muskets to the volunteers.

Ed joined his gray-clad E Company volunteers at the south end of the field, a quarter mile down from the battlefield, while at the same time Sam Barry and his Union troops moved into position to lie in ambush behind improvised cover on the hillside. Beau worked with the Rebs, and Buddy with the Yanks to supervise the loading of black powder and patch by the senior reenactors who had been designated as shooters, while the younger volunteers carried unloaded weapons.

Standing at attention after the commands to fall in and shoulder arms, the forty strong E company troops, now carrying authentic Civil War weapons, felt chills move down their spines. The lighthearted spirit of horseplay from the drill was gone. Suddenly, this was a serious and sacred memorial service to honor the valor of men who had risked everything to preserve their land, homes, families, and heritage from an invading army. When Jack Bradford unfurled the red, white, and blue Battle Flag of the Confederacy, many of the men in ranks wiped tears from their eyes.

Ed solemnly quoted Stonewall Jackson, "Who could not conquer with such troops as these," and followed with Isaiah 43.6, "I will say to the north, Give up, and to the south, Do not withhold." When a bugle sounded again in the distance, Ed called, "Forward march," and the men began to move up the field smartly in step, with adrenaline surging.

*****

Spectators on the road in front of Roseanna rose from their chairs and craned their necks to catch a first glimpse of the Confederate column moving up the valley, while simultaneously watching the Yanks lying silently behind cover on the hillside like waiting predators.

Laura whispered to Margaret, "I hope our troops spot those blue bellied Yankees before they come any closer," pretending she had forgotten that Sam was one of the men in blue positioned on the hillside.

Margaret replied with mock offense, "Rebel rednecks ought to watch who they call blue bellies."

"I don't like this," Lizzie fretted. "I'm afraid Daddy and Doug are going to get hurt."

Jonah, who had been standing beside Daniel, quietly moved behind Lizzie and gently put his calloused hands on her shoulders. She glanced back at the gentle giant now watching over her, and with a reassured smile, went back to watching the scene unfold.

The first sign that the reenactment had achieved an incredible degree of realism came from Hazel Spiller, whose grandfather and two great uncles had been killed in General Pickett's charge on Cemetery Ridge at Gettysburg. She stood and gasped, "Oh, Lord, here they come. Our poor boys are going to be slaughtered."

Mamie Tarter clutched her sister's arm and said in a hushed voice, "I want to stand and scream, 'Stop! You're marching into a trap.'"

Evelyn's eyes were riveted to the action. "Someone ought to yell out a warning," she agreed, squeezing Mamie's hand with white knuckles.

*****

The WESP camera crew stood poised at the top of cemetery hill waiting for the action to begin, Vince taking the lead for the broadcast team, speaking into his microphone to record the battle reenactment as if it were a football game.

"I can see the Confederate column moving up the field into sight below the Union forces concealed on the hillside. The Rebs have no idea that they're marching into an ambush. I wonder what's going through the minds of those men in blue crouching out of sight. The suspense of sitting and waiting must be unbearable. I imagine their hearts are pounding a mile a minute while they wait for the battle to begin.

"The Rebs are only a few hundred feet away, marching

forward at a quick cadence. I keep expecting the Yanks to spring their ambush, but they're still lying low, patiently waiting while the enemy comes closer and closer. Major Horace Dunford is using the same strategy that William Prescott used at the Battle of Bunker Hill, instructing his troops, 'Don't fire until you can see the whites of their eyes.' Captain Jason Taylor Early's company of Confederate troops is now only a hundred feet from the hillside, and closing.

"Major Dunford just ordered, 'Open fire!' Union soldiers all across the hillside are shifting into shooting positions with fire and black smoke spewing from their muskets. I can hear a delayed boom following each muzzle flash.

"Captain Taylor commanded his troops to break ranks, form a skirmish line, and take the hill. The Rebs are advancing under withering fire to engage the Yanks at close range. It's inconceivable that anyone could show such courage. The Yanks are picking them off like they're shooting fish in a barrel. I can see six men of Company E down on the ground already.

"Captain Taylor is leading the charge with drawn saber. The Lieutenant beside him is carrying the red, white, and blue Confederate battle flag right into the middle of the Union forces. The blue and gray soldiers are battling hand to hand all across the hillside. This is the most incredible sight I've ever seen. All I can hear is gunfire and shouting, and there's so much smoke in the air that it's hard for me to see what's going on.

"My heart's in my throat watching these troops fighting for their lives. The action's getting more and more intense. Several of the men in blue are slumping to the ground, wounded or dead."

*****

Ed and Jack knew that they were at the climax of the battle reenactment as they moved further up the hill to engage Sam and his men. The Confederate and Union flag bearers were to clash, and at that moment Ed was to be shot from behind by one of his own men and feign death, triggering the panicked retreat of Company E. Ed looked at Sam, and saw the nod of acknowledgment from his Yankee counterpart. Everything was coming together exactly as planned.

At that moment, Ed was struck in the thigh and knocked to the ground, a searing pain radiating from his leg. A second later, Jack dropped the Confederate battle flag and sprawled in the dirt beside him, holding his right shoulder with his left hand, writhing in agony. Sam watched both men fall, admiring their performances, thinking it was part of the scripted action. That was until he saw the spreading red stains on Ed and Jack's gray uniforms. "What's wrong?" he shouted.

The reply was the last thing Sam expected to hear. "We've been shot," Ed grimaced. "Tell everyone to cease firing. We need help."

*****

Vince was still speaking into the microphone when he sensed something was wrong.

"Wait a minute! Something's happened! Captain Taylor and his flag bearer have both fallen to the ground. It's so realistic that you would swear they've really been hit. Hold on! Someone called out a command to cease fire. There are soldiers in blue and gray huddling around those downed men. I believe that the two on the ground are Ed Housman and Jack Bradford. Something serious has happened. I'm hearing people calling for a doctor. It looks like they've actually been wounded."

*****

For a while, Vickie was mesmerized by the action unfolding below her, listening to Vince's description of the skirmish. She was snapped back to reality when she heard a voice call loudly from the hillside below, "Housman and Bradford have been shot! They're both bleeding badly! We need a doctor down here right now!"

A movement near the base of the nearby oak tree caught her eye, and again she saw the soldier in the long blue overcoat, but now he was trying to conceal something beneath it. If he had been a little quicker, it might have gone unnoticed. But the protruding box magazine of his .30 caliber M1 carbine snagged in the front opening of the coat before he could hide it. Vickie knew that that this was no reenactor with a Civil War muzzle loader. She realized that she was staring into the face of a sniper with a modern military rifle. Reacting without taking time to think of the consequences, she screamed out to him, "Stop!"

Travis Barker pulled the rifle from beneath his coat and pointed it at Vickie's head with a clear unspoken message. Turning on his heel, he sprinted for a truck parked below by the road.

Running to the Wagoneer with her full skirt gathered in her hands, Vickie slid behind the wheel and started the engine. Accelerating quickly, taking a line down the hill toward the truck, she watched Travis pull out. Foot to the floor, Vickie caught up to him as he was speeding away, slamming the Wagoneer into his vehicle just behind the driver's door. She didn't get off the gas until she had crushed the truck like a tin can, driving it sideways across the road into the ditch.

The impact from the collision left both Vickie and Travis unconscious. Daniel, Jonah, and Gertrude were the first to reach the scene, gently helping Vickie from the wrecked vehicle. "How do you feel?" Gertrude asked anxiously. "You appear to have had a concussion, but don't show any signs of broken bones," she added, drawing on her RN experience.

"I have a splitting headache, but I can move my arms and legs OK. Have you heard anything about Doug's dad and Jack Bradford? The man in the truck is the one who shot them."

"We heard that Dr. Jannsen's with them now, but we don't have any report on how they're doing. The driver of the truck appears to be in bad shape. Medical help is on the way here now. We're not going to move him until they arrive."

Mike and Freddie trotted up, out of breath. Mike spoke urgently, "An ambulance just took Ed and Jack to the hospital.

Doug, Laura, and Lizzie followed them over in their car. It looks like both of them are going to be OK."

An ambulance arrived a few minutes later to carry Vickie to the hospital, while a doctor supervised the sheriff and his deputies in removing a badly injured Travis Barker from the truck to transport him under armed guard to the hospital for surgery.

The television crew kept the camera rolling throughout the entire reenactment right up to the aborted ending. They also caught the action scene that followed: their own news anchor, an avenging angel in a Civil War era gown, running down a fleeing Union gunman in a spectacular collision.

Later, as the chase scene was replayed across the country near the end of the NBC Huntley-Brinkley Report, the latest battle of Eden Springs found an audience far larger than the friends on the hill. The two famous commentators summed it up in closing.

"You certainly don't want to get those West Virginia ladies riled up."

"Not that blonde reporter in the ball gown."

"Good night, David."

"Good night, Chet."

CHAPTER 57

"**How are you doing, old** timer?" Doug asked as he entered his parents' house on Saturday, affectionately putting his arm around his dad's shoulder. "Is the leg feeling OK?

"Yeah, but I'll never be able to make the Olympic track team," Ed returned.

"That'll probably cost the United States a gold medal in the one hundred meter event," Doug rejoined. "Oh, well, you already have all those other medals. What's one more to a track and field legend like you?" Glancing around the house, he asked, "Where are Mom and Lizzie this afternoon?"

"Your mother's helping Lizzie with her Halloween costume. I think they're in the bedroom making a Daisy Duck outfit out of a couple of pillows, some cardboard boxes, and fabric remnants. Before you run off looking for them, grab us a couple of Cokes, and have a seat here with me for a minute so I can tell you what I learned in my meeting with Sam yesterday. There's a lot going on right now in the DA's office, and also with the law enforcement agencies, that I think you'll be interested to hear."

Doug returned from the kitchen, handed a cold bottle to his dad, and sat down across from him on the sofa. "Fire away, Pop."

"I'll start with the latest information about the Barker family. Apparently, Robert's body has been buried in the family cemetery plot outside of Beckley. His only son, Travis, was released from the hospital and indicted for attempted murder. He'll be tried in January. And from what can be pieced together, it seems that Robert's right hand man, William Thorpe, has skipped the country with his wife. The authorities think they may be hiding out somewhere down in the Caribbean."

"Good riddance to the lot of them," Doug responded vehemently. "You've been going head-to-head with Barker Mining off and on for seven years. What about that mess that their company, Mountain Ventures, left behind in the landfill, and what about those other two bodies that turned up out there?"

"The State Police were able to identify both of the bodies by fingerprints. It turns out that they're a couple of career criminals out of New Jersey, with a string of convictions and ties to organized crime. The FBI is starting an investigation to see if any crimes were conducted across state lines, which would result in federal jurisdiction. I suspect that we may be looking at the tip of the iceberg, but we won't know for a while longer. Sam told me that the FBI thinks that there's a big bootleg whiskey operation in this part of the state that has ties to the New Jersey Mafia"

"So who will clean up the mess along Stony Creek and reclaim the land, Madison County or the state of West Virginia?" Doug inquired. "Where will all of that toxic material finally end up?"

"I think Madison County will have to foot the bill for closing the landfill, since it was approved by the county government. But the hazardous waste? I don't know for sure. I have a feeling that with very little publicity, it will end up buried at the bottom of an abandoned mine shaft somewhere out in the boondocks."

"Any progress in identifying the people who hurt you in that hit and run, or who sabotaged Sam Bradford's plane?"

"None at all. There wasn't much evidence for the law enforcement people to work with in either of those investigations. Maybe sometime down the road, new evidence will turn up, or a witness will come forward and talk, but for now, they're both cold cases."

Doug drained the last of his Coke, saying, "Thanks for filling me in, Dad. I'm glad to see you're making a good recovery from the gunshot."

"Thanks, son. Run on in the other room and see what your mother and Lizzie are up to. They may need some engineering help with that Daisy Duck costume."

It was probably good that Doug had been tipped off as to what the costume was intended to represent, since it took a bit of imagination to visualize the Walt Disney character from what Laura and Lizzie had assembled. A pillow tied to Lizzie's backside portrayed Daisy's generous bottom. A red vest and large matching hair bow looked like something that Daisy really might have selected. But the orange cardboard duck bill, and the red shoebox pumps were a bit of a stretch. "How do I look, Doug?" Lizzie inquired.

"Squirt, you'd make the great Walt Disney stand up and take notice," Doug replied cryptically. "Mom, I didn't know you were a professional costume artist."

Laura winked at him, replying with a laugh, "I do my best. After all, Lizzie's going out trick or treating after supper with Leon Conklin, and he'll be dressed as Donald Duck. Lizzie says all of the girls in the second grade are in love with Leon, so I've got to get her Daisy Duck costume exactly right, or I may spoil her chances at romance with the biggest heartthrob in Mrs. Mallory's class."

Lizzie quickly defended herself. "He has a crush on me. I don't have a crush on him. I don't have a crush on any boy."

Doug returned Laura's wink, saying to Lizzie, "Oh, but you will someday. Don't believe everything you hear about snakes and snails and puppy dog tails. See y'all later. Good luck with the candy collection tonight, sis."

"Where are you off to now?" Laura asked.

"I'm picking up Vickie and meeting Freddie, Marilyn,

Mike, and Ginny out at the Russo farm. Freddie says Mr. Russo's interested in selling off a twenty acre piece of land, and we're trying to see whether we could go in together to buy it and then subdivide it into three home sites. I'd better roll. Vickie's probably watching for me."

Their friends were waiting with Hiram Russo when Doug and Vickie arrived. For the next hour, the three couples walked over the property with the owner, deciding that the acreage could indeed be subdivided into three very attractive home sites, each with a spectacular view. "May I talk privately with my buddies for a minute, Mr. Russo?" Freddie inquired.

"He's only asking ten grand for this property," Freddie told them excitedly. "By the time we survey it, subdivide it, and close, it will be still be less that four thousand each. I think we ought to handshake on a deal with Mr. Russo today, before someone finds out we're interested in buying the land and bids up the price. What do the rest of you think? Can you swing it? I'll handle all of the paperwork."

The three couples immediately and unanimously decided to buy the tract, and shook hands with Mr. Russo to seal the agreement. Later, they stopped by Gil's for burgers and chocolate shakes.

"So what about the plans for your big weddings coming up?" Ginny inquired.

Vickie surprised the others when she said to Ginny, "I took Sandra's rabbit to the vet's last week, and while I was there, Marilyn and I talked about the possibility of a double wedding. We've all become as close as kin. Doug told me that Freddie's like a second son to his mom."

Marilyn picked up where Vickie stopped, "We think you have an exciting idea, Ginny. When you suggested a double wedding, we realized that it would work out well for the four of us."

When the three couples split up, Ginny was in an up-beat mood all the way home, thinking that Jane Austen couldn't have written about lives any happier than those now unfolding for her best friends.

Chapter 58

"You look beautiful," Ingrid Vicelli said with loving pride, as she looked at Vickie in her white bridal gown, standing before the full length mirror in the hallway. "I remember wearing that same dress twenty-five years ago, when your grandfather gave me in marriage to your daddy. Maybe some day you'll have a daughter, and she'll wear it, too. Time goes by so fast."

Vickie turned to give her mother a hug. She had been up since the crack of dawn, checking and rechecking to see that everything had been done. She had talked to Doug, and later to Marilyn, who was going through the same activities at her apartment, where her mother, father, sister, and two college suitemates were staying during their visit.

"Were you as nervous before your wedding as I am?" Vickie asked. "I wasn't as anxious before my first news broadcast as I am now. I'm wondering why I should feel this way, since I've been going with Doug since our sophomore year in high school."

"That's because most people marry only once, and it's for life," Ingrid answered gently. "Even if you and Doug had gone together longer, it would still be the same. Getting married is the biggest commitment of your entire life. No one enters into

287

marriage lightly, or without a bit of nervous anticipation. I felt exactly the same way on my wedding day."

"You make me feel better, Mom. I guess Daddy and TJ are both dressed by now. I've never seen either of them wearing a white dinner jacket before. I bet Daddy would rather be wearing his usual work clothes and store apron right now."

"They were both downstairs when I came up to see you, and I think that they're going to survive and do fine in formal wear. I don't know whether or not you noticed, but your brother was bowled over when he met Marilyn's pretty seventeen-year old sister Sarah at the rehearsal dinner. I could tell that TJ was doing everything he could to get her attention all evening long. If there'd been a playground swing in the room, I'm sure he would have hung upside down from the top bar to impress her."

"Doug and I both noticed that, Mom," Vickie said, laughing. "Doug said that the Nelson ladies seemed to have a devastating attraction for boys like Freddie and TJ. Then he told me that I have the same effect on him. It was pretty sweet."

"I'll slip on out and let you finish getting dressed, honey. You call me if you need me."

"I will, Mom. I love you."

*****

A similar scene was unfolding in Marilyn's apartment across town. The quarters were crowded, with Marilyn and Sarah sharing the three rooms with her parents, Tom and Belinda, and her vet school suitemates, Betty Wilson and Becky Harper.

"Your mother and I like all of your new friends," Tom commented to Marilyn, as her mother made a final adjustment to the fit of her dress with needle and thread. "Dr. Rollins and his wife Joyce seem like fine folks, the kind of people we'd like to have for next-door neighbors. As for the friends closer to your age, I haven't met one yet that I wouldn't like to have living in our neighborhood. But you got the pick of the litter with Freddie. When you bring him down to our place in Georgia, I'm going to make a bass fisherman out of him. That boy and I are going to have some great times together."

"I'm glad you like him, Pop. Freddie's the finest man I've ever met. He doesn't have a lot of college degrees on the wall, but when you talk to him, you know right away that he's very intelligent. He's good at what he does, working in the real estate business here in the valley. Laura Housman told me that her business had doubled since he'd come to work for her. But most importantly, he's kind, loving, generous, and so much fun to be with. Remind me to tell you sometime what kind of stunt he pulled after we first met to get me to go out with him."

"Remind me to tell you what kind of stunt your father pulled when he bumped into me for the first time at a frat party after a Georgia-Alabama football game," Belinda commented. "There's a side to your father that you've never seen."

"Never mind getting into that right now, honey," Tom said quickly. "You can bring all of the skeletons that you want out of this old elk's closet some day, but at least wait until after I've gone to my reward."

"Don't worry, Pop," Marilyn said, starting to laugh. "Mom told me years ago that you talk a good game, but that you're really harmless."

"She said that about me?" Tom said, with mock incredulity. "That woman!"

"Enough of our silly talk," Belinda said to her husband. "Let's move on and discuss something other than our college romance. I imagine that our beautiful daughter has other things that she would prefer to talk about on her wedding day."

"Yeah, it might be a good time to change the subject," Marilyn laughed. "I picked up on something involving my baby sister that's kind of sweet. Keep an eye on Sarah when we get over to the reception this afternoon. I was watching her last night, and I noticed that she's really got an eye for Vickie's kid brother, TJ."

*****

"I guess it's time for us to put the old ball and chain on the two new victims," Mike joked, as Doug, Freddie, and the other male members of the wedding party gathered at the Eden Springs Resort, waiting for the ceremony to begin.

"Tell us how you like married life, Mike," Doug countered, smiling. "I never heard you say."

"Yeah, we never got a report after you and Ginny came back from your honeymoon," Freddie chimed in. "We'd like to hear all about it."

"I'd tell both of you everything, but TJ's standing here beside me listening, and he hasn't turned eighteen yet," Mike countered. "You'll have to wait and find out what married life's like for yourselves. It won't be long now 'til you know."

"Getting married's the best thing that'll ever happen to you," Vince interjected. "Mark my words."

At that moment, Ed and Freddie's father joined them, and Ed said, "The ministers have asked for the grooms and their best men to join them up front."

*****

Vickie and Marilyn had moved into a small hallway behind the Regency Room, out of sight of the waiting grooms, talking with Ingrid and Belinda, trying to dispel their growing nervousness as they waited. Then Kathleen Edwards, the wedding planner, approached with a big smile. "The ushers are ready to escort the mothers of the brides and grooms to their seats. Vickie, Marilyn, your fathers are standing outside to walk you up the aisle. The curtain's going up, ladies. Y'all look beautiful!"

Shortly afterward, the pianists struck up the wedding march, and the two young women, on their fathers' arms for the last time, started up the aisle toward the front of the room where Doug and Freddie, their fathers, and the two ministers, stood waiting.

Doug had expected to feel nervous, but found himself completely at ease as Vickie approached wearing the beautiful smile he had missed so much during their five years apart. Looking to his side, he could see that Freddie was equally relaxed, eyes focused on Marilyn, as if in disbelief that the beautiful woman coming toward him would soon be his wife.

Doug could see his mother and other family members seated at the front, and behind them his best friends. Lizzie caught his eye, the pretty red-haired flower girl in the white taffeta dress. Beside her sat Gertrude, Dan, and Jonah Buchanan, both brothers wearing suits and ties for the first time in their lives. Behind them were his two favorite high school teachers, Sam and Margaret Barry, looking at him with smiles of encouragement.

Ministers Harold Seymour and Joseph Paulson displayed easy teamwork, starting the double wedding ceremony as soon as everyone was assembled. Doug heard his minister begin with, "Dearly beloved…" He soon found himself holding hands with Vickie, standing face to face, staring deep into her eyes, exchanging wedding vows and rings.

Afterward, he heard the minister announce to each couple in turn, "I now pronounce you husband and wife. You may kiss the bride."

Doug and Vickie embraced, holding each other as though they would never let go. Freddie wrapped his large arms around Marilyn, not seeming to realize that her feet were almost lifted off the floor. Family and friends nearby exchanged smiling glances after overhearing one minister whisper to the other, "I believe both of these marriages will go the distance."

The reception was as boisterous as the newlyweds. When Doug fed Vickie the traditional first bite from the wedding cake, he playfully pulled it away and a large piece of the cake dropped down the bodice of her dress. The wedding photographer caught it all on film, including Vickie rolling her eyes and promising revenge.

Mike observed, "I think that a true gentleman would offer to retrieve it."

Doug countered, "And I think a true gentleman would spend his wedding night sleeping in the doghouse."

Betty Wilson, Becky Harper, and Ginny served champagne punch as if they were competing for promotion in the beverage sales department. Family and friends quickly got into the party mood, and most were on the dance floor to jitterbug to rock and roll favorites, after the newlyweds had slow danced to The Platters hit *Twilight Time*. Ed and Laura, and Tom and Belinda, demonstrated that the old timers could still cut a rug as well as any of the younger generation.

Vickie purposefully tossed her bridal bouquet directly toward her sister, who would go on to marry her VPI sweetheart two years later. Doug received a playful swat on the head from Vickie when he slowly lifted her skirt and slipped off her garter, tossing it to an unmarried friend.

When Freddie removed Marilyn's garter and threw it toward the group of bachelors, TJ almost bowled over several older boys to snag it. He had it in his pocket for good luck when he got up the nerve to invite Sarah Nelson to dance with him for the first time. If he had not been looking down when he asked her, he would have seen her pretty smile as she offered him her hand.

The party broke up when Freddie and Marilyn ran through a shower of rice and the happy calls of well-wishers toward their car, decorated with shoe polish-inscribed messages, off to spend their honeymoon in Niagara Falls.

Doug and Vickie left soon afterwards with an equally lively sendoff, on their way to a beachfront honeymoon cottage in Fort Myers, with Ed, Laura, and their friends waving goodbye as they departed.

Glancing in the rear view mirror, Doug caught sight of a red-haired flower girl flying down the road behind them, excitedly waving her arms, running as fast as she could in her white patent leather Mary Janes. "Looks like Lizzy's giving us a farewell sendoff," Doug observed.

Vickie turned to look, then called out, "Stop the car, Doug.

I think she wants to tell us something." Doug pulled over and parked, allowing time for the breathless young girl to catch up.

"I didn't get to tell you goodbye," Lizzie said, running toward them, almost in tears.

Doug and Vickie got out of the car, and Vickie picked up Lizzie to hold her close. "How could I have failed to say goodbye to my new kid sister?" After a long, affectionate farewell, Lizzie ran back to her parents, smiling, and Doug and Vickie continued on their way.

The wedding day was forever captured in memories, engraved with smiles, good wishes, and loving embraces, with double the excitement and double the promise of long, happy marriages to follow.

CHAPTER 59

"**Only six more days 'til** Christmas," Laura said, turning to face Lizzie, who was seated behind Ed in the family car. "Tell me again, what do you want Santa to bring you this year?"

"Oh, Mom!" Lizzie replied. "I'm not a child any more. Leon told me that there's no such thing as Santa Claus."

"I think that Leon has a very big mouth," Ed interjected. "If there's no Santa Claus, then who keeps filling my stocking every Christmas with tangerines, pecans, hard candy, and chocolate treats?"

"I think you're sitting right beside her, Daddy," Lizzie replied, seeming wise beyond her seven years. "I still look forward to Christmas, even though I know that there's no Santa to come down the chimney with a sack full of toys."

Laura sensed that it was time to let Santa go. "I'm glad you suggested that we drive out to Roseanna this afternoon and take a fruitcake to Gertrude, Daniel and Jonah. They always enjoy seeing Lizzie so much. I think those two men feel like they're her surrogate uncles."

"I like both of them," Lizzie chimed in. "And I like Aunt Gertrude, too." Ed and Laura smiled to hear their daughter call

Gertrude "Aunt." She had invited Lizzie to do so that summer, and Lizzie had picked up on it enthusiastically.

When they arrived, they were greeted at the door by all three residents of the old mansion. "Come in the house where it's nice and warm, Mr. and Mrs. Housman, and young Miss Lizzie," Gertrude invited. Ed and Laura had given up trying to get her to call them by their first names, since she seemed more comfortable with old-fashioned formality. After Laura handed her the fruitcake, she continued, "Y'all shouldn't have gone to all the trouble to buy us this nice gift and bring it all the way out here, but I can tell that Dan and Joe are glad you did. They both have quite a sweet tooth, and they don't get many treats like this."

Gertrude inquired about the newlyweds during a conversation in the parlor. "Tell me about those two young couples. I haven't heard anything more from them since they invited the three of us to their wedding."

"All of them have are back in town and have returned to work," Laura answered. "Vickie gave up her apartment and moved in with Doug. Freddie moved out of Mrs. Owen's Boarding House and into Marilyn's apartment. They've gone in together with Mike and Ginny Rhodes to purchase a parcel of land from Hiram Russo, and subdivided it into three tracts for future home sites, hoping to build in the spring."

Noticing the time, Ed commented, "This Tuesday will be the winter solstice, the shortest day of the year. I expect that we should be running on before it gets dark. But before we go, could we walk up on cemetery hill and look around? That hilltop has a lot of memories for all of us."

"Certainly, Mr. Housman," Gertrude replied obligingly. "We'll grab our coats and stretch our legs with you."

The sun was setting, and the temperature was becoming chilly by the time the six approached the top. Lizzie walked between Daniel and Jonah as though they were her protective book-ends, holding their hands and chatting cheerily along the way. Laura continued beside Ed to stand near the giant oak tree. "Look! You can see Venus, the evening star, lined up next to the crescent moon."

As they stood near the soldiers' final resting place, stillness enveloped the group. Daniel held up his hand, saying softly, "Listen. You can hear a whippoorwill and an owl. An old Indian legend says that when both are calling, the Great Spirit is walking on the land."

"Standing here in the twilight, I can believe the legend is true," Ed replied, pausing to listen to the lonesome sounds as the sun slipped further below the distant mountaintop. Then he broke the silence. "It's getting dark, and we don't have a lantern. We'd better head back to our car, and let y'all get home where it's warm."

Ed and Laura walked side by side down the darkening hillside with their arms intertwined, while Lizzie skipped along in front of the others, singing softly to herself.

Ed turned to Laura, and whispered, "She's such a happy little nightingale. Can you recognize her song?"

"I think it's her version of my favorite hymn, one with a prayer that's finally been answered."

"What's that hymn?"

"*Peace in the Valley.*"